SIDNEY SHELDON is the author of *The Other Side of Midnight*, *A Stranger in the Mirror*, *Bloodline*, *Rage of Angels*, *Master of the Game*, *If Tomorrow Comes*, *Windmills of the Gods*, *The Sands of Time* and *Memories of Midnight*, all Number One international bestsellers. His first book, *The Naked Face*, was acclaimed by the *New York Times* as 'the best first mystery novel of the year' Mr Sheldon has won a Tony award for Broadway's *Redhead* and an Academy Award for *The Bachelor and the Bobby Soxer*. *Rage of Angels*, *Master of the Game* and *Windmills of the Gods* have been made into highly successful television mini-series.

He has written the screenplays for twenty-three motion pictures, including *Easter Parade* (with Judy Garland) and *Annie Get Your Gun*. He also created four long-running television series, including *Hart to Hart* and *I Dream of Jeannie*, which he produced and directed. Sidney Sheldon lives in southern California.

available in Indus by the same author

Rage of Angels
The Other Side of Midnight
Windmills of the Gods
The Sands of Time
Bloodline
Memories of Midnight

also by Sidney Sheldon

If Tomorrow Comes
Master of the Game
The Naked Face

SIDNEY SHELDON

A Stranger in the Mirror

HarperCollins *Publishers*

HarperCollins *Publishers* India

by arrangement with
HarperCollins *Publishers* Limited

This is a work of fiction
Except for the names of theatrical personalities,
all characters are imaginary

31st impression 2023

ISBN 13: 978 81 7223 481 2

FICTION

HarperCollins *Publishers*
4th Floor, Tower A, Building No Phase II, DLF Cyber City,
Gurugram, Haryana - 122002
1 London Bridge Street, London, SE1 9GF, United Kingdom
2 Bloor Street East, Toronto, Ontario M4W 1A8, Canada
Lvl 13, 201 Elizabeth Street (PO Box A565, NSW, 1235), Sydney
NSW 2000, Australia
195 Broadway, New York, NY 10007, USA

Printed and bound at
Thomson Press (India) Ltd.

FSC
www.fsc.org
MIX
Paper from
responsible sources
FSC® C010615

This book is produced from independently certified FSC® paper
to ensure responsible forest management.

Acknowledgements

I wish to express my appreciation for their generous assistance to the following motion-picture and television producers: Seymour Berns, Larry Gelbart, Bert Granet, Harvey Orkin, Marty Rackin, David Swift, Robert Weitman.

And my deep gratitude for sharing with me their memories and experiences goes to: Marty Allen, Milton Berle, Red Buttons, George Burns, Jack Carter, Buddy Hackett, Groucho Marx, Jan Murray.

THE AUTHOR

Note to the Reader

The art of making others laugh is surely a wondrous gift from the gods. I affectionately dedicate this book to the comedians, the men and women who have that gift and share it with us. And to one of them in particular: my daughter's godfather, Groucho.

If you would seek to find yourself
Look not in a mirror
For there is but a shadow there,
A stranger . . .

SILENIUS, *Odes to Truth*

Prologue

On a Saturday morning in early November in 1969, a series of bizarre and inexplicable events occurred aboard the fifty-five-thousand-ton luxury liner SS *Bretagne* as it was preparing to sail from the Port of New York to Le Havre.

Claude Dessard, chief purser of the *Bretagne*, a capable and meticulous man, ran, as he was fond of saying, a 'tight ship'. In the fifteen years Dessard had served aboard the *Bretagne*, he had never encountered a situation he had not been able to deal with efficiently and discreetly. Considering that the SS *Bretagne* was a French ship, this was high tribute, indeed. However, on this particular summer day it was as though a thousand devils were conspiring against him. It was of small consolation to his sensitive Gallic pride that the intensive investigations conducted afterwards by the American and French branches of Interpol and the steamship line's own security forces failed to turn up a single plausible explanation for the extraordinary happenings of that day.

Because of the fame of the persons involved, the story was told in headlines all over the world, but the mystery remained unsolved.

As for Claude Dessard, he retired from the Cie Transatlantique and opened a bistro in Nice, where he never tired of reliving with his patrons that strange, unforgettable November day.

It had begun, Dessard recalled, with the delivery of flowers from the President of the United States.

One hour before sailing time, an official black limousine bearing government licence plates had driven up to Pier 92 on the lower Hudson River. A man wearing a charcoal-grey suit had disembarked from the car, carrying a bouquet of thirty-six Sterling Silver roses. He had made his way to the foot of the gangplank and exchanged a few words with Alain Safford, the *Bretagne*'s officer on duty. The flowers were ceremoniously transferred to Janin, a junior deck officer, who delivered them and then sought out Claude Dessard.

'I thought you might wish to know, Janin reported. 'Roses from the President to Mme Temple.'

Jill Temple. In the last year, her photograph had appeared on the front pages of daily newspapers and on magazine covers from New York to Bangkok and Paris to Leningrad. Claude Dessard recalled reading that she had been number one in a recent poll of the world's most admired women, and that a large number of newborn girls were being christened Jill. The United States of America had always had its heroines. Now, Jill Temple had become one. Her courage and the fantastic battle she had won and then so ironically lost had captured the imagination of the world. It was a great love story, but it was much more than that: it contained all the elements of classic Greek drama and tragedy.

Claude Dessard was not fond of Americans, but in this case he was delighted to make an exception. He had tremendous admiration for Mme Toby Temple. She was – and this was the highest accolade Dessard could tender

– *galante*. He resolved to see to it that her voyage on his ship would be a memorable one.

The chief purser turned his thoughts away from Jill Temple and concentrated on a final check of the passenger list. There was the usual collection of what the Americans referred to as VIPs, an acronym Dessard detested, particularly since Americans had such barbaric ideas about what made a person important. He noted that the wife of a wealthy industrialist was travelling alone. Dessard smiled knowingly and scanned the passenger list for the name of Matt Ellis, a black football star. When he found it, he nodded to himself, satisfied. Dessard was also interested to note that in adjoining cabins were a prominent senator and Carlina Rocca, a South American stripper, whose names had been linked in recent news stories. His eyes moved down the list.

David Kenyon. Money. An enormous amount of it. He had sailed on the *Bretagne* before. Dessard remembered David Kenyon as a good-looking, deeply tanned man with a lean, athletic body. A quiet, impressive man. Dessard put a CT, for captain's table, after David Kenyon's name.

Clifton Lawrence. A last-minute booking. A small frown appeared on the chief purser's face. Ah, here was a delicate problem. What did one do with Monsieur Lawrence? At one time the question would not even have been raised, for he would automatically have been seated at the captain's table, where he would have regaled everyone with amusing anecdotes. Clifton Lawrence was a theatrical agent who in his day represented many of the major stars in the entertainment business. But, alas, M. Lawrence's day was over. Where once the agent had always insisted on the luxurious Princess Suite, on this voyage he had booked a single room on a lower deck. First class, of course, but still . . . Claude Dessard decided he would reserve his decision until he had gone through the other names.

There was minor royalty aboard, a famous opera singer and a Nobel Prize-declining Russian novelist.

A knock at the door interrupted Dessard's concentration. Antoine, one of the porters, entered.

'Yes – what?' Claude Dessard asked.

Antoine regarded him with rheumy eyes. 'Did you order the theatre locked?'

Dessard frowned. 'What are you talking about?'

'I assumed it was you. Who else would do it? A few minutes ago I checked to see everything was in order. The doors were locked. It sounded like someone was inside the theatre, running a movie.'

'We never run films in port,' Dessard said firmly. 'And at no time are those doors locked. I'll look into it.'

Ordinarily, Claude Dessard would have investigated the report immediately, but now he was harassed by dozens of urgent last-minute details that had to be attended to before the twelve o'clock sailing. His supply of American dollars did not tally, one of the best suites had been booked twice by mistake, and the wedding gift ordered by Captain Montaigne had been delivered to the wrong ship. The captain was going to be furious. Dessard stopped to listen to the familiar sound of the ship's four powerful turbines starting. He felt the movement of the SS *Bretagne* as she slipped away from the pier and began backing her way into the channel. Then Dessard once again became engrossed in his problems.

Half an hour later, Léon, the chief veranda-deck

steward, came in. Dessard looked up, impatiently. 'Yes, Léon?'

'I'm sorry to bother you, but I thought you should know . . .'

'Hmm?' Dessard was only half listening, his mind on the delicate task of completing the seating arrangements for the captain's table for each night of the voyage. The captain was not a man gifted with social graces, and having dinner with his passengers every night was an ordeal for him. It was Dessard's task to see that the group was *agréable*.

'It's about Mme Temple . . .' Léon began.

Dessard instantly laid down his pencil and looked up, his small black eyes alert. 'Yes?'

'I passed her cabin a few minutes ago, and I heard loud voices and a scream. It was difficult to hear clearly through the door, but it sounded as though she was saying, "You've killed me, you've killed me." I thought it best not to interfere, so I came to tell you.'

Dessard nodded. 'You did well. I shall check to make certain that she is all right.'

Dessard watched the deck steward leave. It was unthinkable that anyone would harm a woman like Mme Temple. It was an outrage to Dessard's Gallic sense of chivalry. He put on his uniform cap, stole a quick look in the wall mirror and started for the door. The telephone rang. The chief purser hesitated, then picked it up. 'Dessard.'

'Claude – ' It was the third mate's voice. 'For Christ's sake, send someone down to the theatre with a mop, would you? There's blood all over the place.'

Dessard felt a sudden sinking sensation in the pit of his stomach. 'Right away,' Dessard promised. He hung up, arranged for a porter, then dialled the ship's physician.

'André? Claude.' He tried to make his voice casual. 'I was just wondering whether anyone has been in for medical treatment . . . No, no. I wasn't thinking of seasick pills. This person would be bleeding, perhaps badly . . . I see. Thank you.' Dessard hung up, filled with a growing sense of unease. He left his office and headed for Jill Temple's suite. He was halfway there when the next singular event occurred. As Dessard reached the boat deck, he felt the rhythm of the ship's motion change. He glanced out at the ocean and saw that they had arrived at the Ambrose Lightship, where they would drop their pilot tug and the liner would head for the open seas. But instead, the *Bretagne* was slowing to a stop. Something out of the ordinary was happening.

Dessard hurried to the railing and looked over the side. In the sea below, the pilot tug had been snugged against the cargo hatch of the *Bretagne*, and two sailors were transferring luggage from the liner to the tug. As Dessard watched, a passenger stepped from the ship's hatch onto the small boat. Dessard could only catch a glimpse of the person's back, but he was sure that he must have been mistaken in his identification. It was simply not possible. In fact, the incident of a passenger leaving the ship in this fashion was so extraordinary that the chief purser felt a small *frisson* of alarm. He turned and hurriedly made his way to Jill Temple's suite. There was no response to his knock. He knocked again, this time a little more loudly. 'Madame Temple . . . This is Claude Dessard, the chief purser. I was wondering if I might be of any service.'

There was no answer. By now, Dessard's internal warning system was screaming. His instincts told him that there was something terribly wrong, and he had a premonition that it centred, somehow, around this woman. A series of wild, outrageous thoughts danced through his brain. She had been murdered or kidnapped or – He tried the handle of the door. It was unlocked. Slowly, Dessard pushed the door open. Jill Temple was standing at the far end of the cabin, looking out the porthole, her back to him. Dessard opened his mouth to speak, but something in the frozen rigidity of her figure stopped him. He stood there awkwardly for a moment, debating whether to quietly withdraw, when suddenly the cabin was filled with an unearthly, keening sound, like an animal in pain. Helpless before such a deep private agony, Dessard withdrew, carefully closing the door behind him.

Dessard stood outside the cabin a moment, listening to the wordless cries from within. Then, deeply shaken, he turned and headed for the ship's theatre on the main deck. A porter was mopping up a trail of blood in front of the theatre.

Mon Dieu, Dessard thought. *What next?* He tried the door to the theatre. It was unlocked. Dessard entered the large, modern auditorium that could seat six hundred passengers. The auditorium was empty. On an impulse, he went to the projection booth. The door was locked. Only two people had keys to this door, he and the projectionist. Dessard opened it with his key and went inside. Everything seemed normal. He walked over to the two Century 35-mm projectors in the room and put his hands on them.

One of them was warm.

In the crew's quarters on D deck, Dessard found the projectionist, who assured him that he knew nothing about the theatre being used.

On the way back to his office, Dessard took a shortcut through the kitchen. The chef stopped him, in a fury. 'Look at this,' he commanded Dessard. 'Just look what some idiot has done!'

On a marble pastry table was a beautiful, six-tiered wedding cake, with delicate, spun-sugar figures of a bride and groom on top.

Someone had crushed in the head of the bride.

'It was at that moment,' Dessard would tell the spellbound patrons at his bistro, 'that I knew something terrible was about to happen.'

BOOK ONE

Chapter One

In 1919, Detroit, Michigan, was the single most successful industrial city in the world. World War I had ended, and Detroit had played a significant part in the Allies' victory, supplying them with tanks and trucks and aeroplanes. Now, with the threat of the Hun over, the automobile plants once again turned their energies to retooling for motorcars. Soon, four thousand automobiles a day were being manufactured, assembled and shipped. Skilled and unskilled labour came from all parts of the world to seek jobs in the automotive industry. Italians, Irish, Germans – they came in a flood tide.

Among the new arrivals were Paul Templarhaus and his bride, Frieda. Paul had been a butcher's apprentice in Munich. With the dowry he received when he married Frieda, he emigrated to New York and opened a butcher's shop, which quickly showed a deficit. He then moved to St Louis, Boston and, finally, Detroit, failing spectacularly in each city. In an era when business was booming and an increasing affluence meant a growing demand for meat, Paul Templarhaus managed to lose money everywhere he opened a shop. He was a good butcher but a hopelessly incompetent businessman. In truth he was more interested in writing poetry than in making money. He would spend hours dreaming up rhymes and poetic images. He would set them down on paper and mail them off to newspapers and magazines. but they never bought any of his masterpieces. To Paul, money was unimportant. He extended credit to everyone, and the word quickly spread; if you had no money and wanted the finest of meats, go to Paul Templarhaus.

Paul's wife, Frieda, was a plain-looking girl who had had no experience with men before Paul had come along and proposed to her – or, rather, as was proper – to her father. Frieda had pleaded with her father to accept Paul's suit, but the old man had needed no urging, for he had been desperately afraid he was going to be stuck with Frieda the rest of his life. He had even increased the dowry so that Frieda and her husband would be able to leave Germany and go to the New World.

Frieda had fallen shyly in love with her husband at first sight. She had never seen a poet before. Paul was thin and intellectual-looking with pale myopic eyes and receding hair, and it was months before Frieda could believe that this handsome young man truly belonged to her. She had no illusions about her own looks. Her figure was lumpy, the shape of an oversized, uncooked potato kugel. Her best feature was her vivid eyes, the colour of gentians, but the rest of her face seemed to belong to other people. Her nose was her grandfather's, large and bulbous, her forehead was an uncle's, high and sloping, and her chin was her father's, square and grim. Somewhere inside Frieda was a beautiful young girl, trapped with a face and body that God had given her as some kind of cosmic joke. But people could see only the formidable exterior. Except for Paul. Her Paul. It was just as well that Frieda never knew that her attraction lay in her dowry, which Paul saw as an escape from the bloody sides of beef and hog brains. Paul's dream had been to go into business for himself and make enough money so that he could devote himself to his beloved poetry.

Frieda and Paul went to an inn outside Salzburg for their honeymoon, a beautiful old castle on a lovely lake, surrounded by meadows and woods. Frieda had gone over the honeymoon-night scene a hundred times in her mind. Paul would lock the door and take her into his arms and murmur sweet endearments as he began to undress her. His lips would find hers and then slowly move down her naked body, the way they did it in all the little green books she had secretly read. His organ would be hard and erect and proud, like a German banner, and Paul would carry her to the bed (perhaps it would be safer if he *walked* her to it) and tenderly lay her down. *Mein Gott, Frieda,* he would say. *I love your body. You are not like those skinny little girls. You have the body of a woman.*

The actuality came as a shock. It was true that when they reached their room, Paul locked the door. After that, the reality was a stranger to the dream. As Frieda watched, Paul quickly stripped off his shirt, revealing a high, thin, hairless chest. Then he pulled down his pants. Between his legs lay a limp, tiny penis, hidden by a foreskin. It did not resemble in any way the exciting pictures Frieda had seen. Paul stretched out on the bed, waiting for her, and Frieda realized that he expected her to undress herself. Slowly, she began to take off her clothes. *Well, size is not everything,* Frieda thought. *Paul will be a wonderful lover.* Moments later, the trembling bride joined her groom on the marital bed. While she was waiting for him to say something romantic, Paul rolled over on top of her, made a few thrusts inside her, and rolled off again. For the stunned bride, it was finished before it began. As for Paul, his few previous sexual experiences had been with the whores of Munich, and he was reaching for his wallet when he remembered that he no longer had to pay for it. From now on it was free. Long after Paul had fallen asleep, Frieda lay in bed, trying not to think about her disappointment. *Sex is not everything,* she told herself. *My Paul will make a wonderful husband.*

As it turned out, she was wrong again.

It was shortly after the honeymoon that Frieda began to see Paul in a more realistic light. Frieda had been reared in the German tradition of a *Hausfrau*, and so she obeyed her husband without question, but she was far from stupid. Paul had no interest in life except his poems, and Frieda began to realize that they were very bad. She could not help but observe that Paul left a great deal to be desired in almost every area she could think of. Where Paul was indecisive, Frieda was firm, where Paul was stupid about business, Frieda was clever. In the beginning, she had sat by, silently suffering, while the head of the family threw away her handsome dowry by his softhearted idiocies. By the time they moved to Detroit, Frieda could stand it no longer. She marched into her husband's butcher's shop one day and took over the cash register. The first thing she did was to put up a sign: NO CREDIT. Her husband was appalled, but that was only the beginning. Frieda raised the prices of meat and began advertising, showering the neighbourhood with pamphlets, and the business expanded overnight From that moment on, it was Frieda who made all the important decisions, and Paul who followed them

Frieda's disappointment had turned her into a tyrant. She found that she had a talent for running things and people, and she was inflexible. It was Frieda who decided how their money was to be invested, where they would live, where they would vacation, and when it was time to have a baby.

She announced her decision to Paul one evening and put him to work on the project until the poor man almost suffered a nervous breakdown. He was afraid too much sex would undermine his health, but Frieda was a woman of great determination. 'Put it in me,' she would command.

'How *can* I?' Paul protested. 'It is not interested.'

Frieda would take his shrivelled little penis and pull back the foreskin, and when nothing happened, she would take it in her mouth – '*Mein Gott,* Frieda! What are you *doing*?' – until it got hard in spite of him, and she would insert it between her legs until Paul's sperm was inside her.

Three months after they began, Frieda told her husband that he could take a rest. She was pregnant. Paul wanted a girl and Frieda wanted a boy, so it was no surprise to any of their friends that the baby was a boy.

The baby, at Frieda's insistence, was delivered at home by a midwife. Everything went smoothly up to and throughout the actual delivery. It was then that those who were gathered around the bed got a shock. The newborn infant was normal in every way, except for its penis. The baby's organ was enormous, dangling like a swollen, outsized appendage between the baby's innocent thighs.

His father's not built like that, Frieda thought with fierce pride.

*

She named him Tobias, after an alderman who lived in their precinct. Paul told Frieda that he would take over the training of the boy. After all, it was the father's place to bring up his son.

Frieda listened and smiled, and seldom let Paul go near the child. It was Frieda who brought the boy up. She ruled him with a Teutonic fist, and she did not bother with the velvet glove. At five, Toby was a thin, spindly-legged child, with a wistful face and the bright, gentian-blue eyes of his mother. Toby adored his mother and hungered for her approval. He wanted her to pick him up and hold him on her big, soft lap so that he could press his head deep into her bosom. But Frieda had no time for such things. She was busy making a living for her family. She loved little Toby, and she was determined that he would not grow up to be a weakling like his father. Frieda demanded perfection in everything Toby did. When he began school, she would supervise his homework, and if he was puzzled by some assignment, his mother would admonish him, 'Come on, boy – roll up your sleeves!' And she would stand over him until he had solved the problem. The sterner Frieda was with Toby, the more he loved her. He trembled at the thought of displeasing her. Her punishment was swift and her praise was slow, but she felt that it was for Toby's own good. From the first moment her son had been placed in her arms, Frieda had known that one day he was going to become a famous and important man. She did not know how or when, but she knew it would happen. It was as though God had whispered it into her ear. Before her son was even old enough to understand what she was saying, Frieda would tell him of his greatness to come, and she never stopped telling him. And so, young Toby grew up knowing that he was going to be famous, but having no idea how or why. He only knew that his mother was never wrong.

Some of Toby's happiest moments occurred when he sat in the enormous kitchen doing his homework while his mother stood at the large old-fashioned stove and cooked. She would make heavenly smelling, thick black bean soup with whole frankfurters floating in it, and platters of succulent bratwurst, and potato pancakes with fluffy edges of brown lace. Or she would stand at the large chopping block in the middle of the kitchen, kneading dough with her thick, strong hands, then sprinkling a light snowflake of flour over it, magically transforming the dough into a mouthwatering *Pflaumenkuchen* or *Apfelkuchen*. Toby would go to her and throw his arms around her large body, his face reaching only up to her waist. The exciting female smell of her would become a part of all the exciting kitchen smells, and an unbidden sexuality would stir within him. At those moments Toby would gladly have died for her. For the rest of his life, the smell of fresh apples cooking in butter brought back an instant, vivid image of his mother.

One afternoon, when Toby was twelve years old, Mrs Durkin, the neighbourhood gossip, came to visit them. Mrs Durkin was a bony-faced woman with black, darting eyes and a tongue that was never still. When she departed, Toby did an imitation of her that had his mother roaring with laughter. It seemed to Toby that it was the first time he had ever heard her laugh. From that moment on, Toby looked for ways to entertain her. He would do devastating imitations of customers who came into the butcher's shop and of teachers and schoolmates, and his mother would go into gales of laughter.

Toby had finally discovered a way to win his mother's approval.

He tried out for a school play, *No Account David,* and was given the lead. On opening night, his mother sat in the front row and applauded her son's success. It was at that moment that Frieda knew how God's promise was going to come true.

It was the early 1930s, the beginning of the Depression, and movie theatres all over the country were trying every conceivable stratagem to fill their empty seats. They gave away dishes and radios, and had keno nights and bingo nights, and hired organists to accompany the bouncing ball while the audience sang along.

And they held amateur contests. Frieda would carefully check the theatrical section of the newspaper to see where contests were taking place. Then she would take Toby there and sit in the audience while he did his imitations of Al Jolson and James Cagney and Eddie Cantor and yell out, '*Mein Himmel!* What a talented boy!' Toby nearly always won first prize.

He had grown taller, but he was still thin, an earnest child with guileless, bright blue eyes set in the face of a cherub. One looked at him and instantly thought: *innocence.* When people saw Toby they wanted to put their arms around him and hug him and protect him from Life. They loved him and on stage they applauded him. For the first time Toby understood what he was destined to be; he was going to be a star, for his mother first, and God second.

Toby's libido began to stir when he was fifteen. He would masturbate in the bathroom, the one place he was assured of privacy, but that was not enough. He decided he needed a girl.

One evening, Clara Connors, the married sister of a classmate, drove Toby home from an errand he was doing for his mother. Clara was a pretty blonde with large breasts, and as Toby sat next to her, he began to get an erection. Nervously, he inched his hand across to her lap and began to fumble under her skirt, ready to withdraw instantly if she screamed. Clara was more amused than angry, but when Toby pulled out his penis and she saw the size of it, she invited him to her house the following afternoon and initiated Toby into the joys of sexual intercourse. It was a fantastic experience. Instead of a soapy hand, Toby had found a soft, warm receptacle that throbbed and grabbed at his penis. Clara's moans and screams made him grow hard again and again, so that he had orgasm after orgasm without ever leaving the warm, wet nest. The size of his penis had always been a source of secret shame to Toby. Now it had suddenly become his glory. Clara could not keep this phenomenon to herself, and soon Toby found himself servicing half a dozen married women in the neighbourhood.

During the next two years, Toby managed to deflower nearly half the girls in his class. Some of Toby's classmates were football heroes, or better looking than he, or rich – but where they failed, Toby succeeded. He was the funniest, cutest thing the girls had ever seen, and it was impossible to say no to that innocent face and those wistful blue eyes.

In Toby's senior year in high school, when he was eighteen, he was summoned to the principal's office. In the room were Toby's mother, grim-faced, – a sobbing sixteen-year-old Catholic girl named Eileen Henegan and her father, a uniformed police sergeant. The moment Toby entered the room, he knew he was in deep trouble.

'I'll come right to the point, Toby,' the principal said. 'Eileen is pregnant. She says you're the father of her child. Have you had a physical relationship with her?'

Toby's mouth suddenly went dry. All he could think of was how much Eileen had enjoyed it, how she had moaned and begged for more. And now this.

'Answer him you little son of a bitch!' Eileen's father bellowed. 'Did you touch my daughter?'

Toby sneaked a look at his mother. That she was here to witness his shame upset him more than anything else. He had let her down, disgraced her. She would be repelled by his behaviour. Toby resolved that if he ever got out of this, if God would only help him this once and perform some kind of miracle, he would never touch another girl as long as he lived. He would go straight to a doctor and have himself castrated, so that he would never even think about sex again, and . . .

'Toby . . .' His mother was speaking, her voice stern and cold, 'Did you go to bed with this girl?'

Toby swallowed, took a deep breath and mumbled, 'Yes, Mother.'

'Then you will marry her.' There was finality in her tone. She looked at the sobbing, puffy-eyed girl. 'Is that what you want?'

'Y-yes,' Eileen cried. 'I love Toby.' She turned to Toby. 'They *made* me tell. I didn't want to give them your name.'

Her father, the police sergeant, announced to the room at large, 'My daughter's only sixteen. It's statutory rape. He could be sent to jail for the rest of his miserable life. But if he's going to marry her . . .'

They all turned to look at Toby. He swallowed again and said, 'Yes, sir. I – I'm sorry it happened.'

During the silent ride home with his mother, Toby sat at her side, miserable, knowing how much he had hurt her. Now he would have to find a job to support Eileen and the child. He would probably have to go to work in the butcher's shop and forget his dreams, all his plans for the future. When they reached the house, his mother said to him, 'Come upstairs.'

Toby followed her to his room, steeling himself for a lecture. As he watched, she took out a suitcase and began packing his clothes. Toby stared at her, puzzled. 'What are you doing, Mama?'

'Me? I'm not doing anything. *You* are. You're going away from here.'

She stopped and turned to face him. 'Did you think I was going to let you throw your life away on that nothing of a girl? So you took her to bed and she's going to have a baby. That proves two things – that *you're* human, and *she's* stupid! Oh, no – no one traps my son into marriage. God meant you to be a big man, Toby. You'll go to New York, and when you're a famous star, you'll send for me.'

He blinked back tears and flew into her arms, and she cradled him in her enormous bosom. Toby suddenly felt lost and frightened of leaving her. And yet, there was an excitement within him, the exhilaration of embarking on a new life. He was going to be in Show Business. He was going to be a star; he was going to be famous.

His mother had said so.

Chapter Two

In 1939, New York City was a mecca for the theatre. The Depression was over. President Franklin Roosevelt had promised that there was nothing to fear but fear itself, that America would be the most prosperous nation on earth, and so it was. Everyone had money to spend. There were thirty shows playing on Broadway, and all of them seemed to be hits.

Toby arrived in New York with a hundred dollars his mother had given him. Toby knew he was going to be rich and famous. He would send for his mother and they would live in a beautiful penthouse and she would come to the theatre every night to watch the audience applaud him. In the meantime, he had to find a job. He went to the stage doors of all the Broadway theatres and told them about the amateur contests he had won and how talented he was. They threw him out. During the weeks that Toby hunted for a job, he sneaked into theatres and night-clubs and watched the top performers work, particularly the comedians. He saw Ben Blue and Joe E. Lewis and Frank Fay. Toby knew that one day he would be better than all of them.

His money running out, he took a job as a dishwasher. He telephoned his mother every Sunday morning, when the rates were cheaper. She told Toby about the furore caused by his running away.

'You should see them,' his mother said. 'The

policeman comes over here in his squad car every night. The way he carries on, you would think we were all gangsters. He keeps asking where you are.'

'What do you tell him?' Toby asked anxiously.

'The truth. That you slunk away like a thief in the night, and that if I ever got my hands on you I would personally wring your neck.'

Toby laughed aloud.

During the summer, Toby managed to get a job as an assistant to a magician, a beady-eyed, untalented mountebank who performed under the name of the Great Merlin. They played a series of second-rate hotels in the Catskills, and Toby's primary job was to haul the heavy paraphernalia in and out of Merlin's station wagon, and to guard the props, which consisted of six white rabbits, three canaries and two hamsters. Because of Merlin's fears that the props would 'get eaten', Toby was forced to live with them in rooms the size of broom closets, and it seemed to Toby that the whole summer consisted of one overpowering stench. He was in a state of physical exhaustion from carrying the heavy cabinets with trick sides and bottoms and running after props that were constantly escaping. He was lonely and disappointed. He sat staring at the dingy, little rooms, wondering what he was doing here and how this was going to get him started in show business. He practised his imitations in front of the mirror, and his audience consisted of Merlin's smelly little animals.

One Sunday as the summer was drawing to a close, Toby made his weekly telephone call home. This time it was his father who answered.

'It's Toby, Pop. How are you?'

There was a silence.

'Hello! Are you there?'

'I'm here, Toby.' Something in his father's voice chilled Toby.

'Where's Mom?'

'They took her to the hospital last night.'

Toby clutched the receiver so hard that it almost broke in his fist. 'What happened to her?'

'The doctor said it was a heart attack.'

No! Not his mother! 'She's going to be all right,' Toby demanded. 'Isn't she?' He was screaming into the mouthpiece. 'Tell me she's going to be all right, goddamn you!'

From a million miles away he could hear his father crying. 'She – she died a few hours ago, son.'

The words washed over Toby like white-hot lava, burning him, scalding him, until his body felt as though it were on fire. His father was lying. She *couldn't* be dead. They had a pact. Toby was going to be famous and his mother was going to be at his side. There was a beautiful penthouse waiting for her, and a limousine and chauffeur and furs and diamonds . . . He was sobbing so hard he could not breathe. He heard the distant voice saying, 'Toby! Toby!'

'I'm on my way home. When is the funeral?'

'Tomorrow,' his father said. 'But you mustn't come here. They'll be expecting you, Toby. Eileen is going to have her baby soon. Her father wants to kill you. They'll be looking for you at the funeral.'

So he could not even say goodbye to the only person in the world he loved. Toby lay in his bed all that day, remembering. The images of his mother were so vivid and alive. She was in the kitchen, cooking, telling him what an important man he was going to be, and at the theatre, sitting in the front row and calling out, '*Mein Himmel!* What a talented boy!'

And laughing at his imitations and jokes. And packing his suitcase. *When you're a famous star, you'll send for me.* He lay there, numbed with grief, thinking, *I'll never forget this day. Not as long as I live. August the fourteenth, 1939. This is the most important day of my life.*

He was right. Not because of the death of his mother but because of an event that was taking place in Odessa, Texas, fifteen hundred miles away.

The hospital was an anonymous four-story building, the colour of charity. Inside was a rabbit warren of cubicles designed to diagnose sickness, alleviate it, cure it or sometimes bury it. It was a medical supermarket, and there was something there for everyone.

It was four a.m., the hour of quiet death or fitful sleep. A time for the hospital staff to have a respite before girding for the battles of another day.

The obstetrical team in Operating Room 4 was in trouble. What had started out as a routine delivery had suddenly turned into an emergency. Up until the actual delivery of the baby of Mrs Karl Czinski, everything had been normal. Mrs Czinski was a healthy woman in her prime, with wide peasant hips that were an obstetrician's dream. Accelerated contractions had begun, and things were moving along according to schedule.

'Breech delivery,' Dr Wilson, the obstetrician, announced. The words caused no alarm. Although only three per cent of births are breech deliveries – the lower part of the infant emerging first – they are usually handled with ease. There are three types of breech deliveries: spontaneous, where no help is required; assisted, where the obstetrician lends nature a hand; and a complete 'breakup', where the baby is wedged in the mother's womb.

Dr Wilson noted with satisfaction that this was going to be a spontaneous delivery, the simplest kind. He watched the baby's feet emerge, followed by two small legs. There was another contraction from the mother, and the baby's thighs appeared.

'We're almost there,' Dr Wilson said encouragingly. 'Bear down once more.'

Mrs Czinski did. Nothing happened.

He frowned. 'Try again. Harder.'

Nothing.

Dr Wilson placed his hands on the baby's legs and tugged, very gently. There was no movement. He squeezed his hand past the baby, through the narrow passage into the uterus, and began to explore. Beads of perspiration suddenly appeared on his forehead. The maternity nurse moved close to him and mopped his brow.

'We've got a problem,' Dr Wilson said, in a low voice.

Mrs Czinski heard. 'What's wrong?' she asked.

'Everything's fine.' Dr Wilson reached in farther, gently trying to push the infant downward. It would not budge. He could feel the umbilical cord compressed between the baby's body and the maternal pelvis, cutting off the baby's blood supply.

'Fetoscope!'

The maternity nurse reached for the instrument and applied it to the mother's belly, listening for the baby's heartbeat. 'It's down to thirty,' she reported. 'And there's marked arrhythmia.'

Dr Wilson's fingers were inside the mother's body, like remote antennae of his brain, probing, searching.

'I'm losing the foetal heartbeat – ' There was alarm in the maternity nurse's voice. 'It's negative!'

They had a dying baby inside the womb. There was still a slim chance that baby could be revived if they could get it out in time. They had a maximum of four minutes to deliver it, clear its lungs and get its tiny heart beating again. After four minutes, brain damage would be massive and irreversible.

'Clock it,' Dr Wilson ordered.

Everyone in the room instinctively glanced up as the electric clock on the wall clicked to the twelve o'clock position, and the large red second hand began making its first sweep.

The delivery team went to work. An emergency respiratory tank was wheeled to the table while Dr Wilson tried to dislodge the infant from the pelvic floor. He began the Bracht manoeuvre, trying to shift the infant around, twisting its shoulders so that it could clear the vaginal opening. It was useless.

A student nurse, participating in her first delivery, felt suddenly ill. She hurried out of the room.

Outside the door of the operating room stood Karl Czinski, nervously kneading his hat in his large, calloused hands. This was the happiest day of his life. He was a carpenter, a simple man who believed in early marriage and large families. This child would be their first, and it was all he could do to contain his excitement. He loved his wife very much, and he knew that without her he would be lost. He was thinking about his wife as the student nurse came rushing out of the delivery room, and he called to her, 'How is she?'

The distraught young nurse, her mind preoccupied with the baby, cried, 'She's dead, she's dead!' and hurried away to be sick.

Mr Czinski's face went white. He clutched his chest and began gasping for air. By the time they got him to the emergency ward, he was beyond help.

Inside the delivery room, Dr Wilson was working frantically, racing the clock. He could reach inside and touch the umbilical cord and feel the pressure against it, but there was no way to release it. Every impulse in him screamed for him to pull the half-delivered baby out by force, but he had seen what happened to babies that had been delivered that way. Mrs Czinski was moaning now, half delirious.

'Bear down, Mrs Czinski. Harder! Come on!'

It was no use. Dr Wilson glanced at the clock. Two precious minutes were gone, without any blood circulating through the baby's brain. Dr Wilson faced another problem: what was he going to do if the baby were saved *after* the four minutes had elapsed? Let it live and become a vegetable? Or let it have a merciful, quick death? He put the thought out of his mind and began to move faster. Closing his eyes, working by touch, all his concentration focused on what was happening inside the woman's body. He tried the Mauriceau-Smellie-Veit manoeuvre, a complicated series of moves designed to loosen and free the baby's body. And suddenly there was a shift. He felt it begin to move. 'Piper forceps!'

The maternity nurse swiftly handed him the special forceps and Dr Wilson reached in and placed them around the baby's head. A moment later the head emerged.

The baby was delivered.

This was always the instant of glory, the miracle of a newly created life, red-faced and bawling, complaining of the indignity of being forced out of that quiet, dark womb into the light and the cold.

But not this baby. This baby was blue-white and still. It was a female.

The clock. A minute and a half left. Every move was swiftly mechanical now, the result of long years of practice. Gauzed fingers cleared the back of the infant's pharynx so air could get into the laryngeal opening. Dr Wilson placed the baby flat on its back. The maternity nurse handed him a small-size laryngoscope connecting with an electric suction apparatus. He set it in place and nodded, and the nurse clicked a switch. The rhythmic sucking sound of the machine began.

Dr Wilson looked up at the clock.

Twenty seconds left to go. Heartbeat negative.

Fifteen . . . fourteen . . . Heartbeat negative.

The moment of decision was at hand. It might already be too late to prevent brain damage. No one could ever be really sure about these things. He had seen hospital wards filled with pathetic creatures with the bodies of adults and the minds of children, or worse.

Ten seconds. And no pulse, not even a thread to give him hope.

Five seconds. He made his decision then, and hoped that God would understand and forgive him. He was going to pull the plug, say that the baby could not be saved. No one would question his action. He felt the baby's skin once more. It was cold and clammy.

Three seconds.

He looked down at the infant and he wanted to weep. It was such a pity. She was a pretty baby. She would have grown up to be a beautiful woman. He wondered what her life would have been like. Would she have gotten married and had children? Or perhaps become an artist or a teacher or a business executive? Would she have been rich or poor? Happy or unhappy?

One second. Negative heartbeat.

Zero.

He reached his hand towards the switch, and at that instant the baby's heart began to beat. It was a tentative, irregular spasm, and then another and then it steadied down to a strong, regular beat. There was a spontaneous cheer in the room and cries of congratulation. Dr Wilson was not listening.

He was staring up at the clock on the wall.

Her mother named her Josephine, after her grandmother in Krakow. A middle name would have been pretentious for the daughter of a Polish seamstress in Odessa, Texas.

For reasons that Mrs Czinski did not understand, Dr Wilson insisted that Josephine be brought back to the hospital for an examination every six weeks. The conclusions each time were the same: she *seemed* normal.

Only time would tell.

Chapter Three

On Labour Day, the summer season in the Catskills was over and the Great Merlin was out of a job, and along with him, Toby. Toby was free to go. But where? He was homeless, jobless and penniless. Toby's decision was made for him when a guest offered him twenty-five dollars to drive her and her three young children from the Catskills to Chicago.

Toby left without saying goodbye to the Great Merlin or his smelly props.

Chicago, in 1939, was a prosperous, wide-open city. It was a city with a price, and those who knew their way around could buy anything from women to dope to politicians. There were hundreds of nightclubs that catered to every taste. Toby made the rounds of all of them, from the big, brassy Chez Paree to the little bars on Rush Street. The answer was always the same. No one wanted to hire a young punk as a comic. The sands were running out for Toby. It was time he started to fulfil his mother's dream.

He was almost nineteen years old.

One of the clubs Toby hung around was the Knee High, where the entertainment consisted of a tired three-piece combo, a broken-down, middle-aged drunken comic and two strippers, Meri and Jeri, who were billed as the

Perry Sisters and were, improbably enough, really sisters. They were in their twenties, and attractive in a cheap, blowsy way. Jeri came up to the bar one evening and sat next to Toby. He smiled and said politely, 'I like your act.'

Jeri turned to look at him and saw a naive, baby-faced kid, too young and too poorly dressed to be a mark. She nodded indifferently and started to turn away, when Toby stood up. Jeri stared at the telltale bulge in his pants, then turned to look up at the innocent young face again. 'Jesus Christ,' she said. 'Is that all you?'

He smiled. 'There's only one way to find out.'

At three o'clock that morning, Toby was in bed with both of the Perry Sisters.

Everything had been meticulously planned. One hour before showtime, Jeri had taken the club comic, a compulsive gambler, to an apartment on Diversey Avenue where a crap game was in progress. When he saw the action, he licked his lips and said, 'We can stay only a minute.'

Thirty minutes later, when Jeri slipped away, the comic was rolling the dice, screaming like a maniac, 'An eighter from Decatur, you son of a bitch!' lost in some fantasy world where success and stardom and riches all hung on each roll of the dice.

At the Knee High, Toby sat at the bar, neat and tidy, waiting.

When showtime came and the comic had not appeared, the owner of the club began to rage and curse. 'That bastard's through this time, you hear? I won't have him near my club again.'

'I don't blame you,' Meri said. 'But you're in luck.

There's a new comic sitting at the bar. He just got in from New York.'

'What? Where?' The owner took one look at Toby. 'For chrissakes, where's his nanny? He's a baby!'

'He's great!' Jeri said. And she meant it.

'Try him,' Meri added. 'What can you lose?'

'My fuckin' customers!' But he shrugged and walked over to where Toby was sitting. 'So you're a comic, huh?'

'Yeah,' Toby said casually. 'I just finished doing a gig in the Catskills.'

The owner studied him a moment. 'How old are you?'

'Twenty-two,' Toby lied.

'Horseshit. All right. Get out there. And if you lay an egg, you won't *live* to see twenty-two.'

And there it was. Toby Temple's dream had finally come true. He was standing in the spotlight while the band played a fanfare for him, and the audience, *his* audience, sat there waiting to discover him, to adore him. He felt a surge of affection so strong that the feeling brought a lump to his throat. It was as though he and the audience were one, bound together by some wonderful, magical cord. For an instant he thought of his mother and hoped that wherever she was, she could see him now. The fanfare stopped. Toby went into his routine.

'Good evening, you lucky people. My name is Toby Temple. I guess you all know *your* names.'

Silence.

He went on. 'Did you hear about the new head of the Mafia in Chicago? He's a queer. From now on, the Kiss of Death includes dinner and dancing.'

There was no laughter. They were staring at him, cold and hostile, and Toby began to feel the sharp claws of fear tearing at his stomach. His body was suddenly soaked in perspiration. That wonderful bond with the audience had vanished.

He kept going. 'I just played an engagement in a theatre up in Maine. The theatre was so far back in the woods that the manager was a bear.'

Silence. They hated him.

'Nobody told me this was a deaf-mute convention. I feel like the social director on the *Titanic*. Being here is like walking up the gangplank and there's no ship.'

They began to boo. Two minutes after Toby had begun, the owner frantically signalled to the musicians, who started to play loudly, drowning out Toby's voice. He stood there, a big smile on his face, his eyes stinging with tears.

He wanted to scream at them.

It was the screams that awakened Mrs Czinski. They were high-pitched and feral, eerie in the stillness of the night, and it was not until she sat up in bed that she realized it was the baby screaming. She hurried into the other room where she had fixed up a nursery. Josephine was rolling from side to side, her face blue from convulsions. At the hospital, an intern gave the baby an intravenous sedative, and she fell into a peaceful sleep. Dr Wilson, who had delivered Josephine, gave her a thorough examination. He could find nothing wrong with her. But he was uneasy. He could not forget the clock on the wall.

Chapter Four

Vaudeville had flourished in America from 1881 until its final demise when the Palace Theatre closed its doors in 1932. Vaudeville had been the training ground for all the aspiring young comics, the battlefield where they sharpened their wits against hostile, jeering audiences. However, the comics who won out went on to fame and fortune. Eddie Cantor and W. C. Fields, Jolson and Benny, Abbott and Costello, and Jessel and Burns and the Marx Brothers, and dozens more. Vaudeville was a hamen, a steady pay cheque, but with vaudeville dead, comics had to turn to other fields. The big names were booked for radio shows and personal appearances, and they also played the important nightclubs around the country. For the struggling young comics like Toby, however, it was another story. They played nighclubs, too, but it was a different world. It was called the Toilet Circuit, and the name was a euphemism. It consisted of dirty saloons all over the country where the great unwashed public gathered to guzzle beer and belch at the strippers and destroy the comics for sport. The dressing rooms were stinking toilets, smelling of stale food and spilled drinks and urine and cheap perfume and, overlaying it all, the rancid odour of fear: flop sweat. The toilets were so filthy that the female performers squatted over the dressing room sinks to urinate. Payment varied from an indigestible meal to five, ten or sometimes as much as fifteen dollars a night, depending on the audience reaction.

Toby Temple played them all, and they became his school. The names of the towns were different, but the places were all the same, and the smells were the same, and the hostile audiences were the same. If they did not like a performer, they threw beer bottles at him and heckled him throughout his performance and whistled him off. It was a tough school, but it was a good one, because it taught Toby all the tricks of survival. He learned to deal with drunken tourists and sober hoodlums, and never to confuse the two. He learned how to spot a potential heckler and quiet him by asking him for a sip of his drink or borrowing his napkin to mop his brow.

Toby talked himself into jobs at places with names like Lake Kiamesha and Shawanga Lodge and the Avon. He played Wildwood, New Jersey, and the B'nai B'rith and the Sons of Italy and Moose halls.

And he kept learning.

Toby's act consisted of parodies of popular songs, imitations of Gable and Grant and Bogart and Cagney, and material stolen from the big-name comics who could afford expensive writers. All the struggling comics stole their material, and they bragged about it. 'I'm doing Jerry Lester' – meaning they were using his material – 'and I'm twice as good as he is.' 'I'm doing Milton Berle.' 'You should see my Red Skelton.'

Because material was the key, they stole only from the best.

Toby would try anything. He would fix the indifferent, hard-faced audience with his wistful blue eyes and say, 'Did you ever see an Eskimo pee?' He would put his two hands in front of his fly, and ice cubes would dribble out.

He would put on a turban and wrap himself in a sheet. 'Abdul, the snake charmer,' he would intone. He would play a flute, and out of a wicker basket a cobra began to appear, moving rhythmically to the music as Toby pulled wires. The snake's body was a douche bag, and its head was the nozzle. There was always someone in the audience who thought it was funny.

He did the standards and the stockies and the platters, where you laid the jokes in their laps.

He had dozens of *shticks*. He had to be ready to switch from one *bit* to another, before the beer bottles started flying.

And no matter where he played, there was always the sound of a flushing toilet during his act.

Toby travelled across the country by bus. When he arrived at a new town he would check into the cheapest hotel or boarding house and size up the nightclubs and bars and horse parlours. He stuffed cardboard in the soles of his shoes and whitened his shirt collars with chalk to save on laundry. The towns were all dreary, and the feed was always bad; but it was the loneliness that ate into him. He had no one. There was not a single person in the vast universe who cared whether he lived or died. He wrote to his father from time to time, but it was out of a sense of duty rather than love. Toby desperately needed someone to talk to, someone who would understand him, share his dreams with him.

He watched the successful entertainers leave the big clubs with their entourages and their beautiful, classy girls and drive off in shiny limousines, and Toby envied them. *Someday . . .*

The worst moments were when he flopped, when he was booed in the middle of his act, thrown out before he had a chance to get started. At those times Toby hated the people in the audience; he wanted to kill them. It wasn't only that he had failed, it was that he had failed at the bottom. He could go down no further; he was *there.* He hid in his hotel room and cried and begged God to leave him alone, to take away his desire to stand in front of an audience and entertain them. *God,* he prayed, *let me want to be a shoe salesman or a butcher. Anything but this.* His mother had been wrong. God had not singled him out. He was never going to be famous. Tomorrow, he would find some other line of work. He would apply for a nine-to-five job in an office and live like a normal human being.

And the next night Toby would be on the stage again, doing his imitations, telling jokes, trying to win over the people before they turned on him and attacked.

He would smile at them innocently and say, 'This man was in love with his duck, and he took it to a movie with him one night. The cashier said, "You can't bring that duck in here", so the man went around the corner and stuffed the duck down the front of his trousers, bought a ticket and went inside. The duck started getting restless, so the man opened up his fly and let the duck's head out. Well, next to the man was a lady and her husband. She turned to her husband and said, "Ralph, the man next to me has his penis out." So Ralph said, "Is he bothering you?" "No," she said. "Okay. Then forget it and enjoy the movie." A few minutes later the wife nudged her husband again. "Ralph – his penis – " And her husband said, "I told you to ignore it." And she said, "I can't – it's eating my popcorn!"'

He made one-night appearances at the Three Six Five in San Francisco, Rudy's Rail in New York and Kin Wa Low's in Toledo. He played plumbers' conventions and bar mitzvahs and bowling banquets.

And he learned.

He did four and five shows a day at small theatres named the Gem and the Odeon and the Empire and the Star.

And he learned.

And, finally, one of the things that Toby Temple learned was that he could spend the rest of his life playing the Toilet Circuit, unknown and undiscovered. But an event occurred that made the whole matter academic.

On a cold Sunday afternoon in early December in 1941, Toby was playing a five-a-day act at the Dewey Theater on Fourteenth Street in New York. There were eight acts on the bill, and part of Toby's job was to introduce them. The first show went well. During the second show, when Toby introduced the Flying Kanazawas, a family of Japanese acrobats, the audience began to hiss them. Toby retreated back-stage. 'What the hell's the matter with them out there?' he asked.

'Jesus, haven't you heard? The Japs attacked Pearl Harbor a few hours ago,' the stage manager told him.

'So what?' Toby asked. 'Look at those guys – they're great.'

The next show, when it was the turn of the Japanese troupe, Toby went out on stage and said, 'Ladies and gentlemen, it's a great privilege to present to you, fresh from their triumph in Manila – the Flying Filipinos!' The moment the audience saw the Japanese troupe, they began to hiss. During the rest of the day Toby turned them into the Happy Hawaiians, the Mad Mongolians and, finally, the Eskimo Flyers. But he was unable to save them. Nor, as it turned out, himself. When he telephoned his father that evening, Toby learned that there was a letter waiting for him at home. It began, 'Greetings', and was signed by the President. Six weeks later, Toby was sworn into the United States Army. The day he was inducted, his head was pounding so hard that he was barely able to take the oath.

The headaches came often, and when they happened, little Josephine felt as though two giant hands were squeezing her temples. She tried not to cry, because it upset her mother. Mrs Czinski had discovered religion. She had always secretly felt that in some way she and her baby were responsible for the death of her husband. She had wandered into a revival meeting one afternoon, and the minister had thundered, 'You are all soaked in sin and wickedness. The God that holds you over the pit of Hell like a loathsome insect over a fire abhors you. You hang by a slender thread, every damned one of you, and the flames of His wrath will consume you unless you repent!' Mrs Czinski instantly felt better, for she knew that she was hearing the word of the Lord.

'It's a punishment from God because we killed your father,' her mother would tell Josephine, and while she was too young to understand what the words meant, she knew that she had done something bad, and she wished she knew what it was, so that she could tell her mother that she was sorry.

Chapter Five

In the beginning, Toby Temple's war was a nightmare.

In the army, he was a nobody, a serial number in a uniform like millions of others, faceless, nameless, anonymous.

He was sent to basic training camp in Georgia and then shipped out to England, where his outfit was assigned to a camp in Sussex. Toby told the sergeant he wanted to see the commanding general. He got as far as a captain. The captain's name was Sam Winters. He was a dark-complexioned, intelligent-looking man in his early thirties. 'What's your problem, soldier?'

'It's like this, Captain,' Toby began. 'I'm an entertainer. I'm in show business. That's what I did in civilian life.'

Captain Winters smiled at his earnestness. 'What exactly do you do?' he asked.

'A little of everything,' Toby replied. 'I do imitations and parodies and . . .' He saw the look in the captain's eyes and ended lamely, 'things like that.'

'Where have you worked?'

Toby started to speak, then stopped. It was hopeless. The captain would only be impressed by places like New York and Hollywood. 'No place you would have heard of,' Toby replied. He knew now that he was wasting his time.

Captain Winters said, 'It's not up to me, but I'll see what I can do.'

'Sure,' Toby said. 'Thanks a lot, Captain.' He gave a salute and exited.

Captain Sam Winters sat at his desk, thinking about Toby long after the boy had gone. Sam Winters had enlisted because he felt that this was a war that had to be fought and had to be won. At the same time he hated it for what it was doing to young kids like Toby Temple. But if Temple really had talent, it would come through sooner or later, for talent was like a frail flower growing under solid rock. In the end, nothing could stop it from bursting through and blooming. Sam Winters had given up a good job as a motion-picture producer in Hollywood to go into the army. He had produced several successful pictures for Pan-Pacific Studios and had seen dozens of young hopefuls like Toby Temple come and go. The least they deserved was a chance. Later that afternoon he spoke to Colonel Beech about Toby. 'I think we should let Special Services audition him,' Captain Winters said. 'I have a feeling he might be good. God knows the boys are going to need all the entertainment they can get.'

Colonel Beech stared up at Captain Winters and said coolly, 'Right, Captain. Send me a memo on it.' He watched as Captain Winters walked out the door. Colonel Beech was a professional soldier, a West Point man, and the son of a West Point man. The Colonel despised all civilians, and to him, Captain Winters was a civilian. Putting on a uniform and captain's bars did not make a man a soldier. When Colonel Beech received Captain Winters' memo on Toby Temple, he glanced at it, then savagely scribbled across it, 'REQUEST DENIED', and initialled it.

He felt better.

What Toby missed most was the lack of an audience. He needed to work on his sense of timing, his skills. He would tell jokes and do imitations and routines at every opportunity. It did not matter whether his audience was two GIs doing guard duty with him in a lonely field, a busload of soldiers on their way into town or a dishwasher on KP. Toby had to make them laugh, win their applause.

Captain Sam Winters watched one day as Toby went through one of his routines in the recreation hall. Afterwards, he went up to Toby and said, 'I'm sorry your transfer didn't work out, Temple. I think you have talent. When the war's over, if you get to Hollywood, look me up.' He grinned and added, 'Assuming I still have a job out there.'

The following week Toby's battalion was sent into combat.

In later years, when Toby recalled the war, what he remembered was not the battles. At Saint-Lô he had been a smash doing a mouth-sync act to a Bing Crosby record. At Aachen he had sneaked into the hospital and told jokes to the wounded for two hours before the nurses threw him out. He remembered with satisfaction that one GI had laughed so hard all his stitches had broken open. Metz was where he had bombed out, but Toby felt that that was only because the audience was jittery about the Nazi planes flying overhead.

The fighting that Toby did was incidental. He was cited for bravery in the capture of a German command post. Toby had really had no idea what was going on. He had been playing John Wayne, and had got so carried away that it was all over before he had time to be frightened.

To Toby, it was the entertaining that was important. In Cherbourg he visited a whorehouse with a couple of friends, and while they were upstairs, Toby stayed in the parlour doing a routine for the madame and two of her girls. When he had finished, the madame sent him upstairs, on the house.

That was Toby's war. All in all, it was not a bad war, and time went by very quickly. When the war ended, it was 1945 and Toby was almost twenty-five years old. In appearance he had not aged one day. He had the same sweet face and beguiling blue eyes, and that hapless air of innocence about him.

Everyone was talking about going home. There was a bride waiting in Kansas City, a mother and father in Bayonne, a business in St Louis. There was nothing waiting for Toby. Except Fame.

He decided to go to Hollywood. It was time that God made good on His promise.

'Do you know God? Have you seen the face of Jesus? I have seen Him, brothers and sisters, and I have heard His voice, but He speaks only to those who kneel before Him and confess their sins. God abhors the unrepentant. The bow of God's wrath is bent and the flaming arrow of His righteous anger is pointed at your wicked hearts, and at any moment He will let go and the arrow of His retribution shall smite your hearts! Look up to Him now, before it is too late!'

Josephine looked up towards the top of the tent, terrified, expecting to see a flaming arrow shooting at her. She clutched her mother's hand, but her mother was unaware of it. Her face was flushed and her eyes were bright with fervour.

'Praise Jesus!' the congregation roared.

The revival meetings were held in a huge tent, on the outskirts of Odessa, and Mrs Czinski took Josephine to all of them. The preacher's pulpit was a wooden platform raised six feet above the ground. Immediately in front of the platform was the glory pen, where sinners were brought to repent and experience conversion. Beyond the pen were rows and rows of hard wooden benches, packed with chanting, fanatic seekers of salvation, awed by the threats of Hell and Damnation. It was terrifying for a six-year-old child. The evangelists were Fundamentalists, Holy Rollers and Pentecostalists and Methodists and Adventists, and they all breathed Hellfire and Damnation.

'Get on your knees, O ye sinners, and tremble before the might of Jehovah! For your wicked ways have broken the heart of Jesus Christ, and for that ye shall bear the punishment of His Father's wrath! Look around at the faces of the young children here, conceived in lust and filled with sin.'

And little Josephine would burn with shame, feeling everyone staring at her. When the bad headaches came, Josephine knew that they were a punishment from God. She prayed every night that they would go away, so she would know that God had forgiven her. She wished she knew what she had done that was so bad.

'And I'll sing Hallelujah, and you'll sing Hallelujah, and we'll all sing Hallelujah when we arrive at Home.'

'Liquor is the blood of the Devil, and tobacco is his breath, and fornication is his pleasure. Are you guilty of

trafficking with Satan? Then you shall burn eternally in Hell, damned for ever, because Lucifer is coming to get you!'

And Josephine would tremble and look around wildly, fiercely clutching the wooden bench so that the Devil could not take her.

They sang, 'I want to get to Heaven, my long-sought rest.' But little Josephine misunderstood and sang, 'I want to get to Heaven with my long short dress.'

After the thundering sermons would come the Miracles. Josephine would watch in frightened fascination as a procession of crippled men and women limped and crawled and rode in wheelchairs to the glory pen, where the preacher laid hands on them and willed the powers of Heaven to heal them. They would throw away their canes and their crutches, and some of them would babble hysterically in strange tongues, and Josephine would cower in terror.

The revival meetings always ended with the plate being passed. 'Jesus is watching you – and He hates a miser.' And then it would be over. But the fear would stay with Josephine for a long time.

In 1946, the town of Odessa, Texas, had a dark brown taste. Long ago, when the Indians had lived there, it had been the taste of desert sand. Now it was the taste of oil.

There were two kinds of people in Odessa: Oil People and the Others. The Oil People did not look *down* on the Others – they simply felt sorry for them, for surely God meant everyone to have private planes and Cadillacs and swimming pools and to give champagne parties for a hundred people. That was why He had put oil in Texas.

Josephine Czinski did not know that she was one of the Others. At six, Josephine Czinski was a beautiful child, with shiny black hair and deep brown eyes and a lovely oval face.

Josephine's mother was a skilled seamstress who worked for the wealthy people in town, and she would take Josephine along as she fitted the Oil Ladies and turned bolts of fairy cloth into stunning evening gowns. The Oil People liked Josephine because she was a polite, friendly child, and they liked themselves for liking her. They felt it was democratic of them to allow a poor kid from the other side of town to associate with their children. Josephine was Polish, but she did not look Polish, and while she could never be a member of the Club, they were happy to give her visitors' privileges. Josephine was allowed to play with the Oil Children and share their bicycles and ponies and hundred-dollar dolls, so that she came to live a dual life. There was her life at home in the tiny clapboard cottage with battered furniture and outdoor plumbing and doors that sagged on their hinges. Then there was Josephine's life in beautiful colonial mansions on large country estates. If Josephine stayed overnight at Cissy Topping's or Lindy Ferguson's, she was given a large bedroom all to herself, with breakfast served by maids and butlers. Josephine loved to get up in the middle of the night when everyone was asleep and go down and stare at the beautiful things in the house, the lovely paintings and heavy monogrammed silver and antiques burnished by time and history. She would study them and caress them and tell herself that one day she would have such things, one day she would live in a grand house and be surrounded by beauty.

But in both of Josephine's worlds, she felt lonely. She was afraid to talk to her mother about her headaches and her fear of God because her mother had become a brooding fanatic, obsessed with God's punishment, welcoming it. Josephine did not want to discuss her fears with the Oil Children because they expected her to be bright and gay, as they were. And so, Josephine was forced to keep her terrors to herself.

On Josephine's seventh birthday, Brubaker's Department Store announced a photographic contest for the Most Beautiful Child in Odessa. The entry picture had to be taken in the photograph department of the store. The prize was a gold cup inscribed with the name of the winner. The cup was placed in the department-store window, and Josephine walked by the window every day to stare at it. She wanted it more than she had ever wanted anything in her life. Josephine's mother would not let her enter the contest. – 'Vanity is the devil's mirror,' she said – but one of the Oil Women who liked Josephine paid for her picture. From that moment on, Josephine knew that the gold cup was hers. She could visualize it sitting on her dresser. She would polish it carefully every day. When Josephine found out that she was in the finals, she was too excited to go to school. She stayed in bed all day with an upset stomach, her happiness too much for her to bear. This would be the first time that she had owned anything beautiful.

The following day Josephine learned that the contest had been won by Tina Hudson, one of the Oil Children. Tina was not nearly as beautiful as Josephine, but Tina's father happened to be on the board of directors of the chain that owned Brubaker's Department Store.

When Josephine heard the news, she developed a headache that made her want to scream with pain. She was afraid for God to know how much that beautiful gold cup meant to her, but He must have known because her headaches continued. At night she would cry into her pillow, so that her mother could not hear her.

A few days after the contest ended, Josephine was invited to Tina's home for a weekend. The gold cup was sitting in Tina's room on a mantel. Josephine stared at it for a long time.

When Josephine returned home, the cup was hidden in her overnight case. It was still there when Tina's mother came for it and took it back.

Josephine's mother gave her a hard whipping with a switch made from a long, green twig. But Josephine was not angry with her mother.

The few minutes Josephine had held the beautiful gold cup in her hands had been worth all the pain.

Chapter Six

Hollywood, California, in 1946, was the film capital of the world, a magnet for the talented, the greedy, the beautiful, the hopeful and the weird. It was the land of palm trees and Rita Hayworth and the Holy Temple of the Universal Spirit and Santa Anita. It was the agent who was going to make you an overnight star; it was a con game, a whorehouse, an orange grove, a shrine. It was a magical kaleidoscope, and each person who looked into it saw his own vision.

To Toby Temple, Hollywood was where he was meant to come. He arrived in town with an army duffel bag and three hundred dollars in cash, moving into a cheap boarding house on Cahuenga Boulevard. He had to get into action fast, before he went broke. Toby knew all about Hollywood. It was a town where you had to put up a front. Toby went into a haberdashery on Vine Street, ordered a new wardrobe, and with twenty dollars remaining in his pocket, strolled into the Hollywood Brown Derby, where all the stars dined. The walls were covered with caricatures of the most famous actors in Hollywood. Toby could feel the pulse of show business here, sense the power in the room. He saw the hostess walking towards him. She was a pretty redhead in her twenties and she had a sensational figure.

She smiled at Toby and said, 'Can I help you?'

Toby could not resist it. He reached out with his two

hands and grabbed her ripe melon breasts. A look of shock came over her face. As she opened her mouth to cry out, Toby fixed his eyes in a glazed stare and said apologetically, 'Excuse me, miss – I'm not a sighted person.'

'Oh! I'm sorry!' She was contrite for what she had been thinking, and sympathetic. She conducted Toby to a table, holding his arm and helping him sit down, and arranged for his order. When she came back to his table a few minutes later and caught him studying the pictures on the wall, Toby beamed up at her and said, 'It's a miracle! I can see again!'

He was so innocent and so funny that she could not help laughing. She laughed all through dinner with Toby, and at his jokes in bed that night.

Toby took odd jobs around Hollywood because they brought him to the fringes of show business. He parked cars at Ciro's, and as the celebrities drove up, Toby would open the car door with a bright smile and an apt quip. They paid no attention. He was just a parking boy, and they did not even know he was alive. Toby watched the beautiful girls as they got out of the cars in their expensive, tight-fitting dresses, and he thought to himself, *If you only knew what a big star I'm going to be, you'd drop all those creeps.*

Toby made the rounds of agents, but he quickly learned that he was wasting his time. The agents were all starfuckers. You could not look for *them.* They had to be looking for *you.* The name that Toby heard most often was Clifton Lawrence. He handled only the biggest talent and he made the most incredible deals. *One day,*

Toby thought, *Clifton Lawrence is going to be my agent.*

Toby subscribed to the two bibles of show business: *Daily Variety* and the *Hollywood Reporter*. It made him feel like an insider. *Forever Amber* had been bought by Twentieth Century-Fox, and Otto Preminger was going to direct. Ava Gardner had been signed to star in *Whistle Stop* with George Raft and Jorja Curtright, and *Life with Father* had been bought by Warner Brothers. Then Toby saw an item that made his pulse start pounding. 'Producer Sam Winters has been named Vice-President in Charge of Production at Pan-Pacific Studios.'

Chapter Seven

When Sam Winters returned from the war his job at Pan-Pacific Studios was waiting for him. Six months later, there was a shake-up. The head of the studio was fired, and Sam was asked to take over until a new production head could be found. Sam did such a good job that the search was abandoned, and he was officially made Vice-President in Charge of Production. It was a nerve-racking, ulcer-making job, but Sam loved it more than he loved anything in the world.

Hollywood was a three-ring circus filled with wild, insane characters, a minefield with a parade of idiots dancing across it. Most actors, directors and producers were self-centred megalomaniacs, ungrateful, vicious and destructive. But as far as Sam was concerned, if they had talent, nothing else mattered. Talent was the magic key.

Sam's office door opened and Lucille Elkins, his secretary, came in with the freshly opened mail. Lucille was a permanent fixture, one of the competent professionals who stayed on for ever and watched her bosses come and go.

'Clifton Lawrence is here to see you,' Lucille said.

'Tell him to come in.'

Sam liked Lawrence. He had style. Fred Allen had said, 'All the sincerity in Hollywood could be hidden in a gnat's navel and there'd still be room for four caraway seeds and an agent's heart.'

Cliff Lawrence was more sincere than most agents. He was a Hollywood legend, and his client list ran the gamut of who's who in the entertainment field. He had a one-man office and was constantly on the move, servicing clients in London, Switzerland, Rome and New York. He was on intimate terms with all the important Hollywood executives and played in a weekly gin game that included the production heads of three studios. Twice a year, Lawrence chartered a yacht, gathered half a dozen beautiful 'models' and invited top studio executives for a week's 'fishing trip'. Clifton Lawrence kept a fully stocked beach-house at Malibu that was available to his friends any time they wanted to use it. It was a symbiotic relationship that Clifton had with Hollywood, and it was profitable for everyone.

Sam watched as the door opened and Lawrence bounced in, elegant in a beautifully tailored suit. He walked up to Sam, extended a perfectly manicured hand and said, 'Just wanted to say a quick hello. How's everything, dear boy?'

'Let me put it this way,' Sam said. 'If days were ships, today would be the *Titanic.*'

Clifton Lawrence made a commiserating noise.

'What did you think of the preview last night?' Sam asked.

'Trim the first twenty minutes and shoot a new ending, and you've got yourself a big hit.'

'Bull's-eye.' Sam smiled. 'That's exactly what we're doing. Any clients to sell me today?'

Lawrence grinned. 'Sorry. They're all working.'

And it was true. Clifton Lawrence's select stable of

top stars, with a sprinkling of directors and producers, were always in demand.

'See you for dinner Friday, Sam,' Clifton said. '*Ciao.*' He turned and walked out the door.

Lucille's voice came over the intercom. 'Dallas Burke is here.'

'Send him in.'

'And Mel Foss would like to see you. He said it's urgent.'

Mel Foss was head of the television division of Pan-Pacific Studios.

Sam glanced at his desk calendar. 'Tell him to make it breakfast tomorrow morning. Eight o'clock. The Polo Lounge.'

In the outer office, the telephone rang and Lucille picked it up. 'Mr Winters' office.'

An unfamiliar voice said, 'Hello there. Is the great man in?'

'Who's calling, please?'

'Tell him it's an old buddy of his – Toby Temple. We were in the army together. He said to look him up if I ever got to Hollywood, and here I am.'

'He's in a meeting, Mr Temple. Could I have him call you back?'

'Sure.' He gave her his telephone number, and Lucille threw it into the wastebasket. This was not the first time someone had tried the old-army-buddy routine on her.

Dallas Burke was one of the motion-picture industry's pioneer directors. Burke's films were shown at every college that had a course in movie making. Half a dozen of his earlier pictures were considered classics, and none of his work was less than brilliant and innovative. Burke was in his late seventies now, and his once massive frame had shrunk so that his clothes seemed to flap around him.

'It's good to see you again, Dallas,' Sam said as the old man walked into the office.

'Nice to see you, kid.' He indicated the man with him. 'You know my agent.'

'Certainly. How are you, Peter?'

They all found seats.

'I hear you have a story to tell me,' Sam said to Dallas Burke.

'This one's a beauty.' There was a quavering excitement in the old man's voice.

'I'm dying to hear it, Dallas,' Sam said. 'Shoot.'

Dallas Burke leaned forward and began talking. 'What's everybody in the world most interested in, kid? Love – right? And this idea's about the most holy kind of love there is – the love of a mother for her child.' His voice grew stronger as he became immersed in his story. 'We open in Long Island with a nineteen-year-old girl working as a secretary for a wealthy family. Old money. Gives us a chance for a slick background – know what I mean? High society stuff. The man she works for is married to a tight-assed blueblood. He likes the secretary, and she likes him, even though he's older.'

Only half-listening, Sam wondered whether the story was going to be *Back Street* or *Imitation of Life*. Not that it mattered, because whichever it was, Sam was going to buy it. It had been almost twenty years since anyone had given Dallas Burke a picture to direct. Sam could not blame the industry. Burke's last three pictures had been expensive, old-fashioned and box-office disasters. Dallas Burke was finished for ever as a picture maker. But he was a human being and he was still alive, and somehow he had to be taken care of, because he had not saved a cent. He had been offered a room in the Motion Picture Relief Home, but he had indignantly turned it down. 'I don't want your fucking charity!' he had shouted. 'You're talking to the man who directed Doug Fairbanks and Jack Barrymore and Milton Sills and Bill Farnum. I'm a giant, you pygmy sons of bitches!'

And he was. He was a legend; but even legends had to eat.

When Sam had become a producer, he had telephoned an agent he knew and told him to bring in Dallas Burke with a story idea. Since then, Sam had bought unusable stories from Dallas Burke every year for enough money for the old man to live on, and while Sam had been away in the army, he had seen to it that the arrangement continued.

'. . . so you see,' Dallas Burke was saying, 'the baby grows up without knowing her mother. But the mother keeps track of *her.* At the end, when the daughter marries this rich doctor, we have a big wedding. And do you know what the twist is, Sam? Listen to this – it's great. They won't let the mother in! She has to sneak in to the back of the church to watch her own kid getting married. There won't be a dry eye in the audience. . . Well, that's it. What do you think?'

Sam had guessed wrong. *Stella Dallas.* He glanced at the agent, who averted his eyes and studied the tips of his expensive shoes in embarrassment.

'It's great,' Sam said. 'It's exactly the kind of picture the studio's looking for.' Sam turned to the agent. 'Call Business Affairs and work out a deal with them, Peter. I'll tell them to expect your call.'

The agent nodded.

'Tell them they're gonna have to pay a stiff price for this one, or I'll take it to Warner Brothers,' Dallas Burke said. 'I'm giving you first crack at it because we're friends.'

'I appreciate that,' Sam said.

He watched as the two men left the office. Strictly speaking, Sam knew he had no right to spend the company's money on a sentimental gesture like this. But the motion-picture industry owed something to men like Dallas Burke, for without him and his kind there would have been no industry.

At eight o'clock the following morning, Sam Winters drove up under the portico of the Beverly Hills Hotel. A few minutes later, he was threading his way across the Polo Lounge, nodding to friends, acquaintances and competitors. More deals were made in this room over breakfast, lunch and cocktails than were consummated in all the offices of all the studios combined. Mel Foss looked up as Sam approached.

'Morning, Sam.'

The two men shook hands and Sam slid into the booth across from Foss. Eight months ago Sam had hired Foss to run the television division of Pan-Pacific Studios. Television was the new baby in the entertainment world, and it was growing with incredible rapidity. All the studios that had once looked down on television were now involved in it.

The waitress came to take their orders, and when she had left, Sam said, 'What's the good news, Mel?'

Mel Foss shook his head. 'There is no good news,' he said. 'We're in trouble.'

Sam waited, saying nothing.

'We're not going to get a pickup on "The Raiders".'

Sam looked at him in surprise. 'The ratings are great. Why would the network want to cancel it? It's tough enough to get a hit show.'

'It's not the show,' Foss said. 'It's Jack Nolan.' Jack Nolan was the star of 'The Raiders', and he had been an instant success, both critically and with the public.

'What's the matter with him?' Sam asked. He hated Mel Foss's habit of forcing him to draw information from him.

'Have you read this week's issue of *Peek* magazine?'

'I don't read it any week. It's a garbage pail.' He suddenly realized what Foss was driving at. 'They nailed Nolan!'

'In black and white,' Foss replied. 'The dumb son of a bitch put on his prettiest lace dress and went out to a party. Someone took pictures.'

'How bad is it?'

'Couldn't be worse. I got a dozen calls from the network yesterday. The sponsors and the network want out. No one wants to be associated with a screaming fag.'

'Transvestite,' Sam said. He had been counting heavily on presenting a strong television report at the board meeting in New York next month. The news from Foss would put an end to that. Losing 'The Raiders' would be a blow.

Unless he could do something.

When Sam returned to his office, Lucille waved a sheaf of messages at him. 'The emergencies are on top,' she said. 'They need you – '

'Later. Get me William Hunt at IBC.'

Two minutes later, Sam was talking to the head of the International Broadcasting Company. Sam had known Hunt casually for a number of years, and liked him. Hunt had started as a bright young corporate lawyer and had worked his way to the top of the network ladder. They seldom had any business dealings because Sam was not directly involved with television. He wished now that he had taken the time to cultivate Hunt. When Hunt came on the line, Sam forced himself to sound relaxed and casual. 'Morning, Bill.'

'This is a pleasant surprise,' Hunt said. 'It's been a long time, Sam.'

'Much too long. That's the trouble with this business, Bill. You never have time for the people you like.'

'Too true.'

Sam made his voice sound offhand. 'By the way, did you happen to see that silly article in *Peek?*'

'You know I did,' Hunt said quietly. 'That's why we're cancelling the show, Sam.' The words had a finality to them.

'Bill,' Sam said, 'what would you say if I told you that Jack Nolan was framed?'

There was a laugh from the other end of the line. 'I'd say you should think about becoming a writer.'

'I'm serious,' Sam said, earnestly. 'I *know* Jack Nolan. He's as straight as we are. That photograph was taken at a costume party. It was his girlfriend's birthday, and he put the dress on as a gag.' Sam could feel his palms sweating.

'I can't – '

'I'll tell you how much confidence I have in Jack,' Sam said into the phone. 'I've just set him for the lead in *Laredo,* our big Western feature for next year.'

There was a pause. 'Are you serious, Sam?'

'You're damn right I am. It's a three-million-dollar picture. If Jack Nolan turned out to be a fag, he'd be laughed off the screen. The exhibitors wouldn't touch it. Would I take that kind of gamble if I didn't know what I was talking about?'

'Well . . .' There was hesitation in Bill Hunt's voice.

'Come on, Bill, you're not going to let a lousy gossip sheet like *Peek* destroy a good man's career. You *like* the show, don't you?'

'Very much. It's a damned good show. But the sponsors – '

'It's your network. You've got more sponsors than you have air time. We've given you a hit show. Let's not fool around with a success.'

'Well . . .'

'Has Mel Foss talked to you yet about the studio's plans for "The Raiders" for next season?'

'No . . .'

'I guess he was planning to surprise you,' Sam said. 'Wait until you hear what he has in mind! Guest stars, big-name Western writers, shooting on location – the works! If "The Raiders" doesn't skyrocket to number one, I'm in the wrong business.'

There was a brief hesitation. Then Bill Hunt said, 'Have Mel phone me. Maybe we all got a little panicked here.'

'He'll call you,' Sam promised.

'And, Sam – you understand my position. I wasn't trying to hurt anybody.'

'Of course you weren't,' Sam said, generously. 'I know you too well to think that, Bill. That's why I felt I owed it to you to let you hear the truth.'

'I appreciate that.'

'What about lunch next week?'

'Love it. I'll call you Monday.'

They exchanged goodbyes and hung up. Sam sat there, drained. Jack Nolan was as queer as an Indian dime. Someone should have taken him away in a net long ago. And Sam's whole future depended on maniacs like that. Running a studio was like walking a high wire over Niagara Falls in a blizzard. *Anyone's crazy to do this job,* Sam thought. He picked up his private phone and dialled. A few moments later, he was talking to Mel Foss.

'"The Raiders" stays on the air,' Sam said.

'What?' There was stunned disbelief in Foss's voice.

'That's right. I want you to have a fast talk with Jack Nolan. Tell him if he ever steps out of line again, I'll personally run him out of this town and back to Fire Island! I mean it. If he gets the urge to suck something, tell him to try a banana!'

Sam slammed the phone down. He leaned back in his chair, thinking. He had forgotten to tell Foss about the format changes he had ad-libbed to Bill Hunt. He would have to find a writer who could come up with a Western script called *Laredo.*

The door burst open and Lucille stood there, her face white. 'Can you get right down to Stage Ten? Someone set it on fire.'

Chapter Eight

Toby Temple had tried to reach Sam Winters half a dozen times, but he was never able to get past his bitch of a secretary, and he finally gave up. Toby made the rounds of nightclubs and studios without success. During the next year, he took jobs to support himself. He sold real estate and insurance and haberdashery, and in between he played in bars and obscure nightclubs. But he was not able to get past the studio gates.

'You're going about it the wrong way,' a friend of his told him. 'Make *them* come to *you*.'

'How do I do that?' Toby asked, cynically.

'Get into Actors West.'

'An *acting* school?'

'It's more than that. They put on plays, and every studio in town covers them.'

Actors West had the smell of professionalism. Toby could sense it the moment he walked in the door. On the wall were photographs of graduates of the school. Toby recognized many of them as successful actors.

The blonde receptionist behind the desk said, 'May I help you?'

'Yes. I'm Toby Temple. I'd like to enrol.'

'Have you had acting experience?' she asked.

'Well, no,' Toby said. 'But I – '

She shook her head. 'I'm sorry. Mrs Tanner

won't interview anyone without professional experience.'

Toby stared at her a moment. 'Are you kidding me?'

'No. That's our rule. She never – '

'I'm not talking about that,' Toby said. 'I mean – you really don't know who I am?'

The blonde looked at him and said, 'No.'

Toby let his breath out softly. 'Jesus,' he said. 'Leland Hayward was right. If you work in England, Hollywood doesn't even know you're alive.' He smiled and said apologetically, 'I was joking. I figured you'd know me.'

The receptionist was confused now, not knowing what to believe. 'You *have* worked professionally?'

Toby laughed. 'I'll say I have.'

The blonde picked up a form. 'What parts have you played, and where?'

'Nothing here,' Toby said quickly. 'I've been in England for the past two years, working in rep.'

The blonde nodded. 'I see. Well, let me talk to Mrs Tanner.'

The blonde disappeared into the inner office, returning a few minutes later. 'Mrs Tanner will see you. Good luck.'

Toby winked at the receptionist, took a deep breath and walked into Mrs Tanner's office.

Alice Tanner was a dark-haired woman, with an attractive, aristocratic face. She appeared to be in her middle thirties, about ten years older than Toby. She was seated behind her desk, but what Toby could see of her figure was sensational. *This place is going to be just fine,* Toby decided.

Toby smiled winningly and said, 'I'm Toby Temple.'

Alice Tanner rose from behind the desk and walked towards him. Her left leg was encased in a heavy metal brace and she limped with the practised, rolling walk of someone who has lived with it for a long time.

Polio, Toby decided. He did not know whether to comment on it.

'So you want to enrol in our classes.'

'Very much,' Toby said.

'May I ask why?'

He made his voice sincere. 'Because everywhere I go, Mrs Tanner, people talk about your school and the wonderful plays you put on here. I'll bet you have no idea of the reputation this place has.'

She studied him a moment. 'I do have an idea. That's why I have to be careful to keep out phonies.'

Toby felt his face begin to redden, but he smiled boyishly and said, 'I'll bet. A lot of them must try to crash in here.'

'Quite a few,' Mrs Tanner agreed. She glanced at the card she held in her hand. 'Toby Temple.'

'You probably haven't heard the name,' he explained, 'because for the last couple of years, I've been – '

'Playing repertory in England.'

He nodded. 'Right.'

Alice Tanner looked at him and said quietly, 'Mr Temple, Americans are not permitted to play in English repertory. British Actors Equity doesn't allow it.'

Toby felt a sudden sinking sensation in the pit of his stomach.

'You might have checked first and saved us both this embarrassment. I'm sorry, but we only enrol professional talent here.' She started back towards her desk. The interview was over.

'Hold it!' His voice was like a whiplash.

She turned in astonishment. At that instant, Toby had no idea what he was going to say or do. He only knew that his whole future was hanging in the balance. The woman standing in front of him was the stepping-stone to everything he wanted, everything he had worked and sweated for, and he was not going to let her stop him.

'You don't judge talent by rules, lady! Okay – so I haven't acted. And why? Because people like you won't give me a chance. You see what I mean?' It was W. C. Fields' voice.

Alice Tanner opened her mouth to interrupt him, but Toby never gave her the opportunity. He was Jimmy Cagney telling her to give the poor kid a break, and James Stewart agreeing with him, and Clark Gable saying he was dying to work with the kid and Cary Grant adding that he thought the boy was brilliant. A host of Hollywood stars was in that room, and they were all saying funny things, things that Toby Temple had never thought of before. The words, the jokes poured out of him in a frenzy of desperation. He was a man drowning in the darkness of his own oblivion, clinging to a life raft of words, and the words were all that were keeping him afloat. He was soaked in perspiration, running around the room, imitating the movement of each character who was talking. He was manic, totally outside of himself, forgetting where he was and what he was here for until he heard Alice Tanner saying, 'Stop it! Stop it!'

Tears of laughter were streaming down her face.

'Stop it!' she repeated, gasping for breath.

And slowly, Toby came down to earth. Mrs Tanner

had taken out a handkerchief and was wiping her eyes.

'You – you're insane,' she said. 'Do you know that?'

Toby stared at her, a feeling of elation slowly filling him, lifting, exalting him. 'You liked it, huh?'

Alice Tanner shook her head and took a deep breath to control her laughter and said, 'Not – not very much.'

Toby looked at her, filled with rage. She had been laughing *at* him, not with him. He had been making a fool of himself.

'Then what were you laughing at?' Toby demanded.

She smiled and said quietly, 'You. That was the most frenetic performance I've ever seen. Somewhere, hidden beneath all those movie stars, is a young man with a lot of talent. You don't have to imitate other people. You're naturally funny.'

Toby felt his anger begin to sweep away.

'I think one day you could be really good if you're willing to work hard at it. Are you?'

He gave her a slow, beatific grin and said, 'Let's roll up our sleeves and go to work.'

Josephine worked very hard Saturday morning, helping her mother clean the house. At noon, Cissy and some other friends picked her up to take her on a picnic.

Mrs Czinski watched Josephine being driven off in the long limousine filled with the children of the Oil People. She thought: One day something bad is going to happen to Josephine. I shouldn't let her be with those people. They're the Devil's children. And she wondered if there was a devil in Josephine. She would talk to the Reverend Damian. He would know what to do.

Chapter Nine

Actors West was divided into two sections: the Showcase group, which consisted of the more experienced actors, and the Workshop group. It was the Showcase actors who staged plays that were covered by the studio talent scouts. Toby had been put with the Workshop actors. Alice Tanner had told him that it might be six months or a year before he would be ready to do a Showcase play.

Toby found the classes interesting, but the magic ingredient was missing: the audience, the applauders, the laughter, the people who would adore him.

In the weeks since Toby had begun classes, he had seen very little of the head of the school. Occasionally, Alice Tanner would drop into the Workshop to watch improvisations and give a word of encouragement, or Toby would run into her on his way to class. But he had hoped for something more intimate. He found himself thinking about Alice Tanner a great deal. She was what Toby thought of as a classy dame, and that appealed to him; he felt it was what he deserved. The idea of her crippled leg had bothered him at first, but it had slowly begun to take on a sexual fascination.

Toby talked to her again about putting him in a Showcase play where the critics and talent scouts could see him.

'You're not ready yet,' Alice Tanner told him.

She was standing in his way, keeping him from his success. *I have to do something about that,* Toby decided.

A Showcase play was being staged, and on the opening night Toby was seated in a middle row next to a student named Karen, a fat little character actress from his class. Toby had played scenes with Karen, and he knew two things about her: she never wore underclothes and she had bad breath. She had done everything but send up smoke signals to let Toby know that she wanted to go to bed with him, but he had pretended not to understand. *Jesus,* he thought, *fucking her would be like being sucked into a tub of hot lard.*

As they sat there waiting for the curtain to go up, Karen excitedly pointed out the critics from the Los Angeles *Times* and *Herald-Express,* and the talent scouts from Twentieth Century-Fox, MGM and Warner Brothers. It enraged Toby. They were here to see the actors up on the stage, while *he* sat in the audience like a dummy. He had an almost uncontrollable impulse to stand up and do one of his routines, dazzle them, show them what *real* talent looked like.

The audience enjoyed the play, but Toby was obsessed with the talent scouts, who sat within touching distance, the men who held his future in their hands. Well, if Actors West was the lure to bring them to him, Toby would use it; but he had no intention of waiting six months, or even six weeks.

The following morning, Toby went to Alice Tanner's office.

'How did you like the play?' she asked.

'It was wonderful,' Toby said. 'Those actors are really great.' He gave a self-deprecating smile. 'I see what you mean when you say I'm not ready yet.'

'They've had more experience than you, that's all, but you have a unique personality. You're going to make it. Just be patient.'

He sighed. 'I don't know. Maybe I'd be better off forgetting the whole thing and selling insurance or something.'

She looked at him in quick surprise. 'You mustn't,' she said.

Toby shook his head. 'After seeing those pros last night, I – I don't think I have it.'

'Of course you have, Toby. I won't let you talk like that.'

In her voice was the note he had been waiting to hear. It was not a teacher talking to a pupil now, it was a woman talking to a man, encouraging him, caring about him. Toby felt a small thrill of satisfaction.

He shrugged helplessly. 'I don't know, anymore. I'm all alone in this town. I have no one to talk to.'

'You can always talk to me, Toby. I'd like to be your friend.'

He could hear the sexual huskiness come into her voice. Toby's blue eyes held all the wonder in the world as he gazed at her. As she watched him, he walked over and locked the office door He returned to her, fell on his knees, buried his head in her lap and, as her fingers touched his hair, he slowly lifted her skirt, exposing the poor thigh encased in the cruel steel brace. Gently removing the brace, he tenderly kissed the red marks left by the steel bars. Slowly, he unfastened her garter belt, all the time telling Alice of his love and his need for her, and kissed his way down to the moist lips exposed before him. He carried her to the deep leather couch and made love to her.

That evening, Toby moved in with Alice Tanner.

In bed that night, Toby found that Alice Tanner was a pitifully lonely woman, desperate for someone to talk to, someone to love. She had been born in Boston. Her father was a wealthy manufacturer who had given her a large allowance and paid no further attention to her. Alice had loved the theatre and had studied to be an actress, but in college she had contracted polio and that had put an end to her dream. She told Toby how it had affected her life. The boy she was engaged to had jilted her when he learned the news. Alice had left home and married a psychiatrist, who committed suicide six months later. It was as though all her emotions had been bottled up inside her. Now they poured out in a violent eruption that left her feeling drained and peaceful and marvellously content.

Toby made love to Alice until she almost fainted with ecstasy, filling her with his huge penis and making slow circles with his hips until he seemed to be touching every part of her body. She moaned, 'Oh, darling, I love you so much. Oh, God, how I love this!'

But when it came to school, Toby found that he had no influence with Alice. He talked to her about putting him in the next Showcase play, introducing him to casting directors, speaking to important studio people about him, but she was firm. 'You'll hurt yourself if you push too fast, darling. Rule one: the first impression you make is the most important. If they don't like you the first time, they'll never go back to see you a second time. You've got to be ready.'

The instant the words were out, she became The Enemy. She was against him. Toby swallowed his fury and forced himself to smile at her. 'Sure. It's just that I'm impatient. I want to make it for you as much as for me.'

'Do you? Oh, Toby, I love you so much!'

'I love you, too, Alice.' And he smiled into her adoring eyes. He knew he had to circumvent this bitch who was standing in the way of what he wanted. He hated her and he punished her.

When they went to bed, he made her do things she had never done before, things he had never asked a whore to do, using her mouth and her fingers and her tongue. He pushed her further and further, forcing her into a series of humiliations. And each time he got her to do something more degrading, he would praise her, the way one praises a dog for learning a new trick and she would be happy because she had pleased him. And the more he degraded her, the more degraded he felt. He was punishing himself, and he had not the faintest idea why.

Toby had a plan in mind, and his chance to put it into action came sooner than he had anticipated. Alice Tanner announced that the Workshop class was going to put on a private show for the advanced classes and their guests on the following Friday. Each student could choose his own project. Toby prepared a monologue and rehearsed it over and over.

On the morning of the show, Toby waited until class was over and walked up to Karen, the fat actress who had sat next to him during the play. 'Would you do me a favour?' he asked casually.

'Sure, Toby.' Her voice was surprised and eager.

Toby stepped back to get away from her breath. 'I'm pulling a gag on an old friend of mine. I want you to telephone Clifton Lawrence's secretary and tell her you're Sam Goldwyn's secretary, and that Mr Goldwyn would like Mr Lawrence to come to the show tonight to see a brilliant new comic. There'll be a ticket waiting for him at the box office.'

Karen stared at him. 'Jesus, old lady Tanner would have my head. You know she never allows outsiders at the Workshop shows.'

'Believe me, it'll be all right.' He took her arm and squeezed it. 'You busy this afternoon?'

She swallowed, her breath coming a little faster. 'Not – not if you'd like to do something.'

'I'd like to do something.'

Three hours later, an ecstatic Karen made the phone call.

The auditorium was filled with actors from the various classes and their guests, but the only person Toby had eyes for was the man who sat in an aisle seat in the third row. Toby had been in a panic, fearful that his ruse would not work. Surely a man as clever as Clifton Lawrence would see through the trick. But he had not. He was here.

A boy and girl were on stage now, doing a scene from *The Seagull*. Toby hoped they would not drive Clifton Lawrence out of the theatre. Finally, the scene was finished, and the actors took their bows and left the stage.

It was Toby's turn. Alice suddenly appeared at his side in the wings, whispering, 'Good luck, darling', unaware that his luck was sitting in the audience.

'Thanks, Alice.' Toby breathed a silent prayer, straightened his shoulders, bounced out on stage and smiled boyishly at the audience. 'Hello, there. I'm Toby Temple. Hey, did you ever stop to think about names, and how our parents choose them? It's crazy. I asked my mother why she named me Toby. She said she took one look at my mug, and that was it.'

His look was what got the laugh. Toby appeared so innocent and wistful, standing up there on that stage, that they loved him. The jokes he told were terrible, but somehow that did not matter. He was so vulnerable that they wanted to protect him, and they did it with their applause and their laughter. It was like a gift of love that flowed into Toby, filling him with an almost unbearable exhilaration. He was Edward G. Robinson and Jimmy Cagney, and Cagney was saying, 'You dirty rat! Who do you think you're giving orders to?'

And Robinson's, 'To you, you punk. I'm Little Caesar. I'm the boss. You're nuthin'. Do you know what that means?'

'Yeah, you dirty rat. You're the boss of nuthin'.'

A roar. The audience adored Toby.

Bogart was there, snarling, 'I'd spit in your eye, punk, if my lip wasn't stuck over my teeth.'

And the audience was enchanted.

Toby gave them his Peter Lorre. 'I saw this little girl in her room, playing with it, and I got excited. I don't know what came over me. I couldn't help myself. I crept into her room, and I pulled the rope tighter and tighter, and I broke her yo-yo.'

A big laugh. He was rolling.

He switched over to Laurel and Hardy, and a movement in the audience caught his eye and he glanced up. Clifton Lawrence was walking out of the theatre.

The rest of the evening was a blur to Toby.

When the show was over, Alice Tanner came up to Toby. 'You were wonderful, darling! I . . .'

He could not bear to look at her, to have anyone look at him. He wanted to be alone with his misery, to try to cope with the pain that was tearing him apart. His world had collapsed around him. He had had his chance, and he had failed. Clifton Lawrence had walked out on him, had not even waited for him to finish. Clifton Lawrence was a man who knew talent, a professional who handled the best. If Lawrence did not think Toby had anything . . . He felt sick to his stomach.

'I'm going for a walk,' he said to Alice.

He walked down Vine Street and Gower, past Columbia Pictures and RKO and Paramount. All the gates were locked. He walked along Hollywood Boulevard and looked up at the huge mocking sign on the hill that said, 'HOLLYWOODLAND'. There was no Hollywoodland. It was a state of mind, a phony dream that lured thousands of otherwise normal people into the insanity of trying to become a star. The word *Hollywood* had become a lodestone for miracles, a trap that seduced people with wonderful promises, siren songs of dreams fulfilled, and then destroyed them.

Toby walked the streets all night long, wondering what he was going to do with his life. His faith in himself had been shattered and he felt rootless and adrift. He had never imagined himself doing anything other than entertaining people, and if he could not do that, all that was left for him were dull, monotonous jobs where he would be caged up for the rest of his life. Mr Anonymous. No one would ever know who he was. He thought of the long, dreary years, the bitter loneliness of a thousand nameless towns, of the people who had applauded him and laughed at him and loved him. Toby wept. He wept for the past and for the future.

He wept because he was dead.

It was dawn when Toby returned to the white stucco bungalow he shared with Alice. He walked into the bedroom and looked down at her sleeping figure. He had thought that she would be the open sesame to the magic kingdom. But there was no magic kingdom. Not for him. He would leave. He had no idea where he would go. He was almost twenty-seven years old and he had no future.

He lay down on the couch, exhausted. He closed his eyes, listening to the sounds of the city stirring into life. The morning sounds of cities are the same, and he thought of Detroit. His mother. She was standing in the kitchen cooking apple tarts for him. He could smell her wonderful musky female odour mingled with the smell of apples cooking in butter, and she was saying, *God wants you to be famous.*

He was standing alone on an enormous stage, blinded by floodlights, trying to remember his lines. He tried to speak but he had lost his voice. He grew panicky. There was a great rumbling noise from the audience, and through the blinding lights Toby could see the spectators leaving their seats and running towards the stage to attack him, to kill him. Their love had turned to hate. They were surrounding him, grabbing him, chanting, 'Toby! Toby! Toby!'

Toby suddenly jerked awake, his mouth dry with fright. Alice Tanner was leaning over him, shaking him.

'Toby! Telephone. It's Clifton Lawrence.'

Clifton Lawrence's office was in a small, elegant building on Beverly Drive, just south of Wilshire. French Impressionist paintings hung from the carved *boiserie,* and before the dark green marble fireplace a sofa and some antique chairs were grouped around an exquisite tea table. Toby had never seen anything like it.

A shapely, redheaded secretary was pouring tea. 'How do you like your tea, Mr Temple?'

Mr Temple! 'One sugar, please.'

'There you are.' A little smile and she was gone.

Toby did not know that the tea was a special blend imported from Fortnum and Mason, nor that it was steeping in Irish Belleek, but he knew it tasted wonderful. In fact, everything about this office was wonderful, especially the dapper little man who sat in an armchair studying him. Clifton Lawrence was smaller than Toby had expected, but he radiated a sense of authority and power.

'I can't tell you how much I appreciate your seeing me,' Toby said. 'I'm sorry I had to trick you into –'

Clifton Lawrence threw his head back and laughed. 'Trick me? I had lunch with Goldwyn yesterday. I went to watch you last night because I wanted to see if your talent matched your nerve. It did.'

'But you walked out – ' Toby exclaimed.

'Dear boy, you don't have to eat the entire jar of caviar to know if it's good, right? I knew what you had in sixty seconds.'

Toby felt that sense of euphoria building up in him again. After the black despair of the night before, to be lifted to the heights like this, to have his life handed back to him –

'I have a hunch about you, Temple,' Clifton Lawrence said. 'I think it would be exciting to take someone young and build his career. I've decided to take you on as a client.'

The feeling of joy was exploding inside Toby. He wanted to stand up and scream aloud. *Clifton Lawrence was going to be his agent!*

'. . . handle you on one condition,' Clifton Lawrence was saying. 'That you do exactly as I tell you. I don't stand for temperament. You step out of line just once, and we're finished. Do you understand?'

Toby nodded quickly. 'Yes, sir. I understand.'

'The first thing you have to do is face the truth.' He smiled at Toby and said, 'Your act is terrible. Definitely bottom drawer.'

It was as though Toby had been kicked in the stomach. Clifton Lawrence had brought him here to punish him for that stupid phone call; he was not going to handle him. He . . .

But the little agent continued. 'Last night was amateur night, and that's what you are – an amateur.' Clifton Lawrence rose from his chair and began to pace. 'I'm going to tell you what you have, and

I'm going to tell you what you need to become a star.'

Toby sat there.

'Let's start with your material,' Clifton said. 'You could put butter and salt on it and peddle it in theatre lobbies.'

'Yes, sir. Well, some of it might be a litle corny, but – '

'Next. You have no style.'

Toby felt his hands begin to clench. 'The audience seemed to – '

'Next. You don't know how to move. You're a lox.'

Toby said nothing.

The little agent walked over to him, looked down and said softly, reading Toby's mind, 'If you're so bad, what are you doing here? You're here because you've got something that money can't buy. When you stand up on that stage, the audience wants to eat you up. They love you. Do you have any idea how much that could be worth?'

Toby took a deep breath and sat back. 'Tell me.'

'More than you could ever dream. With the right material and the proper kind of handling, you can be a star.'

Toby sat there, basking in the warm glow of Clifton Lawrence's words, and it was as though everything Toby had done all his life had led to this moment, as though he were *already* a star, and it had all happened. Just as his mother had promised him.

'The key to an entertainer's success is personality,' Clifton Lawrence was saying. 'You can't buy it and you can't fake it. You have to be born with it. You're one of the lucky ones, dear boy.' He glanced at the gold Piaget watch on his wrist. 'I've set up a meeting for you with

O'Hanlon and Rainger at two o'clock. They're the best comedy writers in the business. They work for all the top comics.'

Toby said nervously, 'I'm afraid I haven't much mon – '

Clifton Lawrence dismissed it with a wave of his hand. 'Not to worry, dear boy. You'll pay me back later.'

Long after Toby Temple had left, Clifton Lawrence sat there thinking about him, smiling to himself at that wide-eyed innocent face and those trusting, guileless blue eyes. It had been many years since Clifton had represented an unknown. All his clients were important stars, and every studio fought for their services. The excitement had long since gone. The early days had been more fun, more stimulating. It would be a challenge to take this raw, young kid and develop him, build him into a hot property. Clifton had a feeling that he was really going to enjoy this experience. He liked the boy. He liked him very much indeed.

The meeting took place at the Twentieth Century-Fox studios on Pico Boulevard in West Los Angeles, where O'Hanlon and Rainger had their offices. Toby had expected something lavish, on the order of Clifton Lawrence's suite, but the writers' quarters were drab and dingy, located in a small wooden bungalow on the lot.

An untidy, middle-aged secretary in a cardigan ushered Toby into the inner office. The walls were a dirty apple-green, and the only adornment was a battered dart board and a 'PLAN AHEAD' sign with the last three letters squeezed together. A broken venetian blind partially filtered out the sun's rays that fell across a dirty brown carpet worn down to the canvas. There were two scarred desks, back to back, each littered with papers and pencils and half-empty cartons of cold coffee.

'Hi, Toby. Excuse the mess. It's the maid's day off,' O'Hanlon greeted him. 'I'm O'Hanlon.' He indicated his partner. 'This is – er – ?'

'Rainger.'

'Ah, yes. This is Rainger.'

O'Hanlon was large and rotund and wore horn-rimmed glasses. Rainger was small and frail. Both men were in their early thirties and had been a successful writing team for ten years. In all the time that Toby was to work with them, he always referred to them as 'the boys'.

Toby said, 'I understand you fellas are going to write some jokes for me.'

O'Hanlon and Rainger exchanged a look. Rainger said, 'Cliff Lawrence thinks you might be America's new sex symbol. Let's see what you can do. Have you got an act?'

'Sure,' Toby replied. He remembered what Clifton had said about it. Suddenly, he felt diffident.

The two writers sat down on the couch and crossed their arms.

'Entertain us,' O'Hanlon said.

Toby looked at them. 'Just like that?'

'What would you like?' Rainger asked. 'An introduction from a sixty-piece orchestra?' He turned to O'Hanlon. 'Get the music department on the phone.'

You prick, thought Toby. *You're on my shit list, both of you.* He knew what they were trying to do. They were trying to make him look bad so they could go back to Clifton Lawrence and say, *We can't help him. He's a stiff.* Well, he was not going to let them get away with it. He put on a smile he did not feel, and went into his Abbott and Costello routine. 'Hey, Lou, ain't you ashamed of yourself? You're turnin' into a bum. Why don't you go out and get yourself a job?'

'I got a job.'

'What kind of job?'

'Lookin' for work.'

'You call that a job?'

'Certainly. It keeps me busy all day, I got regular hours, and I'm home in time for dinner every night.'

The two of them were studying Toby now, weighing him, analysing him, and in the middle of his routine they began talking, as though Toby were not in the room.

'He doesn't know how to stand.'

'He uses his hands like he's chopping wood. Maybe we could write a woodchopper act for him.'

'He pushes too hard.'

'Jesus, with that material – wouldn't you?'

Toby was getting more upset by the moment. He did not have to stay here and be insulted by these two maniacs. Their material was probably lousy anyway.

Finally, he could stand it no longer. He stopped, his voice trembling with rage. 'I don't need you bastards! Thanks for the hospitality.' He started for the door.

Rainger stood up in genuine amazement. 'Hey! What's the matter with you?'

Toby turned on him in fury. 'What the fuck do you

think is the matter? You – you –' He was so frustrated, he was on the verge of tears.

Rainger turned to look at O'Hanlon in bewilderment. 'We must have hurt his feelings.'

'Golly.'

Toby took a deep breath. 'Look, you two, I don't care if you don't like me, but – '

'We *love* you!' O'Hanlon exclaimed.

'We think you're darling!' Rainger chimed in.

Toby looked from one to the other in complete bafflement. 'What? You acted like – '

'You know your trouble, Toby? You're insecure. Relax. Sure, you've got a lot to learn, but on the other hand, if you were Bob Hope, you wouldn't be here.'

O'Hanlon added, 'And do you know why? Because Bob's up in Carmel today.'

'Playing golf. Do you play golf?' Rainger asked.

'No.'

The two writers looked at each other in dismay. 'There go all the golf jokes. Shit!'

O'Hanlon picked up the telephone. 'Bring in some coffee, will you, Zsa Zsa?' He put down the phone and turned to Toby. 'Do you know how many would-be comics there are in this quaint little business we're in?'

Toby shook his head.

'I can tell you exactly. Three billion seven hundred and twenty-eight million, as of six o'clock last night. And that's not including Milton Berle's brother. When there's a full moon, they all crawl out of the woodwork. There are only half a dozen really top comics. The others will never make it. Comedy is the most serious business in the world. It's goddamned hard work being funny, whether you're a comic or a comedian.'

'What's the difference?'

'A big one. A comic opens funny doors. A comedian opens doors funny.'

Rainger asked, 'Did you ever stop to think what makes one comedian a smash and another one a failure?'

'Material,' Toby said, wanting to flatter them.

'Buffalo shit. The last new joke was invented by Aristophanes. Jokes are basically all the same. George Burns can tell six jokes that the guy on the bill ahead of him just told, and Burns will get bigger laughs. Do you know why? Personality.' *It was what Clifton Lawrence had told him.* 'Without it, you're nothing, nobody. You start with a personality and you turn it into a character. Take Hope. If he came out and did a Jack Benny monologue, he'd bomb. Why? Because he's built up a character. That's what the audiences expect from him. When Hope walks out, they want to hear those rapid-fire jokes. He's a likeable smart-ass, the big city fellow who gets his lumps. Jack Benny – just the opposite. He wouldn't know what to do with a Bob Hope monologue, but he can take a two-minute pause and make an audience scream. Each of the Marx Brothers has his own character. Fred Allen is unique. That brings us to you. Do you know your problem, Toby? You're a little of everybody. You're imitating all the big boys. Well, that's great if you want to play Elks smokers for the rest of your life. But if you want to move up into the big time, you've got to create a character of your own. When you're out on that stage, before you even open your mouth, the audience has to know that it's Toby Temple up there. Do you read me?'

'Yes.'

O'Hanlon took over. 'Do you know what you've got, Toby? A lovable face. If I weren't already engaged to Clark Gable, I'd be crazy about you. There's a naive sweetness about you. If you package it right, it could be worth a fucking fortune.'

'To say nothing of a fortune in fucking,' Rainger chimed in.

'You can get away with things that the other boys can't. It's like a choirboy saying four-letter words – it's cute because you don't believe he really understands what he's saying. When you walked in here, you asked if we were the fellows who were going to write your jokes. The answer is no. This isn't a joke shop. What we *are* going to do is show you what you've got and how to use it. We're going to tailor a character for you. Well – what do you say?'

Toby looked from one to the other, grinned happily and said, 'Let's roll up our sleeves and go to work.'

Every day after that, Toby had lunch with O'Hanlon and Rainger at the studio. The Twentieth Century-Fox commissary was an enormous room filled with wall-to-wall stars. On any given day, Toby could see Tyrone Power and Loretta Young and Betty Grable and Don Ameche and Alice Faye and Richard Widmark and Victor Mature and the Ritz Brothers, and dozens of others. Some were seated at tables in the large room, and others ate in the smaller executive dining room which adjoined the main commissary. Toby loved watching them all. In a short time, he would be one of *them,* people would be asking for *his* autograph. He was on his way, and he was going to be bigger than any of them.

Alice Tanner was thrilled by what was happening to Toby. 'I know you're going to make it, darling. I'm so proud of you.'

Toby smiled at her and said nothing.

Toby and O'Hanlon and Rainger had long discussions about the new character Toby was to be.

'He should think he's a sophisticated man of the world,' O'Hanlon said. 'But every time he comes to bat, he lays an egg.'

'What's his job?' asked Rainger. 'Mixing metaphors?'

'This character should live with his mother. He's in love with a girl, but he's afraid to leave home to marry her. He's been engaged to her for five years.'

'Ten is a funnier number.'

'Right! Make it ten years. His mother shouldn't happen to a dog. Every time Toby wants to get married, his mother develops a new disease. *Time* Magazine calls *her* every week to find out what's happening in medicine.'

Toby sat there listening, fascinated by the fast flow of dialogue. He had never worked with real professionals before, and he enjoyed it. Particularly since he was the centre of attention. It took O'Hanlon and Rainger three weeks to write an act for Toby. When they finally showed it to him he was thrilled. It was *good.* He made a few suggestions, they added and threw out some lines, and Toby Temple was ready. Clifton Lawrence sent for him.

'You're opening Saturday night at the Bowling Ball.'

Toby stared at him. He had had expectations of being booked into Ciro's or the Trocadero. 'What's – what's the Bowling Ball?'

'A little club on south Western Avenue.'

Toby's face fell. 'I never heard of it.'

'And they never heard of you. That's the point, dear boy. If you should bomb there, no one will ever know it.'

Except Clifton Lawrence.

The Bowling Ball was a dump. There was no other word to describe it. It was a duplicate of ten thousand other sleazy little bars scattered throughout the country, a watering hole for losers. Toby had played there a thousand times, in a thousand cities. The patrons were mostly middle-aged males, blue-collar workers indulging in their ritual get-together with their buddies, ogling the tired waitresses in their tight skirts and low-cut blouses, exchanging dirty jokes over a shot of cheap whisky or a glass of beer. The floor show took place in a small cleared area at the far end of the room, where three bored musicians played. A homosexual singer opened the show, followed by an acrobatic dancer in a leotard, and then a stripper who worked with a somnolent cobra.

Toby sat at a table in the back room with Clifton Lawrence and O'Hanlon and Rainger, watching the other acts, listening to the audience, trying to gauge its mood.

'Beer drinkers,' Toby said contemptuously.

Clifton started to retort, then looked at Toby's face and checked himself. Toby was scared. Clifton knew that Toby had played places like this before, but this time was different. This was the test.

Clifton said gently, 'If you can put the beer drinkers in your pocket, the champagne crowd will be a pushover. These people work hard all day, Toby. When they go out at night, they want their nickel's worth. If you can make *them* laugh, you can make anyone laugh.'

At that moment, Toby heard the bored MC announce his name.

'Give 'em hell, tiger!' O'Hanlon said.

Toby was on.

He stood on the stage, on guard and tense, appraising the audience like a wary animal sniffing for danger in a forest.

An audience was a beast with a hundred heads, each one different; and he had to make the beast laugh. He took a deep breath. *Love me,* he prayed.

He went into his act.

And no one was listening to him. No one was laughing. Toby could feel the flop sweat begin to pop out on his forehead. The act was not working. He kept his smile pasted on and went on talking over the loud noise and conversation. He could not get their attention. They wanted the naked broads back. They had been exposed on too many Saturday nights to too many talentless, unfunny comedians. Toby kept talking, in the face of their indifference. He went on because there was nothing else he could do. He looked out and saw Clifton Lawrence and the boys, watching him with worried expressions.

Toby continued. There was no audience in the room,

just people, talking to one another, discussing their problems and their lives. For all they cared, Toby Temple could have been a million miles away. Or dead. His throat was dry now with fear, and it was becoming hard to get the words out. From the corner of his eye, Toby saw the manager start towards the bandstand. He was going to begin the music, pull the plug on him. It was all over. Toby's palms were wet and his bowels had turned to water. He could feel hot urine trickle down his leg. He was so nervous that he was beginning to mix up his words. He did not dare look at Clifton Lawrence or the writers. He was too filled with shame. The manager was at the bandstand, talking to the musicians. They glanced over at Toby and nodded. Toby went on, talking desperately, wanting it to be over, wanting to run away somewhere and hide.

A middle-aged woman seated at a table directly in front of Toby giggled at one of his jokes. Her companions stopped to listen. Toby kept talking, in a frenzy. The others at the table were listening now, laughing. And then the next table.

And the next. And, slowly, the talking began to die down. They were *listening* to him. The laughs were starting to come, long and regular, and they were getting bigger, and building. And building. The people in the room had become an audience. And he had them. *He fucking had them!* It no longer mattered that he was in a cheap saloon filled with beer-drinking slobs. What mattered was their laughter, and their love. It came out at Toby in waves. First he had them laughing, then he had them screaming. They had never heard anything like him, not in this crummy place, not anywhere. They applauded and they cheered and before they were through, they damned near tore the place apart. They were witnessing the birth of a phenomenon. Of course, they could not know that. But Clifton Lawrence and O'Hanlon and Rainger knew it. And Toby Temple knew it.

God had finally come through.

Reverend Damian shoved the blazing torch into Josephine's face and screamed, 'O God Almighty, burn away the evil in this sinful child,' and the congregation roared 'Amen!' And Josephine could feel the flame licking at her face and the Reverend Damian yelled out, 'Help this sinner exorcise the Devil, O God. We will pray him out, we will burn him out, we will drown him out,' and hands grabbed Josephine, and her face was suddenly plunged into a wooden tub of cold water, and she was held under while voices chanted into the night air, beseeching the Almighty One for His help, and Josephine struggled to get loose, fighting for breath, and when they finally pulled her out, half-conscious, the Reverend Damian declared, 'We thank you, sweet Jesus, for your mercy. She is saved! She is saved!' And there was great rejoicing, and everyone was raised in spirit. Except Josephine, whose headaches became worse.

Chapter Ten

'I've gotten you a booking in Las Vegas,' Clifton Lawrence told Toby. 'I've arranged for Dick Landry to work on your act. He's the best nightclub director in the business.'

'Fantastic! Which hotel? The Flamingo? The Thunderbird?'

'The Oasis.'

'The Oasis?' Toby looked at Cliff to see if he was joking. 'I never –'

'I know.' Cliff smiled. 'You never heard of it. Fair enough. They never heard of you. They're really not booking you – they're booking me. They're taking my word that you're good.'

'Don't worry,' Toby promised. 'I will be.'

Toby broke the news to Alice Tanner about his Las Vegas booking just before he was to leave. 'I know you're going to be a big star,' she said. 'It's your time. They'll adore you, darling.' She hugged him and said, 'When do you leave, and what do I wear to the opening night of a young comic genius?'

Toby shook his head ruefully. 'I wish I could take you, Alice. The trouble is I'll be working night and day thinking up a lot of new material.'

She tried to conceal her disappointment. 'I understand.' She held him tighter. 'How long will you be gone?'

'I don't know yet. You see, it's kind of an open booking.'

She felt a small stab of worry, but she knew that she was being silly. 'Call me the moment you can,' she said.

Toby kissed her and danced out the door.

It was as though Las Vegas, Nevada, had been created for the sole pleasure of Toby Temple. He felt it the moment he saw the town. It had a marvellous kinetic energy that he responded to, a pulsating power that matched the power burning inside him. Toby flew in with O'Hanlon and Rainger, and when they arrived at the airport, a limousine from the Oasis Hotel was waiting for them. It was Toby's first taste of the wonderful world that was soon to be his. He enjoyed leaning back in the huge car and having the chauffeur ask, 'Did you have a nice flight, Mr Temple?'

It was always the little people who could smell a success even before it happened, Toby thought.

'It was the usual bore,' Toby said carelessly. He caught the smile that O'Hanlon and Rainger exchanged, and he grinned back at them. He felt very close to them. They were all a team, the best goddamned team in show business.

The Oasis was off the glamorous Strip, far removed from the more famous hotels. As the limousine approached the hotel, Toby saw that it was not as large or as fancy as the Flamingo or the Thunderbird, but it had something better, much better. It had a giant marquee in front that read:

OPENING SEPT 4TH
LILI WALLACE
TOBY TEMPLE

Toby's name was in dazzling letters that seemed a hundred feet high. No sight was as beautiful as this in the whole goddamned world.

'Look at that!' he said in awe.

O'Hanlon glanced at the sign and said, 'Yeah! How about that? *Lili Wallace!*' And he laughed. 'Don't worry, Toby. After the opening you'll be on top of her.'

The manager of the Oasis, a middle-aged, sallow-faced man named Parker, greeted Toby and personally escorted him to his suite, fawning all the way. 'I can't tell you how pleased we are to have you with us, Mr Temple. If there's anything at all you need – anything – just give me a call.'

The welcome, Toby realized, was for Clifton Lawrence. This was the first time the fabulous agent had deigned to book one of his clients into this hotel. The manager of the Oasis hoped that now the hotel would get some of Lawrence's really big stars.

The suite was enormous. It consisted of three bedrooms, a large living room, a kitchen, a bar and a terrace. On a table in the living room were bottles of assorted liquors, flowers and a large bowl of fresh fruit and cheeses, compliments of the management.

'I hope this will be satisfactory, Mr Temple,' Parker said.

Toby looked around and thought of all the dreary little cockroach-ridden fleabag hotel rooms he had lived in. 'Yeah. It's okay.'

'Mr Landry checked in an hour ago. I've arranged to clear the Mirage Room for your rehearsal at three o'clock.'

'Thanks.'

'Remember, if there's *anything* at all you need – ' And the manager bowed himself out.

Toby stood there, savouring his surroundings. He was going to live in places like this for the rest of his life. He would have it all – the broads, the money, the applause. Mostly the applause. People sitting out there laughing and cheering and loving him. *That* was his food and drink. He did not need anything else.

Dick Landry was in his late twenties, a slight, thin man with an alopecian head and long, graceful legs. He had started out as a gipsy on Broadway and had graduated from the chorus to lead dancer to choreographer to director. Landry had taste and a sense of what an audience wanted. He could not make a bad act good, but he could make it *look* good, and if he was given a good act, he could make it sensational. Until ten days ago, Landry had never heard of Toby Temple, and the only reason Landry had cut into his frantic schedule to come to Las Vegas and stage Temple's act was because Clifton Lawrence had asked him to. It was Clifton who had given Landry his start.

Fifteen minutes after Dick Landry met Toby Temple, Landry knew he was working with a talent. Listening to Toby's monologue, Landry found himself laughing aloud – something he rarely did. It was not the jokes so much as Toby's wistful way of delivering them. He was so pathetically sincere that it broke your heart. He was an adorable Chicken Little, terrified that the sky was about to fall on his head. You wanted to run up there and hug him and assure him that everything would be all right.

When Toby finished, it was all that Landry could do to keep from applauding. He went up to the stage where Toby stood. 'You're good,' he said enthusiastically. 'Really good.'

Toby said, pleased, 'Thanks. Cliff says you can show me how to be great.'

Landry said, 'I'm going to try. The first thing is for you to learn to diversify your talents. As long as you can only stand up there and tell jokes, you'll never be more than a standup comic. Let me hear you sing.'

Toby grinned. 'Rent a canary. I can't sing.'

'Try it.'

Toby tried. Landry was pleased. 'Your voice isn't much,' he told Toby, 'but you have an ear. With the right songs, you can fake it so that they'll think you're Sinatra. We'll arrange to have some song writers do some special material for you. I don't want you singing the same songs that everyone is doing. Let's see you move.'

Toby moved.

Landry studied him carefully. 'Fair, fair. You'll never be a dancer, but I'm going to make you look like one.'

'Why?' Toby asked. 'Song-and-dance men are a dime a dozen.'

'So are comics,' Landry retorted. 'I'm going to turn you into an entertainer.'

Toby grinned and said, 'Let's roll up our sleeves and go to work.'

*

They went to work. O'Hanlon and Rainger were at every rehearsal, adding lines, creating new routines, watching Landry drive Toby. It was a gruelling schedule. Toby rehearsed until every muscle in his body ached, but he burned off five pounds and became trim and hard. He took a singing lesson every day and vocalized until he was singing in his sleep. He worked on new comedy routines with the boys, then stopped to learn new songs that had been written for him, and it was time to rehearse again.

Almost every day, Toby found a message in his box that Alice Tanner had telephoned. He remembered how she had tried to hold him back. *You're not ready yet.* Well, he was ready now, and he had done it in *spite* of her. To hell with her. He threw the messages away. Finally, they stopped. But the rehearsals went on.

Suddenly it was opening night.

There is a mystique about the birth of a new star. It is as though some telepathic message is instantaneously transmitted to the four corners of the world of show business. Through some magic alchemy, the news spreads to London and Paris, to New York and Sydney; wherever there is theatre, the word is carried.

Five minutes after Toby Temple walked onto the stage of the Oasis Hotel, the word was out that there was a new star on the horizon.

Clifton Lawrence flew in for Toby's opening and stayed for the supper show. Toby was flattered. Clifton was neglecting his other clients for him. When Toby finished the show, the two of them went to the hotel's all-night coffee shop.

'Did you see all the celebrities out there?' Toby asked. 'When they came back to my dressing room, I damn near died.'

Clifton smiled at Toby's enthusiasm. It was such a pleasant change from all his other, jaded, clients. Toby was a pussycat. A sweet, blue-eyed pussycat.

'They know talent when they see it,' Clifton said. 'So does the Oasis. They want to make a new deal with you. They want to raise you from six-fifty to a thousand a week.'

Toby dropped his spoon. 'A thousand a week? That's fantastic, Cliff!'

'And I've had a couple of feelers from the Thunderbird and the El Rancho Hotel.'

'Already?' Toby asked, elated.

'Don't wet your pants. It's just to play the lounge.' He smiled. 'It's the old story, Toby. To *me* you're a headliner, and to *you* you're a headliner – but to a *headliner*, are you a headliner?' He stood up. 'I have to catch a plane to New York. I'm flying to London tomorrow.'

'London? When will you be back?'

'In a few weeks.' Clifton leaned forward and said, 'Listen to me, dear boy. You have two more weeks here. Treat it like a school. Every night you're up on that stage, I want you to figure out how you can be better. I've persuaded O'Hanlon and Rainger not to leave. They're willing to work with you day and night. Use them. Landry will come back weekends to see how everything is going.'

'Right,' Toby said. 'Thanks, Cliff.'

'Oh, I almost forgot,' Clifton Lawrence said casually. He pulled a small package from his pocket and handed it to Toby.

Inside was a pair of beautiful diamond cuff-links. They were in the shape of a star.

Whenever Toby had some free time, he relaxed around the large swimming pool at the back of the hotel. There were twenty-five girls in the show and there were always a dozen or so from the chorus line in bathing suits, sunning themselves. They appeared in the hot noon air like late-blooming flowers, one more beautiful than the next. Toby had never had trouble getting girls, but what happened to him now was a totally new experience. The showgirls had never heard of Toby Temple before, but his name was up in lights on the marquee. That was enough. He was a *Star,* and they fought each other for the privilege of going to bed with him.

The next two weeks were marvellous for Toby. He would wake up around noon, have breakfast in the dining room where he was kept busy signing autographs and then rehearse for an hour or two. Afterwards he would pick one or two of the long-legged beauties around the pool and they would go up to his suite for an afternoon romp in bed.

And Toby learned something new. Because of the skimpy costumes the girls wore, they had to get rid of their pubic hair. But they waxed it in such a way that only a curly strip of hair was left in the centre of the mound, making the opening more available.

'It's like an aphrodisiac,' one of the girls confided to Toby. 'A few hours in a pair of tight pants and a girl becomes a raving nymphomaniac.'

Toby did not bother to learn any of their names.

They were all 'baby' or 'honey', and they became a marvellous, sensuous blur of thighs and lips and eager bodies.

During the final week of Toby's engagement at the Oasis, he had a visitor. Toby had finished the first show and was in his dressing-room, creaming off his make-up, when the dining room captain opened the door and said in hushed tones, 'Mr Al Caruso would like you to join his table.'

Al Caruso was one of the big names in Las Vegas. He owned one hotel outright, and it was rumoured that he had points in two or three others. It was also rumoured that he had mob connections, but that was no concern of Toby's. What was important was that if Al Caruso liked him, Toby could get bookings in Las Vegas for the rest of his life. He hurriedly finished dressing and went into the dining room to meet Caruso.

Al Caruso was a short man in his fifties with grey hair, twinkling, soft brown eyes and a little paunch. He reminded Toby of a miniature Santa Claus. As Toby came up to the table, Caruso rose, held out his hand, smiled warmly and said, 'Al Caruso. Just wanted to tell you what I think of you, Toby. Pull up a chair.'

There were two other men at Caruso's table, dressed in dark suits. They were both burly, sipped Coca-Colas and did not say a word during the entire meeting. Toby never learned their names. Toby usually had his dinner after the first show. He was ravenous now, but Caruso had obviously just finished eating, and Toby did not want to appear to be more interested in food than in his meeting with the great man.

'I'm impressed with you, kid,' Caruso said. 'Real

impressed.' And he beamed at Toby with those mischievous brown eyes.

'Thanks, Mr Caruso,' Toby said happily. 'That means a lot to me.'

'Call me Al.'

'Yes, sir – Al.'

'You got a future, Toby. I've seen 'em come and I've seen 'em go. But the ones with talent last a long time. You got talent.'

Toby could feel a pleasant warmth suffusing his body. He fleetingly debated whether to tell Al Caruso to discuss business with Clifton Lawrence; but Toby decided it might be better if he made the deal himself. *If Caruso is this excited about me,* Toby thought, *I can make a better deal than Cliff.* Toby decided he would let Al Caruso make the first offer and then he would do some hard bargaining.

'I almost wet my pants,' Caruso was telling him. 'That monkey routine of yours is the funniest thing I ever heard.'

'Coming from you, that's a real compliment,' Toby said with sincerity.

The little Santa Claus eyes were filled with tears of laughter. He took out a white silk handkerchief and wiped them away. He turned to his two escorts. 'Did I say he's a funny man?'

The two men nodded.

Al Caruso turned back to Toby. 'Tell you why I came to see you, Toby.'

This was the magical moment, his entrance into the big time. Clifton Lawrence was off in Europe somewhere, making deals for has-been clients when he should have been here making *this* deal. Well,

Lawrence would have a real surprise in store for him when he returned.

Toby leaned forward and said, smiling engagingly, 'I'm listening, Al.'

'Millie loves you.'

Toby blinked, sure that he had missed something. The old man was watching him, his eyes twinkling.

'I – I'm sorry,' Toby said, in confusion. 'What did you say?'

Al Caruso smiled warmly. 'Millie loves you. She told me.'

Millie? Could that be Caruso's wife? His daughter? Toby started to speak, but Al Caruso interrupted.

'She's a great kid. I been keepin' her for three, four years.' He turned to the other two men. 'Four years?'

They nodded.

Al Caruso turned to Toby. 'I love that girl, Toby. I'm really crazy about her.'

Toby could feel the blood beginning to drain from his face. 'Mr Caruso –'

Al Caruso said, 'Millie and me got a deal. I don't cheat on her except with my wife, and she don't cheat on me unless she tells me.' He beamed at Toby, and this time Toby saw something beyond the cherubic smile that turned his blood to ice.

'Mr Caruso –'

'You know somethin', Toby? You're the first guy she ever cheated on me with.' He turned to the two men at the table. 'Is that the honest truth?'

They nodded.

When Toby spoke, his voice was trembling. 'I – I swear to God I didn't know Millie was your girlfriend. If I had even *dreamed* it, I wouldn't have touched her. I wouldn't have come within a mile of her, Mr Caruso – '

The Santa Claus beamed at him. 'Al. Call me Al.'

'Al.' It came out as a croak. Toby could feel the perspiration running down under his arms. 'Look, Al,' he said. 'I'll – I'll never see her again. *Ever.* Believe me, I – '

Caruso was staring at him. 'Hey! I don't think you were listening to me.'

Toby swallowed. 'Yes. Yes, I was. I heard every word you said. And you don't ever have to worry about – '

'I said the kid loves you. If she wants you, then I want her to have you. I want her to be happy. Understand?'

'I – ' Toby's brain was spinning. For a crazy moment he had actually thought that the man sitting across from him was looking for revenge. Instead Al Caruso was offering him his girlfriend. Toby almost laughed aloud with relief. 'Jesus, Al,' Toby said. 'Sure. Whatever you want.'

'Whatever Millie wants.'

'Yeah. Whatever Millie wants.'

'I knew you were a nice man,' Al Caruso said. He turned to the two men at the table. 'Did I say Toby Temple was a nice man?'

They nodded and silently sipped their Cokes.

Al Caruso rose, and the two men with him were instantly on their feet, one positioned on either side of him. 'I'm gonna give the wedding myself,' Al Caruso said. 'We'll take over the big banquet room at the Morocco. You don't have to worry about nothin'. I'll take care of everything.'

The words came at Toby as though filtered, from a far distance. His mind registered what Al Caruso was saying, but it made no sense to him.

'Wait a minute,' Toby protested. 'I can't – '

Caruso put a powerful hand on Toby's shoulder. 'You're a lucky man,' Caruso said. 'I mean, if Millie hadn't convinced me that you two really love each other, if I thought you were just laying her like she was some two-dollar hoor, this whole thing coulda had a different ending. You get my meaning?'

Toby found himself involuntarily looking up at the two men in black, and they both nodded.

'You finish up here Saturday night,' Al Caruso said. 'We'll make the wedding Sunday.'

Toby's throat had gone dry again. 'I – the thing is, Al, I'm afraid I have some bookings. I – '

'They'll wait,' the cherubic face beamed. 'I'm gonna pick out Millie's wedding dress myself. Night, Toby.'

Toby stood there, staring in the direction of the three figures long after they had disappeared.

He did not have the faintest notion who Millie was.

By the next morning, Toby's fears had evaporated. The unexpectedness of what had happened had thrown him off guard. But this was not the era of Al Capone. No one could force him to marry anyone he did not want to marry. Al Caruso was not some cheap, strong-arm hoodlum; he was a respectable hotel owner. The more Toby thought about the situation, the funnier it became. He kept embellishing it in his mind, building up the laughs. He had not really let Caruso scare him, of course, but he would tell it as though he had been terrified. *I go up to this table, and there's Caruso sitting with these six gorillas, see? They've all got big bulges where they're carrying guns.* Oh, yes, it would make a great story. He might even get a hilarious routine out of it.

For the rest of the week Toby stayed away from the swimming pool and the casino and avoided all the girls. He was not afraid of Al Caruso, but why take unnecessary chances? Toby had planned to leave Las Vegas by plane Sunday noon. Instead, he arranged for a rental car to be delivered to the back of the hotel parking lot Saturday night. The car would be waiting for him there. He packed his bags before he went downstairs to do his last show, so that he would be ready to leave for Los Angeles the moment he finished. He would stay away from Las Vegas for a while. If Al Caruso was really serious, Clifton Lawrence could straighten things out.

Toby's closing performance was sensational. He got a standing ovation, the first one he had ever received. He stood on the stage, feeling the waves of love coming from the audience, bathing him in a warm, soft glow. He did one encore, begged off and hurried upstairs. This had been the greatest three weeks of his life. In that short period of time, he had gone from a nobody who slept with waitresses and cripples to a Star who had laid Al Caruso's mistress. Beautiful girls were begging him to take them to bed, audiences admired him and the big hotels wanted him. He had it made, and he knew that this was only the beginning. He took out the key to his door. As he opened it, a familiar voice called out, 'Come on in, kid.'

Slowly, Toby entered the room. Al Caruso and his two friends were inside. A quick shiver of apprehension went down Toby's back. But it was all right. Caruso was beaming and saying, 'You were great tonight, Toby, really great.'

Toby began to relax. 'It was a good audience.'

Caruso's brown eyes twinkled and he said, 'You *made* them a good audience, Toby. I told you – you got talent.'

'Thanks, Al.' He wished they would all leave, so he could be on his way.

'You work hard,' Al Caruso said. He turned to his two lieutenants. 'Did I say I never seen nobody work so hard?'

The two men nodded.

Caruso turned back to Toby. 'Hey – Millie was kinda upset you didn't call her. I told her it was because you was workin' so hard.'

'That's right,' Toby said quickly. 'I'm glad you understand, Al.'

Al smiled benignly. 'Sure. But you know what I don't understand? You didn't call to find out what time the wedding is.'

'I was going to call in the morning.'

Al Caruso laughed and said chidingly, 'From LA?'

Toby felt a small pang of anxiety. 'What are you talking about, Al?'

Caruso regarded him reproachfully. 'You got your suitcases all packed in there.' He pinched Toby's cheek playfully. 'I told you I'd kill anyone who hurt Millie.'

'Wait a minute! Honest to God, I wasn't – '

'You're a good kid, but you're stupid, Toby. I guess that's part of bein' a genius, huh?'

Toby stared at the chubby, beaming countenance, not knowing what to say.

'You gotta believe me,' Al Caruso said warmly, 'I'm your friend. I wanna make sure nothin' bad happens to you. For Millie's sake. But if you won't listen to me, what can I do? You know how you get a mule to pay attention?'

Toby shook his head dumbly.

'First, you hit it over the head with a two-by-four.'

Toby felt fear rising in his throat.

'Which is your good arm?' Caruso asked.

'My – my right one,' Toby mumbled.

Caruso nodded genially and turned to the two men. 'Break it,' he said.

From out of nowhere, a tyre iron appeared in the hands of one of the men. The two of them began closing in on Toby. The river of fear became a sudden flood that made his whole body shake.

'For Christ's sake,' Toby heard himself say, inanely. 'You can't do this.'

One of the men hit him hard in the stomach. In the next second, Toby felt excruciating pain as the tyre iron slammed against his right arm, shattering bones. He fell to the floor, writhing in an unbearable agony. He tried to scream, but he could not catch his breath. Through tear-filled eyes, he looked up and saw Al Caruso standing over him, smiling.

'Have I got your attention?' Caruso asked softly.

Toby nodded, in torment.

'Good,' Caruso said. He turned to one of the men. 'Open up his pants.'

The man leaned down and unzipped Toby's fly. He took the tyre iron and flicked out Toby's penis.

Caruso stood there a moment, looking down at it. 'You're a lucky man, Toby. You're really hung.'

Toby was filled with a dread such as he had never known. 'Oh, God . . . please . . . don't . . . don't do it to me,' he croaked.

'I wouldn't hurt you,' Caruso told him. 'As long as you're good to Millie, you're my friend. If she ever tells me you did anything to hurt her – anything – you understand me?' He nudged Toby's broken arm with the toe of his shoe and Toby screamed aloud. 'I'm glad we understand each other,' Caruso beamed. 'The wedding is at one o'clock.'

Caruso's voice was fading in and out as Toby felt himself slipping into unconsciousness. But he knew he had to hang on. 'I can't,' he whimpered. 'My arm . . .'

'Don't worry about that,' Al Caruso said. 'There's a doc on his way up to take care of you. He's gonna set your arm and give you some stuff so you won't feel no pain. The boys will be here tomorrow to pick you up. You be ready, huh?'

Toby lay there in a nightmare of agony, staring up at Santa Claus's smiling face, unable to believe that any of this was really happening. He saw Caruso's foot moving towards his arm again.

'S-sure,' Toby moaned. 'I'll be ready . . .'

And he lost consciousness.

Chapter Eleven

The wedding, a gala event, was held in the ballroom of the Morocco Hotel. It seemed that half of Las Vegas was there. There were entertainers and owners from all the other hotels and showgirls and, in the centre of it all, Al Caruso and a couple of dozen of his friends, quiet, conservatively dressed men, most of whom did not drink. There were lavish arrangements of flowers everywhere, strolling musicians, a gargantuan buffet and two fountains that flowed champagne. Al Caruso had taken care of everything.

Everyone sympathized with the groom, whose arm was in a cast as a result of an accidental fall down some stairs. But they all commented on what a marvellous-looking couple the bride and groom made and what a wonderful wedding it was.

Toby had been in such a daze from the opiates that the doctor had given him that he had walked through the ceremony almost oblivious to what was going on. Then, as the drugs began to wear off and the pain began to take hold again, the anger and hate flooded back into him. He wanted to scream out to everyone in the room the unspeakable humiliation that had been forced upon him.

Toby turned to look at his bride across the room. He remembered Millie now. She was a pretty girl in her twenties, with honey-blonde hair and a good figure.

Toby recalled that she had laughed louder than the others at his stories and had followed him around. Something else came back to him, too. She was one of the few who had refused to go to bed with him, which had only served to whet Toby's appetite. It was *all* coming back to him now.

'I'm crazy about you,' he had said. 'Don't you like me?'

'Of course I do,' she had replied. 'But I have a boyfriend.'

Why hadn't he listened to her! Instead, he had coaxed her up to his room for a drink and then had started telling her funny stories. Millie was laughing so hard that she hardly noticed what Toby was doing until he had her undressed and in bed.

'Please, Toby,' she had begged. 'Don't. My boyfriend will be angry.'

'Forget about him. I'll take care of the jerk later,' Toby had said. 'I'm going to take care of *you*, now.'

They had had a wild night of lovemaking. In the morning, when Toby had awakened, Millie was lying beside him, crying. In a benevolent mood, Toby had taken her in his arms and said, 'Hey, baby, what's the matter? Didn't you enjoy it?'

'You know I did. But – '

'Come on, stop that,' Toby had said. 'I love you.'

She had propped herself up on her elbows, looked into his eyes and said, 'Do you really, Toby? I mean, *really*?'

'Damned right I do.' All she needed was what he would give her right now. It proved to be a real cheerer-upper.

She had watched him return from the shower,

towelling his still wet hair and humming snatches of his theme song. Happy, she had smiled and said, 'I think I loved you from the first moment I saw you, Toby.'

'Hey, that's wonderful. Let's order breakfast.'

And that had been the end of that . . . Until now. Because of a stupid broad he had fucked only one night, his whole life was turned topsy-turvy.

Now, Toby stood there, watching Millie coming towards him in her long, white wedding gown, smiling at him, and he cursed himself and he cursed his cock and he cursed the day he was born.

In the limousine, the man in the front seat chuckled and said admiringly, 'I sure gotta hand it to you, boss. The poor bastard never knew what hit him.'

Caruso smiled benignly. It had worked out well. Ever since his wife, who had the temper of a virago, had found out about his affair with Millie, Caruso had known that he would have to find a way to get rid of the blonde showgirl.

'Remind me to see that he treats Millie good,' Caruso said softly.

Toby and Millie moved into a small home in Benedict Canyon. In the beginning, Toby spent hours scheming about ways to get out of his marriage. He would make Millie so miserable that she would ask for a divorce. Or he would frame her with another guy and then demand a divorce. Or he would simply leave her and defy Caruso to do something about it. But he changed his mind after a talk with Dick Landry, the director.

They were having lunch at the Bel Air Hotel a few

weeks after the wedding, and Landry asked, 'How well do you really know Al Caruso?'

Toby looked at him. 'Why?'

'Don't get mixed up with him, Toby. He's a killer. I'll tell you something I know for a fact. Caruso's kid brother married a nineteen-year-old girl fresh out of a convent. A year later, the kid caught his wife in bed with some guy. He told Al about it.'

Toby was listening, his eyes fastened on Landry. 'What happened?'

'Caruso's goons took a meat cleaver and cut off the guy's prick. They soaked it in gasoline and set it on fire while the guy watched. Then they left him to bleed to death.'

Toby remembered Caruso saying, *Open up his pants,* and the hard hands fumbling at his zipper, and Toby broke out in a cold sweat. He felt suddenly sick to his stomach. He knew now with an awful certainty that there was no escape.

Josephine found an escape when she was ten. It was a door to another world where she could hide from her mother's punishment and the constant threat of Hellfire and Damnation. It was a world filled with magic and beauty. She would sit in the darkened movie house hour after hour and watch the glamorous people on the screen. They all lived in beautiful houses and wore lovely clothes, and they were all so happy. And Josephine thought, I will go to Hollywood one day and live like that. She hoped that her mother would understand.

Her mother believed that movies were the thoughts of the Devil, so Josephine had to sneak away to the theatre, using money she earned by baby-sitting. The picture that was playing today was a love story, and Josephine leaned forward in joyous anticipation as it began. The credits came on first. They read, 'Produced by Sam Winters.'

Chapter Twelve

There were days when Sam Winters felt as though he were running a lunatic asylum instead of a motion-picture studio, and that all the inmates were out to get him. This was one of those days, for the crises were piled a foot high. There had been another fire at the studio the night before – the fourth; the sponsor of 'My Man Friday' had been insulted by the star of the series and wanted to cancel the show; Bert Firestone, the studio's boy-genius director, had shut down production in the middle of a five-million-dollar picture; and Tessie Brand had walked out on a picture that was scheduled to start shooting in a few days.

The fire marshal and the studio comptroller were in Sam's office.

'How bad was last night's fire?' Sam asked.

The comptroller said, 'The sets are a total loss, Mr Winters. We're going to have to rebuild Stage Fifteen completely. Sixteen is fixable, but it will take us three months.'

'We haven't got three months,' Sam snapped. 'Get on the phone and rent some space at Goldwyn. Use this weekend to start building new sets. Get everybody moving.'

He turned to the fire marshal, a man named Reilly, who reminded Sam of George Bancroft, the actor.

'Somebody sure as hell don't like you, Mr Winters,'

Reilly said. 'Each fire has been a clear case of arson. Have you checked on grunts?'

Grunts were disgruntled employees who had been recently fired or felt they had a grievance against their employer.

'We've gone through all the personnel files twice,' Sam replied. 'We haven't come up with a thing.'

'Whoever is setting these babies knows exactly what he's doing. He's using a timing device attached to a homemade incendiary. He could be an electrician or a mechanic.'

'Thanks,' Sam said. 'I'll pass that on.'

'Roger Tapp is calling from Tahiti.'

'Put him on,' Sam said. Tapp was the producer of 'My Man Friday', the television series being shot in Tahiti, starring Tony Fletcher.

'What's the problem?' Sam asked.

'You won't fucking believe this, Sam. Philip Heller, the chairman of the board of the company that's sponsoring the show, is visiting here with his family. They walked on the set yesterday afternoon, and Tony Fletcher was in the middle of a scene. He turned to them and insulted them.'

'What did he say?'

'He told them to *get off his island*.'

'Jesus Christ!'

'That's who he thinks he is. Heller's so mad he wants to cancel the series.'

'Get over to Heller and apologize. Do it right now. Tell him Tony Fletcher's having a nervous breakdown. Send Mrs Heller flowers, take them to dinner. I'll talk to Tony Fletcher myself.'

*

The conversation lasted thirty minutes. It began with Sam saying, 'Hear this, you stupid cocksucker. . . ' and ended with, 'I love you, too, baby. I'll fly over there to see you as soon as I can get away. And for God's sake, Tony, don't lay Mrs Heller!'

The next problem was Bert Firestone, the boy-genius director who was breaking Pan-Pacific Studios. Firestone's picture, *There's Always Tomorrow,* had been shooting for a hundred and ten days, and was more than a million dollars over budget. Now Bert Firestone had shut the production down, which meant that, besides the stars, there were a hundred and fifty extras sitting around on their asses doing nothing. Bert Firestone. A thirty-year-old whiz kid who came from directing prize-winning television shows at a Chicago station to directing movies in Hollywood. Firestone's first three motion pictures had been mild successes, but his fourth one had been a box-office smash. On the basis of that moneymaker, he had become a hot property. Sam remembered his first meeting with him. Firestone looked a not-yet-ready-to-shave fifteen. He was a pale, shy man with black horn-rimmed glasses that concealed tiny, myopic pink eyes. Sam had felt sorry for the kid. Firestone had not known anyone in Hollywood, so Sam had gone out of his way to have him to dinner and to see that he was invited to parties. When they had first discussed *There's Always Tomorrow*, Firestone was very respectful. He told Sam that he was eager to learn. He hung on every word that Sam said. He could not have agreed more with Sam. If he were signed for this picture, he told Sam, he would certainly lean heavily on Mr Winter's expertise.

That was *before* Firestone signed the contract. *After* he signed it, he made Adolf Hitler look like Albert Schweitzer. The little apple-cheeked kid turned into a killer overnight. He cut off all communication. He completely ignored Sam's casting suggestions, insisted on totally rewriting a fine script that Sam had approved, and he changed most of the shooting locales that had already been agreed upon. Sam had wanted to throw him off the picture, but the New York office had told Sam to be patient. Rudolph Hergershorn, the president of the company, was hypnotized by the enormous grosses on Firestone's last movie. So Sam had been forced to sit tight and do nothing. It seemed to him that Firestone's arrogance grew day by day. He would sit quietly through a production meeting, and when all the experienced department heads had finished speaking, Firestone would begin chopping down everyone. Sam gritted his teeth and bore it. In no time at all, Firestone acquired the nickname of the Emperor, and when his co-workers were not calling him that, they referred to him as Kid Prick from Chicago. Somebody said about him, 'He's a hermaphrodite. He could probably fuck himself and give birth to a two-headed monster.'

Now, in the middle of shooting, Firestone had closed down the company.

Sam went over to see Devlin Kelly, the head of the art department. 'Give it to me fast,' Sam said.

'Right, Kid Prick ordered – '

'Cut that out. It's *Mr* Firestone.'

'Sorry. *Mr Firestone* asked me to build a castle set for him. He drew sketches himself. You okayed them.'

'They were good. What happened?'

'What happened was that we built him exactly what the little – what he wanted, and when he took a look at it yesterday, he decided he didn't want it anymore. A half-million bucks down the –'

'I'll talk to him,' Sam said.

Bert Firestone was outside, in back of Stage Twenty-three playing basketball with the crew. They had rigged up a court and had painted in boundary lines and put up two baskets.

Sam stood there, watching a moment. The game was costing the studio two thousand dollars an hour. 'Bert!'

Firestone turned, saw Sam, smiled and waved. The ball came to him, he dribbled it, feinted, and sank a basket. Then he strolled over to Sam. 'How are things?' As though nothing were wrong.

As Sam looked at the boyish, smiling young face, it occurred to him that Bert Firestone was a psycho. Talented, maybe even a genius, but a certifiable lunatic. And five million dollars of the company's money was in his hands.

'I hear there's a problem with the new set,' Sam said. 'Let's straighten it out.'

Bert Firestone smiled lazily and said, 'There's nothing to straighten out, Sam. The set won't work.'

Sam exploded. 'What the hell are you talking about? We gave you exactly what you ordered. You did the sketches yourself. Now you tell me what's wrong with it!'

Firestone looked at him and blinked. 'Why, there's nothing wrong with it. It's just that I've changed my mind. I don't want a castle. I've decided that's not the right ambience. Do you know what I mean? This is Ellen and Mike's farewell scene. I'd like to have Ellen come to visit Mike on the deck of his ship as he's getting ready to sail.'

Sam stared at him. 'We don't have a ship set, Bert.'

Bert Firestone stretched his arms and smiled lazily and said, 'Build one for me, Sam.'

'Sure, I'm pissed off, too,' Rudolph Hergershorn said, over the long-distance line, 'but you *can't* replace him, Sam. We're in too deep now. We have no stars in the picture. *Bert Firestone*'s our star.'

'Do you know how far over the budget he's – '

'I know. And like Goldwyn said, "I'll never use the son of a bitch again, until I need him." We need him to finish this picture.'

'It's a mistake,' Sam argued. 'He shouldn't be allowed to get away with this.'

'Sam – do you like the stuff Firestone has shot so far?'

Sam had to be honest. 'It's great.'

'Build him his ship.'

The set was ready in ten days, and Bert Firestone put the *There's Always Tomorrow* company back into production. It turned out to be the top grosser of the year.

The next problem was Tessie Brand.

Tessie was the hottest singer in show business. It had been a coup when Sam Winters had managed to sign her to a three-picture deal at Pan-Pacific Studios. While the other studios were negotiating with Tessie's agents, Sam had quietly flown to New York, seen Tessie's show and taken her out to supper afterwards. The supper had lasted until seven o'clock the following morning.

Tessie Brand was one of the ugliest girls Sam had ever seen, and probably the most talented. It was the talent that won out. The daughter of a Brooklyn tailor, Tessie had never had a singing lesson in her life. But when she walked onto a stage and began belting out a song in a voice that rocked the rafters, audiences went wild. Tessie had been an understudy in a flop Broadway musical that had lasted only six weeks. On closing night, the ingenue made the mistake of phoning in sick and staying home. Tessie Brand made her debut that evening, singing her heart out to the sprinkling of people in the audience. Among them happened to be Paul Varrick, a Broadway producer. He starred Tessie in his next musical. She turned the show, which was fair, into a smash. The critics ran out of superlatives trying to describe the incredible, ugly Tessie and her amazing voice. She recorded her first single record. Overnight it became number one. She did an album, and it sold two million copies in the first month. She was Queen Midas, for everything she touched turned to gold. Broadway producers and record companies were making their fortunes with Tessie Brand, and Hollywood wanted in on the action. Their enthusiasm dimmed when they got a look at Tessie's face, but her box-office figures gave her an irresistible beauty.

After spending five minutes with her, Sam knew how he was going to handle her.

'What makes me nervous,' Tessie confessed to Sam the first night they met, 'is how I'm gonna look on that great big screen. I'm ugly enough *life-sized,* right? All the studios tell me they can make me look beautiful, but I think that's a load of horseshit.'

'It *is* a load of horseshit,' Sam said. Tessie looked at him in surprise. 'Don't let anyone try to change you, Tessie. They'll ruin you.'

'Yeah?'

'When MGM signed Danny Thomas, Louie Mayer wanted him to get a nose job. Instead, Danny quit the studio. He knew that what he had to sell was *himself*. That's what *you* have to sell – Tessie Brand, not some plastic stranger up there.'

'You're the first one who's levelled with me,' Tessie said. 'You're a real *Mensch*. You married?'

'No,' Sam said.

'Do you fool around?'

Sam laughed. 'Never with singers – I have no ear.'

'You wouldn't need an ear.' Tessie smiled. 'I like you.'

'Do you like me well enough to make some movies with me?'

She looked at him and said, 'Yeah.'

'Wonderful. I'll work out the deal with your agent.'

She stroked Sam's hand and said, 'Are you sure you don't fool around?'

Tessie Brand's first two pictures went through the box-office roof. She received an Academy nomination for the first one and was awarded the golden Oscar for the second. Audiences all over the world lined up at motion-picture theatres to see Tessie and to hear that incredible voice. She had everything. She was funny, she could sing and she could act. Her ugliness turned out to be an asset, because audiences identified with it. Tessie Brand became a surrogate for all the unattractive, the unloved, the unwanted.

Tessie married the leading man in her first picture, divorced him after the retakes and married the leading man in her next picture. Sam had heard rumours that this marriage too was sinking, but Hollywood was a hotbed of gossip. He paid no attention, for he felt that it was none of his business.

As it turned out, he was mistaken.

Sam was talking on the phone to Barry Herman, Tessie's agent. 'What's the problem, Barry?'

'Tessie's new picture. She's not happy, Sam.'

Sam felt his temper rising. 'Hold it! Tessie approved the producer, the director and the shooting script. We've got the sets built and we're ready to roll. There's no way she can walk away now. I'll – '

'She doesn't want to walk away.'

Sam was taken aback. 'What the hell *does* she want?'

'She wants a new producer on the picture.'

Sam yelled into the phone. 'She *what*?'

'Ralph Dastin doesn't understand her.'

'Dastin's one of the best producers in the business. She's lucky to have him.'

'I couldn't agree with you more, Sam. But the chemistry's wrong. She won't make the picture unless he's out.'

'She's got a contract, Barry.'

'I know that, sweetheart. And, believe me, Tessie has every intention of honouring it. As long as she's physically able. It's just that she gets nervous when she's unhappy and she can't seem to remember her lines.'

'I'll call you back,' Sam said savagely. He slammed down the phone.

The goddamned bitch! There was no reason to fire Dastin from the picture. He had probably refused to go to bed with her, or something equally ridiculous. He said to Lucille, 'Ask Ralph Dastin to come up here.'

Ralph Dastin was an amiable man in his fifties. He had started as a writer and had eventually become a producer. His movies had taste and charm.

'Ralph,' Sam began, 'I don't know how to – '

Dastin held up his hand. 'You don't have to say it, Sam. I was on my way up here to tell you I'm quitting.'

'What the hell's going on?' Sam demanded.

Dastin shrugged. 'Our star's got an itch. She wants someone else to scratch it.'

'You mean she has your replacement already picked out?'

'Jesus, where have you been – on Mars? Don't you read the gossip columns?'

'Not if I can help it. Who is he?'

'It's not a he.'

Sam sat down, slowly. *'What?'*

'It's the costume designer on Tessie's picture. Her name is Barbara Carter – like the little liver pills.'

'Are you sure about this?' Sam asked.

'You're the only one in the entire Western Hemisphere who doesn't know it.'

Sam shook his head. 'I always thought Tessie was straight.'

'Sam, life's a cafeteria. Tessie's a hungry girl.'

'Well, I'm not about to put a goddamned female costume designer in charge of a four-million-dollar picture.'

Dastin grinned. 'You just said the wrong thing.'

'What does *that* mean?'

'It means that part of Tessie's pitch is that women aren't given a fair chance in this business. Your little star has become very feminist-minded.'

'I won't do it,' Sam said.

'Suit yourself. But I'll give you some free advice. It's the only way you're ever going to get this picture made.'

Sam telephoned Barry Herman. 'Tell Tessie that Ralph Dastin walked off the picture,' Sam said.

'She'll be pleased to hear that.'

Sam gritted his teeth, then asked, 'Did she have anyone else in mind to produce the picture?'

'As a matter of fact, she did,' Herman said smoothly. 'Tessie has discovered a very talented young girl who she feels is ready for a challenge like this. Under the guidance of someone as brilliant as you, Sam – '

'Cut out the commercial,' Sam said. 'Is that the bottom line?'

'I'm afraid it is, Sam. I'm sorry.'

Barbara Carter had a pretty face and a good figure and, as far as Sam could tell, was completely feminine. He watched her as she took a seat on the leather couch in his office and daintily crossed her long, shapely legs. When she spoke, her voice sounded a trifle husky, but that may have been because Sam was looking for some kind of sign. She studied him with soft grey eyes and said, 'I seem to be in a terrible spot, Mr Winters. I had no intention of putting anyone out of work. And yet' – she raised her hands helplessly – 'Miss Brand says she simply won't make the picture unless I produce it. What do you think I should do?'

For an instant, Sam was tempted to tell her. Instead, he said, 'Have you had any experience with show business – besides being a costume designer?'

'I've ushered, and I've seen lots of movies.'

Terrific! 'What makes Miss Brand think you can produce a motion picture?'

It was as though Sam had touched a hidden spring. Barbara Carter was suddenly full of animation. 'Tessie and I have talked a lot about this picture.' No more '*Miss Brand*', Sam noticed. 'I feel there are a lot of things wrong with the script, and when I pointed them out to her, she agreed with me.'

'Do you think you know more about writing a script than an Academy Award-winning writer who's done half a dozen successful pictures and Broadway plays?'

'Oh, no, Mr Winters! I just think I know more about *women.*' The grey eyes were harder now, the tone a little tougher. 'Don't you think it's ridiculous for men to always be writing women's parts? Only *we* really know how we feel. Doesn't that make sense to you?'

Sam was tired of the game. He knew he was going to hire her, and he hated himself for it, but he was running a studio, and his job was to see that pictures got made. If Tessie Brand wanted her pet squirrel to produce this picture, Sam would start ordering nuts. A Tessie Brand picture could easily mean a profit of from twenty to thirty million dollars. Besides, Barbara Carter couldn't do anything to really hurt the picture. Not now. It was too close to shooting for any major changes to be made.

'You've convinced me,' Sam said, with irony. 'You've got the job. Congratulations.'

The following morning, the *Hollywood Reporter* and

Variety announced on their front pages that Barbara Carter was producing the new Tessie Brand movie. As Sam started to throw the papers in his wastebasket, a small item at the bottom of the page caught his eye: 'TOBY TEMPLE SIGNED FOR LOUNGE AT TAHOE HOTEL.'

Toby Temple. Sam remembered the eager young comic in uniform, and the memory brought a smile to Sam's face. Sam made a mental note to see his act if Temple ever played in town.

He wondered why Toby Temple had never gotten in touch with him.

Chapter Thirteen

In a strange way, it was Millie who was responsible for Toby Temple's rise to stardom. Before their marriage, he had been just another up-and-coming comic, one of dozens. Since the wedding, a new ingredient had been added: hatred. Toby had been forced into a marriage with a girl he despised, and there was such rage in him that he could have killed her with his bare hands.

Although Toby did not realize it, Millie was a wonderful, devoted wife. She adored him and did everything she could to please him. She decorated the house in Benedict Canyon, and did it beautifully. But the more Millie tried to please Toby, the more he loathed her. He was always meticulously polite to her, careful never to do or say anything that might upset her enough to call Al Caruso. As long as he lived, Toby would not forget the awful agony of that tyre iron smashing into his arm, or the look on Al Caruso's face when he said, 'If you ever hurt Millie . . .'

Because Toby could not take out his aggressions on his wife, he turned his fury on his audiences. Anyone who rattled a dish, or rose to go to the washroom or dared to talk while Toby was on stage was the instant object of a savage tirade. Toby dealt it with such wide-eyed, naive charm that the audiences adored it, and when Toby ripped apart some hapless victim, people laughed until they cried. The combination of his innocent, guileless face and his wicked, funny tongue made him irresistible. He could say the most outrageous things and get away with them. It became a mark of distinction to be singled out for a tongue lashing by Toby Temple. It never occurred to his victims that Toby meant every word he said. Where before Toby had been just another promising young comedian, now he became the talk of the entertainment circuit.

When Clifton Lawrence returned from Europe, he was amazed to learn that Toby had married a showgirl. It had seemed out of character, but when he asked Toby about it, Toby looked him in the eye and said, 'What's there to tell, Cliff? I met Millie, fell in love with her and that was that.'

Somehow, it had not rung true. And there was something else that puzzled the agent. One day in his office, Clifton told Toby, 'You're really getting hot. I've booked you into the Thunderbird for a four-week gig. Two thousand a week.'

'What about that tour?'

'Forget it. Las Vegas pays ten times as much, and everybody will see your act.'

'Cancel Vegas. Get me the tour.'

Clifton looked at him in surprise. 'But Las Vegas is –'

'Get me the tour.' There was a note in Toby's voice that Clifton Lawrence had never heard before. It was not arrogance or temperament; it was something beyond that, a deep, controlled rage.

What made it frightening was that it emanated from a face that had grown more genial and boyish than ever.

*

From that time on, Toby was on the road constantly. It was his only escape from his prison. He played nightclubs and theatres and auditoriums, and when those bookings ran out, he badgered Clifton Lawrence to book him into colleges. Anywhere, to get away from Millie.

The opportunities to go to bed with eager, attractive women were limitless. It was the same in every town. They waited in Toby's dressing room before and after the show and waylaid him in his hotel lobby.

Toby went to bed with none of them. He thought of the man's penis being hacked off and set on fire and Al Caruso saying to Toby, *You're really hung . . . I wouldn't hurt you. You're my friend. As long as you're good to Millie . . .* And Toby turned all the women away.

'I'm in love with my wife,' he would say shyly. And they believed him and admired him for it, and the word spread, as Toby meant it to spread: Toby Temple did not fool around; he was a real family man.

But the lovely, nubile young girls kept coming after him, and the more Toby refused, the more they wanted him. And Toby was so hungry for a woman that he was in constant physical pain. His groin ached so much that sometimes it was difficult for him to work. He started to masturbate again. Each time he did, he thought of all the beautiful girls waiting to go to bed with him, and he cursed and raged against fate.

Because Toby could not have it, sex was on his mind all the time. Whenever he returned home after a tour, Millie was waiting for him, eager and loving and ready. And the moment Toby saw her, all his sexual desire drained away. She was the enemy, and Toby despised her for what she was doing to him. He forced himself to go to bed with her, but it was Al Caruso he was satisfying. Whenever Toby took Millie, it was with a savage brutality that forced gasps of pain from her. He pretended that he thought they were sounds of pleasure, and he pounded into her harder and harder, until finally he came in an explosion of fury that poured his venomous semen into her. He was not making love.

He was making hate.

In June, 1950, the North Koreans moved across the 38th Parallel and attacked the South Koreans, and President Truman ordered United States troops in. No matter what the rest of the world thought about it, to Toby the Korean War was the best thing that ever happened.

In early December, there was an announcement in *Daily Variety* that Bob Hope was getting ready to make a Christmas tour to entertain the troops in Seoul. Thirty seconds after he read it, Toby was on the telephone, talking to Clifton Lawrence.

'You've got to get me on it, Cliff.'

'What for? You're almost thirty years old. Believe me, dear boy, those tours are no fun. I – '

'I don't give a damn whether they're fun or not,' Toby shouted into the phone. 'Those soldiers are out there risking their lives. The least I can do is give them a few laughs.'

It was a side of Toby Temple that Clifton had not seen before. He was touched and pleased.

'Okay. If you feel that strongly about it, I'll see what I can do,' Clifton promised.

An hour later he called Toby back. 'I talked to Bob. He'd be happy to have you. But if you should change your mind – '

'No chance,' Toby said, hanging up.

Clifton Lawrence sat there a long time, thinking about Toby. He was very proud of him. Toby was a wonderful human being, and Clifton Lawrence was delighted to be his agent, delighted to be the man helping to shape his growing career.

Toby played Taegu and Pusan and Chonju, and he found solace in the laughter of the soldiers. Millie faded into the background of his mind.

Then Christmas was over. Instead of returning home, Toby went to Guam. The boys there loved him. He went to Tokyo and entertained the wounded in the army hospital. But finally, it was time to return home.

In April, when Toby came back from a ten-week tour in the Midwest, Millie was waiting at the airport for him. Her first words were, 'Darling – I'm going to have a baby!'

He stared at her, stunned. She mistook his expression for happiness.

'Isn't it wonderful?' she exclaimed. 'Now, when you're away, I'll have the baby to keep me company. I hope it's a boy so that you can take him to baseball games and . . .'

Toby did not hear the rest of the stupidities she was mouthing. It was as though her words were being filtered from far away. Somewhere in the back of his mind, Toby had believed that someday, somehow, there would be an escape for him. They had been married two years, and it seemed like an eternity. Now this. Millie would *never* let him go.

Never.

The baby was due around Christmas time. Toby had made arrangements to go to Guam with a troupe of entertainers, but he had no idea whether Al Caruso would approve of his being away while Millie was having the baby. There was only one way to find out. Toby called Las Vegas.

Caruso's cheerful, familiar voice came on the line immediately and said, 'Hi, kid. Good to hear your voice.'

'It's good to hear yours, Al.'

'I hear you're gonna be a father. You must be real excited.'

'Excited isn't the word for it,' Toby said truthfully. He let his voice take on a note of careful concern. 'That's the reason I'm calling you, Al. The baby's going to be born around Christmas, and – ' He had to be very careful. 'I don't know what to do. I want to be here with Millie when the kid's born, but they asked me to go back to Korea and Guam to entertain the troops.'

There was a long pause. 'That's a tough spot.'

'I don't want to let our boys down, but I don't want to let Millie down, either.'

'Yeah.' There was another pause. Then, 'I'll tell you what I think, kid. We're all good Americans, right? Those kids are out there fighting for us, right?'

Toby felt his body suddenly relax. 'Sure. But I hate to – '

'Millie'll be okay,' Caruso said. 'Women have been havin' babies a hell of a long time. You go to Korea.'

Six weeks later, on Christmas Eve, as Toby walked off a stage to thunderous applause at the army post in Pusan, he was handed a cable, informing him that Millie had died while giving birth to a stillborn son.

Toby was free.

Chapter Fourteen

August 14, 1952, was Josephine Czinski's thirteenth birthday. She was invited to a party by Mary Lou Kenyon, who had been born on the same day. Josephine's mother had forbidden her to go. 'Those are wicked people,' Mrs Czinski admonished her. 'You'll be better off stayin' home and studyin' your Bible.'

But Josephine had no intention of remaining at home. Her friends were *not* wicked. She wished that there was some way she could make her mother understand. As soon as her mother left, Josephine took five dollars that she had earned by baby-sitting and went downtown, where she bought a lovely white bathing suit. Then she headed for Mary Lou's house. She had a feeling it was going to be a wonderful day.

Mary Lou Kenyon lived in the most beautiful of all the Oil People mansions. Her home was filled with antiques and priceless tapestries and beautiful paintings. On the grounds were guest cottages, stables, a tennis court, a private landing strip and two swimming pools, an enormous one for the Kenyons and their guests and a smaller one in back for the staff.

Mary Lou had an older brother, David, of whom Josephine had caught glimpses from time to time. He was the most handsome boy Josephine had ever seen. He seemed about ten feet tall with broad, football shoulders and teasing grey eyes. He was an All-American halfback and had been given a Rhodes scholarship Mary Lou had also had an older sister, Beth, who had died when Josephine was a little girl.

Now, at the party, Josephine kept looking around hopefully for David, but she did not see him anywhere. In the past, he had stopped to speak to her several times, but each time Josephine had reddened and stood there, tongue-tied.

The party was a big success. There were fourteen boys and girls. They had eaten an enormous lunch of barbecue beef, chicken, chilli and potato salad and lemonade, served on the terrace by uniformed butlers and maids. Then Mary Lou and Josephine opened their presents, while everyone stood around and commented on them.

Mary Lou said, 'Let's all go for a swim.'

Everyone made a dash for the dressing rooms at their side of the pool. As Josephine changed into her new bathing suit, she thought that she had never been so happy. It had been a perfect day, spent with her friends. She was one of them, sharing the beauty that surrounded them everywhere. There was nothing evil about it. She wished she could stop time and freeze this day so that it would never end.

Josephine stepped out into the bright sunlight. As she walked towards the pool, she became aware that the others were watching her, the girls with open envy, the boys with sly, covert looks. In the past few months Josephine's body had matured dramatically. Her breasts were firm and full, straining against her bathing suit, and her hips hinted at the lush, rounded curves of a woman. Josephine dived into the pool, joining the others.

'Let's play Marco Polo,' someone called out.

Josephine loved the game. She enjoyed moving around in the warm water with her eyes tightly closed. She would call out 'Marco!' and the others would have to reply, 'Polo!' Josephine would dive after the sound of their voices before they got away, until she tagged someone, and then that person became 'it'.

They began the game. Cissy Topping was 'it'. She went after the boy she liked, Bob Jackson, but could not get him, so she tagged Josephine. Josephine closed her eyes tightly and listened for the telltale sound of splashes.

'Marco!' she called out.

There was a chorus of 'Polo!' Josephine made a dive for the nearest voice. She felt around in the water. There was no one there.

'Marco!' she called.

Again, a chorus of 'Polo!' She made a blind grab but reached only thin air. It did not matter to Josephine that they were faster than she; she wanted this game to go on for ever, as she wanted this day to last until eternity.

She stood still, straining to hear a splash, a giggle, a whisper. She moved around in the pool, eyes closed, hands outstretched, and reached the steps. She took a step up to quiet the sound of her own movements.

'Marco!' she called out.

And there was no answer. She stood there, still.

'Marco!'

Silence. It was as though she were in a warm, wet deserted world, alone. They were playing a trick on her. They had decided that no one would answer her. Josephine smiled and opened her eyes.

She was alone on the pool steps. Something made her look down. The bottom of her white bathing suit was stained with red, and there was a thin trickle of blood coming from between her thighs. The children were all standing on the sides of the pool, staring at her. Josephine looked up at them, stricken. 'I – ' She stopped, not knowing what to say. She quickly moved down the steps into the water, to cover her shame.

'We don't do that in the swimming pool,' Mary Lou said.

'Polacks do,' someone giggled.

'Hey, let's go take a shower.'

'Yeah. I feel icky.'

'Who wants to swim in *that?*'

Josephine closed her eyes again and heard them all moving towards the poolhouse, leaving her. She stayed there, keeping her eyes squeezed closed, pressing her legs together to try to stop the shameful flow. She had never had her period before. It had been totally unexpected. They would all come back in a moment and tell her that they had only been teasing, that they were still her friends, that the happiness would never stop. They would return and explain that it was all a game. Perhaps they were back already to play. Eyes tightly shut, she whispered, 'Marco', and the echo died on the afternoon air. She had no idea how long she stood there in the water with her eyes closed.

We don't do that in the swimming pool.

Polacks do.

Her head had begun pounding violently. She felt nauseous, and her stomach was suddenly cramping.

But Josephine knew that she must keep standing there with her eyes tightly shut. Just until they returned and told her it was a joke.

She heard footsteps and a rustling sound above her and she suddenly knew that everything was all right. They had come back. She opened her eyes and looked up.

David, Mary Lou's older brother, was standing at the side of the pool, a terrycloth robe in his hands.

'I apologize for all of them,' he said, his voice tight. He held out the robe. 'Here. Come out and put this on.'

But Josephine closed her eyes and stayed there, rigid. She wanted to die as quickly as possible.

Chapter Fifteen

It was one of Sam Winters' good days. The rushes on the Tessie Brand picture were wonderful. Part of the reason, of course, was that Tessie was breaking her neck to vindicate her behaviour. But whatever the reason, Barbara Carter was going to emerge as the hottest new producer of the year. It was going to be a terrific year for costume designers.

The television shows produced by Pan-Pacific were doing well, and 'My Man Friday' was the biggest of them all. The network was talking to Sam about a new five-year contract for the series.

Sam was preparing to leave for lunch when Lucille hurried in and said, 'They just caught someone setting a fire in the prop department. They're bringing him over here now.'

The man sat in a chair facing Sam in silence, two studio guards standing behind him. His eyes were bright with malice. Sam had still not gotten over his shock. 'Why?' he asked. 'For God's sake – why?'

'Because I didn't want your fucking charity,' Dallas Burke said. 'I hate you and this studio and the whole rotten business. I *built* this business, you son of a bitch. I paid for half the studios in this lousy town. Everybody got rich off me. Why didn't you give me a picture to direct instead of trying to pay me off by pretending to buy a bunch of fucking stolen fairy tales? You would have bought the phone book from me, Sam. I didn't want any favours from you – I wanted a job. You're making me die a failure, you prick, and I'll never forgive you for that.'

Long after they had taken Dallas Burke away, Sam sat there thinking about him, remembering the great things Dallas had done, the wonderful movies he had made. In any other business, he would have been a hero, the chairman of the board or would have been retired with a nice, fat pension and glory.

But this was the wonderful world of show business.

Chapter Sixteen

In the early 1950s, Toby Temple's success was growing. He played the top nightclubs – the Chez Paree in Chicago, the Latin Casino in Philadelphia, the Copacabana in New York. He played benefits and children's hospitals and charity affairs – he would play for anybody, anywhere, at any time. The audience was his lifeblood. He needed the applause and the love. He was totally absorbed in show business. Major events were occurring around the world, but to Toby they were merely grist for his act.

In 1951, when General MacArthur was fired and said, 'Old soldiers don't die – they just fade away,' Toby said, 'Jesus – we must use the same laundry.'

In 1952, when the hydrogen bomb was dropped, Toby's response was, 'That's nothing. You should have caught my opening in Atlanta.'

When Nixon made his 'Checkers' speech, Toby said, 'I'd vote for him in a minute. Not Nixon – Checkers.'

Ike was President and Stalin died and young America was wearing Davy Crockett hats and there was a bus boycott in Montgomery.

When he delivered his zingers with that wide-eyed look of baffled innocence, the audiences screamed.

Toby's whole life consisted of punch lines. '. . . so he said, "Wait a minute; I'll get my hat and go with you . . ."' and '. . . to tell the truth, it looked so good I ate it myself!' and '. . . it's a candystore, but they'll call me . . .' and '. . . I would have been a Shamus . . .' and '. . . now I've got you and there's no ship . . .' and 'Just my luck. I get the part that eats . . .' and on and on, with the audiences laughing until they cried. His audiences loved him, and he fed on their love and battened on it and climbed ever higher.

But there was a deep, wild restlessness in Toby. He was always looking for something more. He could never enjoy himself because he was afraid he might be missing a better party somewhere, or playing to a better audience, or kissing a prettier girl. He changed girls as frequently as he changed his shirts. After the experience with Millie, he was afraid to become deeply involved with anyone. He remembered when he had played the Toilet Circuit and envied the comics with the big limousines and the beautiful women. He had made it, and he was as lonely now as he had been then. Who was it who had said, 'When you get there, there is no there . . .'?

He was dedicated to becoming Number One and he knew he would make it. His one regret was that his mother would not be there to watch her prediction come true.

The only reminder left of her was his father.

The nursing home in Detroit was an ugly brick building from another century. Its walls held the sweet stench of old age and sickness and death.

Toby Temple's father had suffered a stroke and was almost a vegetable now, a man with listless, apathetic eyes and a mind that cared for nothing except Toby's visits. Toby stood in the dingy green-carpeted hall of the home that now held his father. The nurses and inmates crowded adoringly around him.

'I saw you on the Harold Hobson show last week, Toby. I thought you were just marvellous. How do you think of all those clever things to say?'

'My writers think of them,' Toby said, and they laughed at his modesty.

A male nurse was coming down the corridor, wheeling Toby's father. He was freshly shaved and had his hair slicked down. He had let them dress him in a suit in honour of his son's visit.

'Hey, it's Beau Brummel!' Toby called, and everyone turned to look at Mr Temple with envy, wishing that they had a wonderful, famous son like Toby to come and visit them.

Toby walked over to his father, leaned down and gave him a hug. 'Who you trying to kid?' Toby asked. He pointed to the male nurse. '*You* should be wheeling *him* around, Pop.'

Everyone laughed, filing the quip away in their minds so that they could tell their friends what they had heard Toby Temple say. *I was with Toby Temple the other day and he said . . . I was standing as close as I am to you, and I heard him . . .*

He stood around entertaining them, insulting them gently, and they loved it. He kidded them about their sex lives and their health and their children, and for a little while they were able to laugh at their own problems. Finally, Toby said ruefully, 'I hate to leave you, you're the best-looking audience I've had in years' – *they would remember that, too* – 'but I have to spend a little time alone with Pop. He promised to give me some new jokes.'

They smiled and laughed and adored him.

Toby was alone in the small visitors' room with his father. Even this room had the smell of death, and yet, *that was what this place was all about, wasn't it?* Toby thought. *Death?* It was filled with used-up mothers and fathers who were in the way. They had been taken out of the small back bedrooms at home, out of the dining rooms and parlours where they were becoming an embarrassment whenever there were guests, and had been sent to this nursing home by their children, nieces and nephews. *Believe me, it's for your own good, Father, Mother, Uncle George, Aunt Bess. You'll be with a lot of very nice people your own age. You'll have company all the time. You know what I mean?* What they really meant was, *I'm sending you there to die with all the other useless old people. I'm sick of your drooling at the table and telling the same stories over and over and pestering the children and wetting your bed.* The Eskimos were more honest about it. They sent their old people out onto the ice and abandoned them there.

'I'm sure glad you came today,' Toby's father said. His speech was slow. 'I wanted to talk to you. I got some good news. Old Art Riley next door died yesterday.'

Toby stared at him. '*That's* good news?'

'It means I can move into his room,' his father explained. 'It's a single.'

And that was what old age was all about: Survival, hanging on to the few creature comforts that still remained. Toby had seen people here who would have been better off dead, but they clung to life, fiercely. *Happy Birthday, Mr Dorset. How do you feel about being ninety-five years old today? . . . When I think of the alternative, I feel great.*

At last, it was time for Toby to leave.

'I'll be back to see you as soon as I can,' Toby promised. He gave his father some cash and handed out lavish tips to all the nurses and attendants. 'You take good care of him, huh? I need the old man for my act.'

And Toby was gone. The moment he walked out the door, he had forgotten them all. He was thinking about his performance that evening.

For weeks they would talk about nothing but his visit.

Chapter Seventeen

At seventeen, Josephine Czinski was the most beautiful girl in Odessa, Texas. She had a golden, tanned complexion and her long black hair showed a hint of auburn in the sunlight, and her deep brown eyes held flecks of gold. She had a stunning figure, with a full, rounded bosom, a narrow waist that tapered to gently swelling hips, and long, shapely legs.

Josephine did not socialize with the Oil People anymore. She went out with the Others now. After school she worked as a waitress at the Golden Derrick, a popular drive-in. Mary Lou and Cissy Topping and their friends came there with their dates. Josephine always greeted them politely, but everything had changed.

Josephine was filled with a restlessness, a yearning for something she had never known. It was nameless, but it was there. She wanted to leave this ugly town, but she did not know where she wanted to go or what she wanted to do. Thinking about it too long made her headaches begin.

She went out with a dozen different boys and men. Her mother's favourite was Warren Hoffman.

'Warren'd make you a fine husband. He's a regular churchgoer, he earns good money as a plumber and he's half out of his head about you.'

'He's twenty-five years old and he's fat.'

Her mother studied Josephine. 'Poor Polack girls don't find no knights in shinin' armour. Not in Texas and not no-place else. Stop foolin' yourself.'

Josephine would permit Warren Hoffman to take her to the movies once a week. He would hold her hand in his big, sweaty, calloused palms and keep squeezing it throughout the picture. Josephine hardly noticed. She was too engrossed in what was happening on the screen. What was up there was an extension of the world of beautiful people and things that she had grown up with, only it was even bigger and even more exciting. In some dim recess of her mind, Josephine felt that Hollywood could give her everything she wanted: the beauty, the fun, the laughter and happiness. Aside from marrying a rich man, she knew there was no other way she would ever be able to have that kind of life. And the rich boys were all taken, by the rich girls.

Except for one.

David Kenyon. Josephine thought of him often. She had stolen a snapshot of him from Mary Lou's house long ago. She kept it hidden in her closet and took it out to look at whenever she was unhappy. It brought back the memory of David standing by the side of the pool saying, *I apologize for all of them,* and the feeling of hurt had gradually disappeared and been replaced by his gentle warmth. She had seen David only once after that terrible day at his swimming pool when he had brought her a robe. He had been in a car with his family, and Josephine later heard that he had been driven to the train depot. He was on his way to Oxford, England. That had been four years ago, in 1952. David had returned home for summer vacations and at Christmas, but their paths had never crossed. Josephine often heard the other girls discussing him. In addition to the estate David had inherited from his father, his grandmother had left him a trust fund of five million dollars. He was a real catch. *But not for the Polish daughter of a seamstress.*

Josephine did not know that David Kenyon had returned from Europe. It was a late Saturday evening in July, and Josephine was working at the Golden Derrick. It seemed to her that half the population of Odessa had come to the drive-in to defeat the hot spell with gallons of lemonade and ice cream and sodas. It had been so busy that Josephine had been unable to take a break. A ring of autos constantly circled the neon-lighted drive-in like metallic animals lined up at some surrealistic water hole. Josephine delivered a car tray with what seemed to her to be her millionth order of cheeseburgers and Cokes, pulled out a menu and walked over to a white sports car that had just driven up.

'Good evening,' Josephine said cheerfully. 'Would you like to look at a menu?'

'Hello, stranger.'

At the sound of David Kenyon's voice, Josephine's heart suddenly began to pound. He looked exactly as she remembered him, only he seemed even more handsome. There was a maturity now, a sureness, that being abroad had given him. Cissy Topping was seated next to him, looking cool and beautiful in an expensive silk skirt and blouse.

Cissy said, 'Hi, Josie. You shouldn't be working on a hot night like this, honey.'

As though it was something Josephine had chosen to

do instead of going to an air-conditioned theatre or riding around in a sports car with David Kenyon.

Josephine said evenly, 'It keeps me off the streets,' and she saw that David Kenyon was smiling at her. She knew that he understood.

Long after they had gone, Josephine thought about David. She went over every word – *Hello, stranger . . . I'll have a pig in a blanket and a root beer – make that coffee. Cold drinks are bad on a hot night . . . How do you like working here? . . . I'm ready for the check . . . Keep the change . . . It was nice seeing you again, Josephine* – looking for hidden meanings, nuances that she might have missed. Of course, he could not have said anything with Cissy seated beside him, but the truth was that he really had nothing to say to Josephine. She was surprised that he had even remembered her name.

She was standing in front of the sink in the little kitchen of the drive-in, lost in her thoughts, when Paco, the young Mexican cook, came up behind her and said, '*¿Que pasa,* Josita? You have that look een your eye.'

She liked Paco. He was in his late twenties, a slim, dark-eyed man with a ready grin and a flip joke when pressure built up and everyone was tense.

'Who ees he?'

Josephine smiled. 'Nobody, Paco.'

'Bueno. Because there are seex hungry cars goin' crazy out there. *Vamos!*'

He telephoned the next morning, and Josephine knew who it was before she lifted the receiver. She had not been able to get him out of her mind all night. It was as though this call was the extension of her dream.

His first words were, 'You're a cliché. While I was

away, you've grown up and become a beauty,' and she could have died of happiness.

He took her out to dinner that evening. Josephine had been prepared for some out-of-the-way little restaurant where David would not be likely to run into any of his friends. Instead they went to his club, where everyone stopped by their table to say hello. David was not only unashamed to be seen with Josephine, he seemed proud of her. And she loved him for it and for a hundred other reasons. The look of him, his gentleness and understanding, the sheer joy of being with him. She had never known that anyone as wonderful as David Kenyon could exist.

Each day, after Josephine finished work, they were together. Josephine had had to fight men off from the time she was fourteen, for there was a sexuality about her that was a challenge. Men were always pawing and grabbing at her, trying to squeeze her breasts or shove their hands up her skirt, thinking that that was the way to excite her, not knowing how much it repelled her.

David Kenyon was different. He would occasionally put his arm around her or touch her casually, and Josephine's whole body would respond. She had never felt this way about anyone before. On the days when she did not see David, she could think of nothing else.

She faced the fact that she was in love with him. As the weeks went by, and they spent more and more time together, Josephine realized that the miracle had happened. David was in love with her.

He discussed his problems with her, and his difficulties with his family. 'Mother wants me to take over the businesses,' David told her, 'but I'm not sure that's how I want to spend the rest of my life.'

The Kenyon interests included, besides oil wells and refineries, one of the largest cattle ranches in the Southwest, a chain of hotels, some banks and a large insurance company.

'Can't you just tell her no, David?'

David sighed. 'You don't know my mother.'

Josephine had met David's mother. She was a tiny woman (it seemed impossible that David had come out of that stick figure) who had borne three children. She had been very ill during and after each pregnancy and had had a heart attack following the third delivery. Over the years she repeatedly described her suffering to her children, who grew up with the belief that their mother had deliberately risked death in order to give each of them life. It gave her a powerful hold on her family, which she wielded unsparingly.

'I want to live my own life,' David told Josephine, 'but I can't do anything to hurt Mother. The truth is – Doc Young doesn't think she's going to be with us much longer.'

One evening, Josephine told David about her dreams of going to Hollywood and becoming a star. He looked at her and said, quietly, 'I won't let you go.' She could feel her heart beating wildly. Each time they were together, the feeling of intimacy between them grew stronger. Josephine's background did not mean a damn to David. He did not have an ounce of snobbery in him. It made the incident at the drive-in one night that much more shocking.

It was closing time, and David was parked in his car, waiting for her. Josephine was in the small kitchen with Paco, hurriedly putting away the last of the trays.

'Heavy date, huh?' Paco said.

Josephine smiled. 'How did you know?'

'Because you look like Chreestmas. Your pretty face ees all lit up. You tell heem for me he's one lucky hombre!'

Josephine smiled and said, 'I will.' On an impulse, she leaned over and gave Paco a kiss on the cheek. An instant later, she heard the roar of a car engine and then the scream of rubber. She turned in time to see David's white convertible smash the fender of another car and race away from the drive-in. She stood there, unbelievingly, watching the tail lights disappear into the night.

At three o'clock in the morning, as Josephine lay tossing in bed, she heard a car pull up outside her bedroom. She hurried to the window and looked out. David was sitting behind the wheel. He was very drunk. Quickly, Josephine put on a robe over her nightgown and went outside.

'Get in,' David commanded. Josephine opened the car door and slid in beside him. There was a long, heavy silence. When David finally spoke, his voice was thick, but it was more than the whisky he had drunk. There was a rage in him, a savage fury that propelled the words out of him like small explosions. 'I don't own you,' David said. 'You're free to do exactly as you please. But as long as you go out with me, I expect you not to kiss any goddamned Mexicans. Y'understand?'

She looked at him, helplessly, then said, 'When I kissed Paco, it was because – he said something that made me happy. He's my friend.'

David took a deep breath, trying to control the emotions that were churning inside him. 'I'm going to tell you something I've never told to a living soul.'

Josephine sat there waiting, wondering what was coming next.

'I have an older sister,' David said. 'Beth. I – I adore her.'

Josephine had a vague recollection of Beth, a blonde fair-skinned beauty, whom Josephine used to see when she went over to play with Mary Lou. Josephine had been eight when Beth passed away. David must have been about fifteen. 'I remember when Beth died,' Josephine said.

David's next words were a shock. 'Beth is alive.'

She stared at him. 'But, I – everyone thought – '

'She's in an insane asylum.' He turned to face her, his voice dead. 'She was raped by one of our Mexican gardeners. Beth's bedroom was across the hall from mine. I heard her screams and I raced into her room. He had ripped off her nightgown and he was on top of her and – ' His voice broke with the memory. 'I struggled with him until my mother ran in and called the police. They finally arrived and took the man to jail. He committed suicide in his cell that night. But Beth had lost her mind. She'll never leave that place. Never. I can't tell you how much I love her, Josie. I miss her so damned much. Ever since that night, I – I – I can't – stand – '

She placed a hand over his and said, 'I'm sorry, David. I understand, I'm glad you told me.'

In some strange way, the incident served to bring them even closer together. They discussed things they had never talked about before. David smiled when Josephine told him about her mother's religious fanaticism. 'I had an uncle like that once,' he said. 'He went off to some monastery in Tibet.'

*

'I'm going to be twenty-four next month,' David told Josephine one day. 'It's an old family tradition that the Kenyon men marry by the time they're twenty-four,' and her heart leaped within her.

The following evening, David had tickets for a play at the Globe Theatre. When he came to pick Josephine up, he said, 'Let's forget the play. We're going to talk about our future.'

The moment Josephine heard the words, she knew that everything she had prayed for was coming true. She could read it in David's eyes. They were filled with love and wanting.

She said, 'Let's drive out to Dewey Lake.'

She wanted it to be the most romantic proposal ever made, so that one day it would become a tale that she would tell her children, over and over. She wanted to remember every moment of this night.

Dewey Lake was a small body of water about forty miles outside of Odessa. The night was beautiful and star-spangled, with a soft, waxing gibbous moon. The stars danced on the water, and the air was filled with the mysterious sounds of a secret world, a microcosm of the universe, where millions of tiny unseen creatures made love and preyed and were preyed upon and died.

Josephine and David sat in the car, silent, listening to the sounds of the night. Josephine watched him, sitting behind the wheel of the car, his handsome face intense and serious. She had never loved him as much as she loved him at that moment. She wanted to do something wonderful for him, to give him something to let him know how much she cared for him. And suddenly she knew what she was going to do.

'Let's go for a swim, David,' she said.

'We didn't bring bathing suits.'

'It doesn't matter.'

He turned to look at her and started to speak, but Josephine was out of the car, running down to the shore of the lake. As she started to undress she could hear him moving behind her. She plunged into the warm water. A moment later David was beside her.

'Josie . . .'

She turned towards him, then into him, her body hurting with wanting, hungry for him. They embraced in the water and she could feel the male hardness of him pressed against her, and he said, 'We can't, Josie.' His voice was choked with his desire for her. She reached down for him and said, 'Yes. Oh, yes, David.'

They were back on the shore and he was on top of her and inside her and one with her and they were both a part of the stars and the earth and the velvet night.

They lay together a long time, holding each other. It was not until much later, after David had dropped her off at home, that Josephine remembered that he had not proposed to her. But it no longer mattered. What they had shared together was more binding than any marriage ceremony. He would propose tomorrow.

Josephine slept until noon the next day. She woke up with a smile on her face. The smile was still there when her mother came into the bedroom carrying a lovely old wedding dress. 'Go down to Brubaker's and get me twelve yards of tulle right away. Mrs Topping just brought me her wedding dress. I have to make it over for Cissy by Saturday. She and David Kenyon are getting married.'

*

David Kenyon had gone to see his mother as soon as he drove Josephine home. She was in bed, a tiny, frail woman who had once been very beautiful.

His mother opened her eyes when David walked into her dimly lit bedroom. She smiled when she saw who it was. 'Hello, son. You're up late.'

'I was out with Josephine, Mother.'

She said nothing, just watching him with her intelligent grey eyes.

'I'm going to marry her,' David said.

She shook her head slowly. 'I can't let you make a mistake like that, David.'

'You don't really know Josephine. She's –'

'I'm sure she's a lovely girl. But she's not suitable to be a Kenyon wife. Cissy Topping would make you happy.' And if you married her, it would make me happy.'

He took her frail hand in his and said, 'I love you very much, Mother, but I'm capable of making my own decisions.'

'Are you really?' she asked softly. 'Do you always do the right thing?'

He stared at her and she said, 'Can you always be trusted to act properly, David? Not to lose your head? Not to do terrible –'

He snatched his hand away.

'Do you always know what you're doing, son?' Her voice was even softer now.

'Mother, for God's sake!'

'You've done enough to this family already, David. Don't burden me any further. I don't think I could bear it.'

His face was white. 'You know I didn't – I couldn't help –'

'You're too old to send away again. You're a man now. I want you to act like one.'

His voice was anguished. 'I – I love her – '

She was seized with a spasm, and David summoned the doctor. Later, he and the doctor had a talk.

'I'm afraid your mother hasn't much longer, David.'

And so the decision was made for him.

He went to see Cissy Topping.

'I'm in love with someone else,' David said. 'My mother always thought that you and I – '

'So did I, darling.'

'I know it's a terrible thing to ask, but – would you be willing to marry me until – until my mother dies, and then give me a divorce?'

Cissy looked at him and said softly, 'If that's what you want, David.'

He felt as though an unbearable weight had been lifted from his shoulders. 'Thank you, Cissy, I can't tell you how much – '

She smiled and said, 'What are old friends for?'

The moment David left, Cissy Topping telephoned David's mother. All she said was, 'It's all arranged.'

The one thing David Kenyon had not anticipated was that Josephine would hear about the forthcoming marriage before he could explain everything to her. When David arrived at Josephine's home, he was met at the door by Mrs Czinski.

'I'd like to see Josephine,' he said.

She glared at him with eyes filled with malicious triumph. 'The Lord Jesus shall overcome and smite down His enemies, and the wicked shall be damned for ever.'

David said patiently, 'I want to talk to Josephine.'

'She's gone,' Mrs Czinski said. 'She's gone away!'

Chapter Eighteen

The dusty Greyhound Odessa-El Paso-San Bernardino-Los Angeles bus pulled into the Hollywood depot on Vine Street at seven a.m., and somewhere during the fifteen-hundred-mile, two-day journey, Josephine Czinski had become Jill Castle. Outwardly, she looked like the same person. It was inside that she had changed. Something in her was gone. The laughter had died.

The moment she had heard the news, Josephine knew that she must escape. She began to mindlessly throw her clothes into a suitcase. She had no idea where she was going or what she would do when she got there. She only knew that she had to get away from this place at once.

It was when she was walking out of her bedroom and saw the photographs of the movie stars on her wall that she suddenly knew where she was going. Two hours later, she was on the bus for Hollywood. Odessa and everyone in it receded in her mind, fading faster and faster as the bus swept her towards her new destiny. She tried to make herself forget her raging headache. Perhaps she should have seen a doctor about the terrible pains in her head. But now she no longer cared. That was part of her past, and she was sure they would go away. From now on life was going to be wonderful. Josephine Czinski was dead.

Long live Jill Castle.

BOOK TWO

Chapter Nineteen

Toby Temple became a superstar because of the unlikely juxtaposition of a paternity suit, a ruptured appendix and the President of the United States.

The Washington Press Club was giving its annual dinner, and the guest of honour was the President. It was a prestigious affair attended by the Vice-President, senators, Cabinet members, Chief Justices and anyone else who could buy, borrow or steal a ticket. Because the event was always given international press coverage, the job of master of ceremonies had become a highly prized plum. This year, one of America's top comedians had been chosen to emcee the show. One week after he had accepted, he was named defendant in a paternity suit involving a fifteen-year-old girl. On the advice of his attorney, the comedian immediately left the country for an indefinite vacation. The dinner committee turned to their number two choice, a popular motion-picture and television star. He arrived in Washington the night before the dinner. The following afternoon, on the day of the banquet, his agent telephoned to announce that the actor was in the hospital, undergoing emergency surgery for a burst appendix.

There were only six hours left before the dinner. The committee frantically went through a list of possible replacements. The important names were busy doing a movie or a television show, or were too far away to get to Washington in time. One by one, the candidates were eliminated and finally, near the bottom of the list, the name of Toby Temple appeared. A committee member shook his head. 'Temple's a nightclub comic. He's too wild. We wouldn't dare turn him loose on the President.'

'He'd be all right if we could get him to tone down his material.'

The chairman of the committee looked around and said, 'I'll tell you what's great about him, fellows. He's in New York City and he can be here in an hour. The goddamned dinner is tonight!'

That was how the committee selected Toby Temple.

As Toby looked around the crowded banquet hall, he thought to himself that if a bomb were dropped here tonight, the federal government of the United States would be leaderless.

The President was seated in the centre of the speakers' table on the dais. Half a dozen Secret Service men stood behind him. In the last-minute rush of putting everything together, no one had remembered to introduce Toby to the President, but Toby did not mind. *The President will remember me,* Toby thought. He recalled his meeting with Downey, the chairman of the dinner committee. Downey had said, 'We love your humour, Toby. You're very funny when you attack people. However – ' He had paused to clear his throat. 'This is – er – a sensitive group here tonight. Don't get me wrong. It's not that they can't take a little joke on themselves, but everything said in this room tonight is going to be reported by the news media all over the world. Naturally, none of us wants anything said that would hold the President of the United States or members of Congress up to ridicule. In other words, we want you to be funny, but we don't want you to get anyone mad.'

'Trust me.' Toby had smiled.

The dinner plates were being cleared and Downey was standing in front of the microphone. 'Mr President, honoured guests, it's my pleasure to introduce to you our master of ceremonies, one of our brightest young comedians, Mr Toby Temple!'

There was polite applause as Toby rose to his feet and walked over to the microphone. He looked out at the audience, then turned to the President of the United States.

The President was a simple, homespun man. He did not believe in what he called top-hat diplomacy. 'People to people,' he said in a nationwide speech, 'that's what we need. We've got to quit depending on computers and start trusting our instincts again. When I sit down with the heads of foreign powers, I like to negotiate by the seat of my pants.' It had become a popular phrase.

Now Toby looked at the President of the United States and said, his voice choked with pride, 'Mr President, I cannot tell you what a thrill it is for me to be up here on the same podium with the man who has the whole world wired to his ass.'

There was a shocked hush for a long moment, then the President grinned, guffawed, and the audience suddenly exploded with laughter and applause. From that moment on, Toby could do no wrong. He attacked the senators in the room, the Supreme Court, the press. They adored it. They screamed and howled, because they knew Toby did not really mean a word of what he said. It was excruciatingly funny to hear these insults coming from that boyish, innocent face. There were foreign ministers there that night. Toby addressed them in a double-talk version of their own languages that sounded so real that they were nodding in agreement. He was an idiot-savant, reeling off patter that praised them, berated them, and the meaning of his wild gibberish was so clear that every person in the room understood what Toby was saying.

He received a standing ovation. The President walked over to Toby and said, 'That was brilliant, absolutely brilliant. We're giving a little supper at the White House Monday night, Toby, and I'd be delighted . . .'

The following day, all the newspapers wrote about Toby Temple's triumph. His remarks were quoted everywhere. He was asked to entertain at the White House. There, he was an even bigger sensation. Important offers began pouring in from all over the world. Toby played the Palladium in London, he gave a command performance for the Queen, he was asked to conduct symphony orchestras for charity and to serve on the National Arts Committee. He played golf with the President frequently and was invited to dinner at the White House again and again. Toby met legislators and governors and the heads of America's largest corporations. He insulted them all, and the more he attacked them, the more charmed they were. They adored having Toby around, turning his acerbic wit loose on their guests. Toby's friendship became a symbol of prestige among the Brahmins.

The offers that were coming in were phenomenal. Clifton Lawrence was as excited about them as Toby, and Clifton's excitement had nothing to do with business or money. Toby Temple had been the most wonderful thing that had happened to him in years, for he felt as though

Toby were his son. He had spent more time on Toby's career than on any of his other clients, but it had been worth it. Toby had worked hard, had perfected his talent until it shone like a diamond. And he was appreciative and generous, something that was rare in this business.

'Every top hotel in Vegas is after you,' Clifton Lawrence told Toby. 'Money no object. They want you, period. I have scripts on my desk from Fox, Universal, Pan-Pacific – all starring parts. You can do a tour of Europe, any guest shot you want, or you can have your own television show on any of the networks. That would still give you time to do Vegas and a picture a year.'

'How much could I make with my own television show, Cliff?'

'I think I can push them up to ten thousand a week for an hour variety show. They'll have to give us a firm two years, maybe three. If they want you badly enough, they'll go for it.'

Toby leaned back on the couch, exulting. Ten thousand a show, say forty shows a year. In three years, that would come to over one million dollars for telling the world what he thought of it! He looked over at Clifton. The little agent was trying to play it cool, but Toby could see that he was eager. He wanted Toby to make the television deal. Why not? Clifton could pick up a hundred-and-twenty-thousand-dollar commission for Toby's talent and sweat. Did Clifton really deserve that kind of money? He had never had to work his ass off in filthy little clubs or have drunken audiences throw empty beer bottles at him or go to greedy quacks in nameless villages to have a clap treated because the only girls available were the raddled whores around the Toilet Circuit. What did Clifton Lawrence know of the cockroach-ridden rooms and the greasy food and the endless procession of all-night bus rides going from one hell-hole to another? He could never understand. One critic had called Toby an overnight success, and Toby had laughed aloud. Now, sitting in Clifton Lawrence's office, he said, 'I want my own television show.'

Six weeks later, the deal was signed with Consolidated Broadcasting.

'The network wants a studio to do the deficit financing,' Clifton Lawrence told Toby. 'I like the idea because I can parlay it into a picture deal.'

'Which studio?'

'Pan-Pacific.'

Toby frowned. 'Sam Winters?'

'That's right. For my money, he's the best studio head in the business. Besides, he owns a property I want for you, *The Kid Goes West.*'

Toby said, 'I was in the army with Winters. Okay. But he owes me one. Shaft the bastard!'

Clifton Lawrence and Sam Winters were in the steam room in the gymnasium at Pan-Pacific Studios, breathing in the eucalyptus scent of the heated air.

'This is the life,' the little agent sighed. 'Who needs money?'

Sam grinned. 'Why don't you talk like that when we're negotiating, Cliff?'

'I don't want to spoil you, dear boy.'

'I hear that you made a deal with Toby Temple at Consolidated Broadcasting.'

'Yeah. Biggest deal they've ever made.'

'Where are you going to get the deficit financing for the show?'

'Why, Sam?'

'We could be interested. I might even throw in a picture deal. I just bought a comedy called *The Kid Goes West.* It hasn't been announced yet. I think Toby'd be perfect for it.'

Clifton Lawrence frowned and said, 'Shit! I wish I'd known about this earlier, Sam. I've made a deal at MGM.'

'Have you closed yet?'

'Well, practically. I gave them my word . . .'

Twenty minutes later, Clifton Lawrence had negotiated a lucrative arrangement for Toby Temple in which Pan-Pacific Studios would produce 'The Toby Temple Show' and star him in *The Kid Goes West.*

The negotiations could have gone on longer, but the steam room had become unbearably hot.

One of the stipulations in Toby Temple's contract was that he did not have to come to rehearsals. Toby's stand-in would work with the guest stars in the sketches and dance routines, and Toby would appear for the final rehearsal and taping. In this way, Toby could keep his part fresh and exciting.

On the afternoon of the show's premiere, in September, 1956, Toby walked into the theatre on Vine Street where the show would be taped and sat watching the run-through. When it was over, Toby took his stand-in's place. Suddenly the theatre was filled with electricity. The show came to life and crackled and sparkled. And when it was taped that evening and went on the air, forty million people watched it. It was as though television had been made for Toby Temple. In close-up, he was even more adorable, and everyone wanted him in his living room. The show was an instant success. It jumped to number one in the Nielsen Ratings, and there it firmly remained. Toby Temple was no longer a star.

He had become a superstar.

Chapter Twenty

Hollywood was more exciting than Jill Castle had ever dreamed. She went on sightseeing tours and saw the outside of the stars' homes. And she knew that one day she would have a beautiful home in Bel-Air or Beverly Hills. Meanwhile, Jill lived in an old roominghouse, an ugly two-storey wooden structure that had been converted into an even uglier twelve-bedroom house with tiny bedrooms. Her room was inexpensive, which meant that she could stretch out the two hundred dollars she had saved up. The house was located on Bronson, a few minutes from Hollywood and Vine Street, the heart of Hollywood, and was convenient to the motion-picture studios.

There was another feature about the house that attracted Jill. There were a dozen roomers, and all of them were either trying to get into pictures, were working in pictures as extras or bit players or had retired from the Business. The old-timers floated around the house in yellowed robes and curlers, frayed suits and scuffed shoes that would no longer take a shine. The roomers looked used up, rather than old. There was a common living room with battered and sprung furniture where they all gathered in the evening to exchange gossip. Everyone gave Jill advice, most of it contradictory.

'The way to get into pictures, honey, is you find yourself an AD who likes you.' This from a sour-faced lady who had recently been fired from a television series.

'What's an AD?' Jill asked.

'An assistant director.' In a tone that pitied Jill's ignorance. 'He's the one who hires the supes.'

Jill was too embarrassed to ask what the 'supes' were.

'If you want *my* advice, you'll find yourself a horny casting director. An AD can only use you on *his* picture. A casting director can put you into *everything.*' This from a toothless woman who must have been in her eighties.

'Yeah? Most of them are fags.' A balding character actor.

'What's the difference? I mean, if it gets one launched?' An intense, bespectacled young man who burned to be a writer.

'What about starting out as an extra?' Jill asked. 'Central Casting –'

'Forget it. Central Casting's books are closed. They won't even register you unless you're a specialty.'

'I'm – I'm sorry. What's a specialty?'

'It's like if you're an amputee. That pays thirty-three fifty-eight instead of the regular twenty-one fifty. Or if you own dinner clothes or can ride a horse, you make twenty-eight thirty-three. If you know how to deal cards or handle the stick at a crap table, that's twenty-eight thirty-three. If you can play football or baseball, that pays thirty-three fifty-eight – same as an amputee. If you ride a camel or an elephant, it's fifty-five ninety-four. Take my advice, forget about being an extra. Go for a bit part.'

'I'm not sure what the difference is,' Jill confessed.

'A bit player's got at least one line to say. Extras ain't allowed to talk, except the omnies.'

'Than what?'

'The omnies – the ones who make background noises.'

'First thing you gotta do is get yourself an agent.'

'How do I find one?'

'They're listed in the *Screen Actor*. That's the magazine the Screen Actors Guild puts out. I got a copy in my room. I'll get it.'

They all looked through the list of agents with Jill, and finally narrowed it down to a dozen of the smaller ones. The consensus of opinion was that Jill would not have a chance at a large agency.

Armed with the list, Jill began to make the rounds. The first six agents would not even talk to her. She ran into the seventh as he was leaving his office.

'Excuse me,' Jill said. 'I'm looking for an agent.'

He eyed her a moment and said, 'Let's see your portfolio.'

She stared at him blankly. 'My what?'

'You must have just gotten off the bus. You can't operate in this town without a book. Get some pictures taken. Different poses. Glamour stuff. Tits and ass.'

Jill found a photographer in Culver City near the David Selznick Studios, who did her portfolio for thirty-five dollars. She picked up the pictures a week later and was very pleased with them. She looked beautiful. All of her moods had been captured by the camera. She was pensive . . . angry . . . loving . . . sexy. The photographer had bound the pictures together in a book with looseleaf cellophane pages.

'At the front here,' he explained, 'you put your acting credits.'

Credits. That was the next step.

By the end of the next two weeks, Jill had seen, or tried to see, every agent on her list. None of them was remotely interested. One of them told her, 'You were in here yesterday, honey.'

She shook her head. 'No, I wasn't.'

'Well, she looked exactly like you. That's the problem. You all look like Elizabeth Taylor or Lana Turner or Ava Gardner. If you were in any other town trying to get a job in any other business, everybody would grab you. You're beautiful, you're sexy-looking, and you've got a great figure. But in Hollywood, looks are a drug on the market. Beautiful girls come here from all over the world. They starred in their high school play or they won a beauty contest or their boyfriend told them they ought to be in pictures – and whammo! They flock here by the thousands, and they're all the same girl. Believe me, honey, you were in here yesterday.'

The boarders helped Jill make a new list of agents. Their offices were smaller and the locations were in the cheap-rent district, but the results were the same.

'Come back when you've got some acting experience, kid. You're a looker, and for all I know you could be the greatest thing since Garbo, but I can't waste my time finding out. You go and get yourself a screen credit and I'll be your agent.'

'How can I get a screen credit if no one will give me a job?'

He nodded. 'Yeah. That's the problem. Lots of luck.'

There was only one agency left on Jill's list, recommended by a girl she had sat next to at the Mayflower Coffee Shop on Hollywood Boulevard. The Dunning Agency was located in a small bungalow off La Cienega in a residential area. Jill had telephoned for an appointment, and a woman had told her to come in at six o'clock.

Jill found herself in a small office that had once been someone's living room. There was an old scarred desk littered with papers, a fake-leather couch mended with white surgical tape and three rattan chairs scattered around the room. A tall, heavyset woman with a pockmarked face came out of another room and said, 'Hello. Can I help you?'

'I'm Jill Castle. I have an appointment to see Mr Dunning.'

'*Miss* Dunning,' the woman said. 'That's me.'

'Oh,' said Jill, in surprise. 'I'm sorry, I thought –'

The woman's laugh was warm and friendly. 'It doesn't matter.'

But it does matter, Jill thought, filled with a sudden excitement. Why hadn't it occurred to her before? A *woman* agent! Someone who had gone through all the traumas, someone who would understand what it was like for a young girl just starting out. She would be more sympathetic than any man could ever be.

'I see you brought your portfolio,' Miss Dunning was saying. 'May I look at it?'

'Certainly,' Jill said. She handed it over.

The woman sat down, opened the portfolio and began to turn the pages, nodding approval. 'The camera likes you.'

Jill did not know what to say. 'Thank you.'

The agent studied the pictures of Jill in a bathing suit. 'You've got a good figure. That's important. Where you from?'

'Texas,' Jill said. 'Odessa.'

'How long have you been in Hollywood, Jill?'

'About two months.'

'How many agents have you been to?'

For an instant, Jill was tempted to lie, but there was nothing but compassion and understanding in the woman's eyes. 'About thirty, I guess.'

The agent laughed. 'So you finally got down to Rose Dunning. Well, you could have done worse. I'm not MCA or William Morris, but I keep my people working.'

'I haven't had any acting experience.'

The woman nodded, unsurprised. 'If you had, you'd be at MCA or William Morris. I'm a kind of breaking-in station. I get the kids with talent started, and then the big agencies snatch them away from me.'

For the first time in weeks, Jill began to feel a sense of hope. 'Do – do you think you'd be interested in handling me?' she asked.

The woman smiled. 'I have clients working who aren't half as pretty as you. I think I can put you to work. That's the only way you'll ever get experience, right?'

Jill felt a glow of gratitude.

'The trouble with this damned town is that they won't give kids like you a chance. All the studios scream that they're desperate for new talent, and then they put up a big wall and won't let anybody in. Well, we'll fool 'em. I know of three things you might be right for. A daytime soap, a bit in the Toby Temple picture and a part in the new Tessie Brand movie.'

Jill's head was spinning. 'But would they – ?'

'If *I* recommend you, they'll take you. I don't send clients who aren't good. They're just bit parts, you understand, but it will be a start.'

'I can't tell you how grateful I'd be,' Jill said.

'I think I've got the soap-opera script here.' Rose Dunning lumbered to her feet, pushing herself out of her chair, and walked into the next room, beckoning Jill to follow her.

The room was a bedroom with a double bed in a corner under a window and a metal filing cabinet in the opposite corner. Rose Dunning waddled over to the filing cabinet, opened a drawer, took out a script and brought it over to Jill.

'Here we are. The casting director is a good friend of mine, and if you come through on this, he'll keep you busy.'

'I'll come through,' Jill promised fervently.

The agent smiled and said, 'Course, I can't send over a pig in a poke. Would you mind reading for me?'

'No. Certainly not.'

The agent opened the script and sat down on the bed. 'Let's read this scene.'

Jill sat on the bed next to her and looked at the script.

'Your character is Natalie. She's a rich girl who's married to a weakling. She decides to divorce him, and he won't let her. You make your entrance *here*.'

Jill quickly scanned the scene. She wished she had had a chance to study the script overnight or even for an hour. She was desperately anxious to make a good impression.

'Ready?'

'I – I think so,' Jill said. She closed her eyes and tried to think like the character. A rich woman. Like the mothers of the friends that she had grown up with, people who took it for granted that they could have anything they wanted in life, believing that other people were there for their convenience. The Cissy Toppings of the world. She opened her eyes, looked down at the script and began to read. 'I want to talk to you, Peter.'

'Can't it wait?' That was Rose Dunning, cueing her.

'I'm afraid it's waited too long already. I'm catching a plane for Reno this afternoon.'

'Just like that?'

'No. I've been trying to catch that plane for five years, Peter. This time I'm going to make it.'

Jill felt Rose Dunning's hand patting her thigh. 'That's very good,' the agent said, approvingly. 'Keep reading.' She let her hand rest on Jill's leg.

'Your problem is that you haven't grown up yet. You're still playing games. Well, from now on, you're going to have to play by yourself.'

Rose Dunning's hand was stroking her thigh. It was disconcerting. 'Fine. Go on,' she said.

'I – I don't want you to try to get in touch with me ever again. Is that *quite* clear?'

The hand was stroking Jill faster, moving towards her groin. Jill lowered the script and looked at Rose Dunning. The woman's face was flushed and her eyes had a glazed look in them.

'Keep reading,' she said huskily.

'I – I can't,' Jill said. 'If you – '

The woman's hand began to move faster. 'This is to get you in the mood, darling. It's a sexual fight, you see. I want to feel the sex in you.' Her hand was pressing harder now, moving between Jill's legs.

'No!' Jill got to her feet, trembling.

Saliva was dribbling out of the corner of the woman's mouth. 'Be good to me and I'll be good to you.' Her voice was pleading. 'Come here, baby.' She held out her arms and made a grab for her, and Jill ran out of the office.

In the street outside, she vomited. Even when the racking spasms were over and her stomach had quieted down, she felt no better. Her headache had started again.

It was not fair. The headaches didn't belong to her. They belonged to Josephine Czinski.

During the next fifteen months, Jill Castle became a fully fledged member of the Survivors, the tribe of people on the fringes of show business who spent years and sometimes a whole lifetime trying to break into the Business, working at other jobs temporarily. The fact that the temporary jobs sometimes lasted ten or fifteen years did not discourage them.

As ancient tribes once sat around long-ago campfires and recounted sagas of brave deeds, so the Survivors sat around Schwab's Drugstore, telling and retelling heroic tales of show business, nursing cups of cold coffee while they exchanged the latest bits of inside gossip. They were outside the Business, and yet, in some mystérious fashion, they were at the very pulse and heartbeat of it. They could tell you what star was going to be replaced, what producer had been caught sleeping with his director, what network head was about to be kicked upstairs. They knew these things before anyone else did, through their own special kind of jungle drums. For the Business *was* a jungle. They had no illusions about that. Their illusions lay in another direction. They thought they could find a way to get through the studio gates, scale the studio walls. They were artists, they were the Chosen. Hollywood was their Jericho and Joshua would blow his golden trumpet and the mighty gates would fall before them and their enemies would be smitten, and lo, Sam Winters' magic wand would be waved and they would be wearing silken robes and be Movie Stars and adored ever after by their grateful public, Amen. The coffee at Schwab's was heady sacramental wine, and they were the Disciples of the future, huddling together for comfort, warming one another with their dreams, on the very brink of *making it*. They had met an assistant director who told them a producer who said a casting director who promised and any second now, and the reality would be in their grasp.

In the meantime, they worked in supermarkets and garages and beauty parlours and car washes. They lived with each other and married each other and divorced each other, and they never noticed how time was betraying them. They were unaware of the new lines and the greying temples, and the fact that it took half an hour longer in the morning to put on make-up. They had become shopworn without having been used, aged without mellowing, too old for a career with a plastics company, too old to have babies, too old for those younger parts once so coveted.

They were now character actors. But they still dreamed.

The younger and prettier girls were picking up what they called mattress money.

'Why break your ass over some nine-to-five job when all you have to do is lay on your back a few minutes and pick up an easy twenty bucks? Just till your agent calls.'

Jill was not interested. Her only interest in life was her career. A poor Polish girl could never marry a David Kenyon. She knew that now. But Jill Castle, the movie star, could have anybody and anything she wanted. Unless she could achieve that, she would change back into Josephine Czinski again.

She would never let that happen.

Jill's first acting job came through Harriet Marcus, one of the Survivors who had a third cousin whose ex-brother-in-law was a second assistant director on a television medical series shooting at Universal Studios. He agreed to give Jill a chance. The part consisted of one line, for which Jill was to receive fifty-seven dollars, minus deductions for Social Security, withholding taxes and the Motion Picture Relief Home. Jill was to play the part of a nurse. The script called for her to be in a hospital room at a patient's bedside, taking his pulse when the doctor entered.

Doctor: 'How is he, Nurse?'

Nurse: 'Not very good, I'm afraid, Doctor.'

That was it.

Jill was given a single, mimeographed page from the script on a Monday afternoon and told to report for make-up at six a.m. the following morning. She went over the scene a hundred times. She wished the studio had given her the entire script. How did they expect her to figure out what the character was like from *one page?* Jill tried to analyse what kind of a woman the nurse might be. Was she married? Single? She could be secretly in love with the doctor. Or maybe they had had an affair and it was over. How did she feel about the patient? Did she hate the thought of his death? Or would it be a blessing?

'Not very good, I'm afraid, Doctor.' She tried to put concern in her voice.

She tried again. 'Not very good, I'm *afraid*, Doctor.'

Alarmed. He was going to die.

'*Not* very good, I'm afraid, Doctor.' Accusing. It was the doctor's fault. If he had not been away with his mistress . . .

Jill stayed up the entire night working on the part, too keyed-up to sleep, but in the morning, when she reported to the studio, she felt exhilarated and alive. It was still dark when she arrived at the guard's gate off Lankershim

Boulevard, in a car borrowed from her friend Harriet. Jill gave the guard her name and he checked it against a roster and waved her on.

'Stage Seven,' he said. 'Two blocks down, turn right.'

Her name was on the roster. Universal Studios was expecting *her*. It was like a wonderful dream. As Jill drove towards the sound stage, she decided she would discuss the part with the director, let him know that she was capable of giving him any interpretation he wanted. Jill pulled into the large parking lot and went onto Stage Seven.

The sound stage was crowded with people busily moving lights, carrying electrical equipment, setting up the camera, giving orders in a foreign language she did not understand.

'Hit the inky dink and give me a brute . . . I need a scrim here . . . Kill the baby . . .'

Jill stood there watching, savouring the sights and smells and sounds of show business. This was her world, her future. She would find a way to impress the director, show him that she was someone special. He would get to know her as a person, not as just another actress.

The second assistant director herded Jill and a dozen other actors over to Wardrobe, where Jill was handed a nurse's uniform and sent back to the sound stage, where she was made up with all the other bit players in a corner of the sound stage. Just as they finished with her, the assistant director called her name. Jill hurried on to the hospital-room set where the director stood near the camera, talking to the star of the series. The star's name was Rod Hanson, and he played a surgeon full of compassion and wisdom. As Jill approached them, Rod Hanson was saying, 'I have a German shepherd that can fart better dialogue than this shit. Why can't the writers ever give me some character, for Christ's sake?'

'Rod, we've been on the air five years. Don't improve a hit. The public loves you the way you are.'

The cameraman walked up to the director. 'All lit, chief.'

'Thanks, Hal,' the director said. He turned to Rod Hanson. 'Can we make this, baby? We'll finish the discussion later.'

'One of these days, I'm going to wipe my ass with this studio,' Hanson snapped. He strode away.

Jill turned to the director, who was now alone. This was her opportunity to discuss the interpretation of the character, to show him that she understood his problems and was there to help make the scene great. She gave him a warm, friendly smile. 'I'm Jill Castle,' she said. 'I'm playing the nurse. I think she can really be very interesting and I have some ideas about –'

He nodded absently and said, 'Over by the bed,' and walked away to speak to the cameraman.

Jill stood looking after him, stunned. The second assistant director, Harriet's third cousin's ex-brother-in-law, hurried up to Jill and said in a low voice, 'For Chrissakes, didn't you hear him? Over by the bed!'

'I wanted to ask him –'

'Don't blow it!' he whispered fiercely. 'Get out there!'

Jill walked over to the patient's bed.

'All right, Let's have it quiet, everybody.' The assistant director looked at the director. 'Do you want a rehearsal, chief?'

'For this? Let's go for a take.'

'Give us a bell. Settle down, everybody. Nice and quiet. We're rolling. Speed.'

Unbelievingly, Jill listened to the sound of the bell. She looked frantically towards the director, wanting to ask him how he would like her to interpret the scene, what her relationship was to the dying man, what she was –

A voice called, 'Action!'

They were all looking at Jill expectantly. She wondered whether she dare ask them to stop the cameras for just a second, so she could discuss the scene and –

The director yelled, 'Jesus Christ! Nurse! This isn't a morgue – it's a hospital. Feel his goddamned pulse before he dies of old age!'

Jill looked anxiously into the circle of bright lights around her. She took a deep breath, lifted the patient's hand and took his pulse. If they would not help her, she would have to interpret the scene in her own way. The patient was the father of the doctor. The two of them had quarrelled. The father had been in an accident and the doctor had just been notified. Jill looked up and saw Rod Hanson approaching. He walked up to her and said, 'How is he, Nurse?'

Jill looked into the doctor's eyes and read the concern there. She wanted to tell him the truth, that his father was dying, that it was too late for them to make up their quarrel. Yet she had to break it to him in such a way that it would not destroy him and –

The director was yelling, 'Cut! Cut! Cut! Goddamn it, the idiot's got *one* line, and she can't even remember it. Where did you find her – in the Yellow Pages?'

Jill turned towards the voice shouting from the darkness, aflame with embarrassment. 'I – I know my line,' she said shakily. 'I was just trying to – '

'Well, if you know it, for Chrissakes, would you *mind saying it?* You could drive a train through that pause.

When he *asks* you the fucking question, *answer it*. Okay?'

'I was just wondering if I should – '

'Let's go again, right away. Give us a bell.'

'We're on a bell. Hold it down. We're rolling.'

'Speed.'

'Action.'

Jill's legs were trembling. It was as though she was the only one here who cared about the scene. All she had wanted to do was create something beautiful. The hot lights were making her dizzy, and she could feel the perspiration running down her arms, ruining the crisp, starched uniform.

'Action! Nurse!'

Jill stood over the patient and put her hand on his pulse. If she did the scene wrong again, they would never give her another chance. She thought of Harriet and of her friends at the rooming-house and of what they would say.

The doctor entered and walked up to her. 'How is he, Nurse?'

She would no longer be one of them. She would be a laughing-stock. Hollywood was a small town. Word got around fast.

'Not very good, I'm afraid, Doctor.'

No other studio would touch her. It would be her last job. It would be the end of everything, her whole world.

The doctor said, 'I want this man put in intensive care immediately.'

'Good!' the director called. 'Cut and print.'

Jill was hardly aware of the people rushing past her, starting to dismantle the set to make room for the next one. She had done her first scene – and she had been thinking about something else. She could not believe it was over. She wondered whether she should find the director and thank him for the opportunity, but he was at the other end of the stage talking to a group of people. The second assistant director came up to her and squeezed her arm and said, 'You did okay, kid. Only next time, learn your lines.'

There was film on her; she had her first credit.

From now on, Jill thought, *I'll be working all the time.*

Jill's next acting job was thirteen months later, when she did a bit part at MGM. In the meantime, she held a series of civilian jobs. She became the local Avon lady, she worked behind a soda fountain and – briefly – she drove a taxi.

With her money running low, Jill decided to share an apartment with Harriet Marcus. It was a two-bedroom apartment and Harriet kept her bedroom working overtime. Harriet worked at a downtown department store as a model. She was an attractive girl with short dark hair, black eyes, a model's boyish figure and a sense of humour.

'When you come from Hoboken,' she told Jill, 'you'd *better* have a sense of humour.'

In the beginning, Jill had been a bit daunted by Harriet's cool self-sufficiency, but she soon learned that underneath that sophisticated façade, Harriet was a warm, frightened child. She was in love constantly. The first time Jill met her, Harriet said, 'I want you to meet Ralph. We're getting married next month.'

A week later, Ralph had left for parts unknown, taking with him Harriet's car.

A few days after Ralph had departed, Harriet met Tony. He was in import-export and Harriet was head-over-heels in love with him.

'He's very important,' Harriet confided to Jill. But someone obviously did not think so, because a month later, Tony was found floating in the Los Angeles River with an apple stuffed in his mouth.

Alex was Harriet's next love.

'He's the best-looking thing you've seen,' Harriet confided to Jill.

Alex *was* handsome. He dressed in expensive clothes, drove a flashy convertible and spent a lot of time at the racetracks. The romance lasted until Harriet started running out of money. It angered Jill that Harriet had so little sense about men.

'I can't help it,' Harriet confessed. 'I'm attracted to guys who are in trouble. I think it's my mother instinct.' She grinned and added, 'My mother was an idiot.'

Jill watched a procession of Harriet's fiancés come and go. There was Nick and Bobby and John and Raymond, until finally Jill could no longer keep track of them.

A few months after they had moved in together, Harriet announced that she was pregnant.

'I think it's Leonard,' she quipped, 'but you know – they all look alike in the dark.'

'Where is Leonard?'

'He's either in Omaha or Okinawa. I always was lousy at geography.'

'What are you going to do?'

'I'm going to have my baby.'

Because of her slight figure, Harriet's pregnancy became obvious in a matter of weeks and she had to give up her modelling job. Jill found a job in a supermarket so that she could support the two of them.

One afternoon when Jill returned home from work, she found a note from Harriet. It read: 'I've always wanted my baby to be born in Hoboken. Have gone back home to my folks. I'll bet there's a wonderful guy there, waiting for me. Thanks for everything.' It was signed: 'Harriet, The Nun.'

The apartment had suddenly become a lonely place.

Chapter Twenty-one

It was a heady time for Toby Temple. He was forty-two years old and owned the world. He joked with kings and golfed with Presidents, but his millions of beer-drinking fans did not mind because they knew Toby was one of *them*, their champion who milked all the sacred cows, ridiculed the high and mighty, shattered the shibboleths of the Establishment. They loved Toby, just as they knew that Toby loved them.

He spoke about his mother in all his interviews, and each time she became more saintlike. It was the only way Toby could share his success with her.

Toby acquired a beautiful estate in Bel-Air. The house was Tudor, with eight bedrooms and an enormous staircase and hand-carved panelling from England. It had a movie theatre, a games room, a wine cellar, and on the grounds were a large swimming pool, a housekeeper's cottage and two guest cottages. He bought a lavish home in Palm Springs, a string of racehorses and a trio of stooges. Toby called them all 'Mac' and they adored him. They ran errands, chauffeured him, got him girls at any hour of the day or night, took trips with him, gave him massages. Whatever the master desired, the three Macs were always there to give him. They were the jesters to the Nation's Jester. Toby had four secretaries, two just to handle the enormous flow of fan mail. His private secretary was a pretty twenty-one-year-old honey-blonde named Sherry. Her body had been designed by a sex maniac, and Toby insisted that she wear short skirts with nothing under them. It saved them both a lot of time.

The premiere of Toby Temple's first movie had gone remarkably well. Sam Winters and Clifton Lawrence were at the theatre. Afterwards they all went to Chasen's to discuss the picture.

Toby had enjoyed his first meeting with Sam after the deal had been made. 'It would have been cheaper if you had returned my phone calls,' Toby said, and he told Sam of how he had tried to reach him.

'My tough luck,' Sam said, ruefully.

Now, as they sat in Chasen's, Sam turned to Clifton Lawrence. 'If you don't take an arm and a leg, I'd like to make a new three-picture deal for Toby.'

'Just an arm. I'll give you a call in the morning,' the agent said to Sam. He looked at his watch. 'I have to run along.'

'Where you going?' Toby asked.

'I'm meeting another client. I *do* have other clients, dear boy.'

Toby looked at him oddly, then said, 'Sure.'

The reviews the next morning were raves. Every critic predicted that Toby Temple was going to be as big a star in movies as he was in television.

Toby read all the reviews, then got Clifton Lawrence on the phone.

'Congratulations, dear boy,' the agent said. 'Did you see the *Reporter* and *Variety?* Those reviews were love letters.'

'Yeah. It's a green-cheese world, and I'm a big fat rat. Can I have any more fun than that?'

'I told you you'd own the world one day, Toby, and now you do. It's all yours.' There was a deep satisfaction in the agent's voice.

'Cliff, I'd like to talk to you. Can you come over?'

'Certainly. I'll be free at five o'clock and –'

'I meant now.'

There was a brief hesitation, then Clifton said, 'I have appointments until –'

'Oh, if you're too busy, forget it.' And Toby hung up.

One minute later, Clifton Lawrence's secretary called and said, 'Mr Lawrence is on his way to see you, Mr Temple.'

Clifton Lawrence was seated on Toby's couch. 'For God's sake, Toby, you know I'm never too busy for you. I had no idea you would want to see me today, or I wouldn't have made other appointments.'

Toby sat there staring at him, letting him sweat it out. Clifton cleared his throat and said, 'Come on! You're my favourite client. Didn't you know that?'

And it was true, Clifton thought. *I made him. He's my creation. I'm enjoying his success as much as he is.*

Toby smiled. 'Am I really, Cliff?' He could see the tension easing out of the dapper little agent's body. 'I was beginning to wonder.'

'What do you mean?'

'You've got so many clients that sometimes I think you don't pay enough attention to me.'

'That's not true. I spend more time –'

'I'd like you to handle just me, Cliff.'

Clifton smiled. 'You're joking.'

'No. I'm serious.' He watched the smile leave Clifton's face. 'I think I'm important enough to have my own agent – and when I say my own agent, I don't mean someone who's too busy for me because he has a dozen other people to take care of. It's like a group fuck, Cliff. Somebody always gets left with a hard-on.'

Clifton studied him a moment, then said, 'Fix us a drink.' While Toby went over to the bar, Clifton sat there, thinking. He knew what the real problem was, and it was not Toby's ego, or his sense of importance.

It had to do with Toby's loneliness. Toby was the loneliest man Clifton had ever known. Clifton had watched Toby buy women by the dozens and try to buy friends with lavish gifts. No one could ever pick up a check when Toby was around. Clifton once heard a musician say to Toby, 'You don't have to *buy* love, Toby. Everybody loves you, anyway.' Toby winked and said, 'Why take a chance?'

The musician never worked on Toby's show again.

Toby wanted *all* of everybody. He had a need, and the more he acquired the bigger his need grew.

Clifton had heard that Toby went to bed with as many as half a dozen girls at a time, trying to appease the hunger in him. But of course, it did not work. What Toby needed was *one* girl, and he had not found her. So he went on playing the numbers game.

He had a desperate need to have people around him all the time.

Loneliness. The only time it was not there was when Toby was in front of an audience, when he could hear the applause and feel the love. *It was all really very simple,* Clifton thought. When Toby was not on stage, he carried his audience with him. He was always surrounded by musicians and stooges and writers and showgirls and down-and-out comics, and everyone else he could gather into his orbit.

And now he wanted Clifton Lawrence. *All* of him.

Clifton handled a dozen clients, but their total income was not a great deal more than Toby's income from nightclubs, television and motion pictures, for the deals Clifton had been able to make for Toby were phenomenal. Nevertheless, Clifton did not make his decision on the basis of money. He made it because he loved Toby Temple, and Toby needed him. Just as *he* needed Toby. Clifton remembered how flat his life had been before Toby came into it. There had been no new challenges for years. He had been coasting on old successes. And he thought now of the electric excitement around Toby, the fun and laughter and the deep camaraderie the two of them shared.

When Toby came back to Clifton and handed him his drink, Clifton raised his glass in a toast and said, 'To the two of us, dear boy.'

It was the season of successes and fun and parties, and Toby was always 'on'. People expected him to be funny. An actor could hide behind the words of Shakespeare or Shaw or Molière, and a singer could count on the help of Gershwin or Rodgers and Hart or Cole Porter. But a comedian was naked. His only weapon was his wit.

Toby Temple's ad libs quickly became famous around Hollywood. At a party for the elderly founder of a studio, someone asked Toby, 'Is he really ninety-one years old?'

Toby replied, 'Yep. When he reaches one hundred, they're going to split him two-for-one.'

At dinner one evening, a famous physician who took

care of many of the stars told a long and laboured joke to a group of comedians.

'Doc,' Toby pleaded, 'don't amuse us – save us!'

One day the studio was using lions in a movie, and as Toby saw them being trucked by, he yelled, 'Christians – ten minutes!'

Toby's practical jokes became legend. A Catholic friend of his went to the hospital for a minor operation. While he was recuperating, a beautiful young nun stopped by his bed. She stroked his forehead. 'You feel nice and cool. Such soft skin.'

'Thank you, Sister.'

She leaned over him and began straightening his pillows, her breasts brushing against his face. In spite of himself, the poor man began to get an erection. As the Sister started to straighten the blankets, her hand brushed against him. He was in an agony of mortification.

'Good Lord,' the nun said. 'What have we here?' And she pulled the covers back, revealing his rock-hard penis.

'I'm terribly sorry, Sister,' he stammered. 'I – '

'Don't be sorry. It's a great cock,' the nun said, and began to go down on him.

It was six months before he learned that it was Toby who had sent the hooker in to him.

As Toby was stepping out of an elevator one day, he turned to a pompous network executive and said, 'By the way, Will, how did you ever come out on that morals charge?' The elevator door closed and the executive was left with half a dozen people eyeing him warily.

When it came time to negotiate a new contract, Toby arranged for a trained panther to be delivered to him at the studio. Toby opened Sam Winters' office door while Sam was in the middle of a meeting.

'My agent wants to talk to you,' Toby said. He shoved the panther inside the office and closed the door.

When Toby told the story later, he said, 'Three of the guys in that office almost had heart attacks. It took them a month to get the smell of panther piss out of that room.'

Toby had a staff of ten writers working for him, headed by O'Hanlon and Rainger. Toby complained constantly about the material his writers gave him. Once Toby made a whore a member of the writing team. When Toby learned that his writers were spending most of their time in the bedroom, he had to fire her. Another time, Toby brought an organ grinder and his monkey to a story conference. It was humiliating and demeaning, but O'Hanlon and Rainger and the other writers took it because Toby turned their material into pure gold. He was the best in the business.

Toby's generosity was profligate. He gave his employees and his friends gold watches and cigarette lighters and complete wardrobes and trips to Europe. He carried an enormous amount of money with him and paid for everything in cash, including two Rolls-Royces. He was a soft touch. Every Friday a dozen hangers-on in the Business would line up for a handout. Once Toby said to one of the regulars, 'Hey, what are you doing here today? I read in *Variety* that you got a job in a picture.' The man looked at Toby and said, 'Hell, don't I get two weeks' notice?'

There were myriad stories about Toby, and nearly all of them were true. One day, during a story conference a writer walked in late, an unforgivable sin. 'I'm sorry I'm late,' he apologized. 'My kid was run over by a car this morning.'

Toby looked at him and said, 'Did you bring the jokes?'

Everyone in the room was shocked. After the meeting, one of the writers said to O'Hanlon, 'That's the coldest son of a bitch in the world. If you were on fire, he'd sell you water.'

Toby flew in a top brain surgeon to operate on the injured boy and paid all the hospital bills. He said to the father, 'If you ever mention this to anyone, you're out on your ass.'

Work was the only thing that made Toby forget his loneliness, the only thing that brought him real joy. If a show went well, Toby was the most amusing companion in the world, but if the show went badly, he was a demon, attacking every target within reach of his savage wit.

He was possessive. Once, during a story conference, he took Rainger's head between his two hands and announced to the room, 'This is mine. It belongs to me.'

At the same time he grew to hate writers, because he needed them and he did not want to need anyone. So he treated them with contempt. On pay day, Toby made aeroplanes of the writers' pay cheques and sailed them through the air. Writers would be fired for the smallest infraction. One day a writer walked in with a tan and Toby immediately had him discharged. 'Why did you do that?' O'Hanlon asked. 'He's one of our best writers.'

'If he was working,' Toby said, 'he wouldn't have had time for a tan.'

A new writer brought in a joke about mothers and was let go.

If a guest on his show got big laughs, Toby would

exclaim, 'You're great! I want you on this show every week.' He would look over at the producer and say, 'You hear me?' and the producer would know that the actor was never to appear on the show again.

Toby was a mass of contradictions. He was jealous of the success of other comics, yet the following happened. One day as Toby was leaving his rehearsal stage, he passed the dressing room of an old-time comedy star, Vinnie Turkel, whose career had long since gone downhill. Vinnie had been hired to do his first dramatic part, in a live television play. He hoped that it would mean a comeback for him. Now, as Toby looked into the dressing room, he saw Vinnie on the couch, drunk. The director of the show came by and said to Toby, 'Let him be, Toby. He's finished.'

'What happened?'

'Well, you know Vinnie's trademark has always been his high, quavery voice. We started rehearsing and every time Vinnie opened his mouth and tried to be serious, everyone began to laugh. It destroyed the old guy.'

'He was counting on this part, wasn't he?' Toby asked.

The director shrugged. 'Every actor counts on every part.'

Toby took Vinnie Turkel home with him and stayed with the old comedy star, sobering him up. 'This is the best role you've ever had in your life. Are you gonna blow it?'

Vinnie shook his head, miserable. 'I've already blown it, Toby. I can't cut it.'

'Who says you can't?' Toby demanded. 'You can play that part better than anyone in the world.'

The old man shook his head. 'They laughed at me.'

'Sure they did. And do you know why? Because you've

made them laugh all your life. They *expected* you to be funny. But if you keep going, you'll win them over. You'll kill them.'

He spent the rest of the afternoon restoring Vinnie Turkel's confidence. That evening, Toby telephoned the director at home. 'Turkel's all right now,' Toby said. 'You have nothing to worry about.'

'I know I haven't,' the director retorted. 'I've replaced him.'

'*Un*-replace him,' Toby said. 'You've got to give him a shot.'

'I can't take the chance, Toby. He'll get drunk again and –'

'Tell you what I'll do,' Toby offered. 'Keep him in. If you still don't want him after dress rehearsal I'll take over his part and do it for nothing.'

There was a pause, and the director said, 'Hey! Are you serious?'

'You bet your ass.'

'It's a deal,' the director said quickly. 'Tell Vinnie to be at rehearsal at nine o'clock tomorrow morning.'

When the show went on the air, it was the hit of the season. And it was Vinnie Turkel whose performance the critics singled out. He won every prize that television had to offer and a new career opened up for him as a dramatic actor. When he sent Toby an expensive gift to show his appreciation, Toby returned it with a note. 'I didn't do it, *you* did.' That was Toby Temple.

A few months later, Toby signed Vinnie Turkel to do a sketch in his show. Vinnie stepped on one of Toby's laugh lines and from that moment on, Toby gave him wrong cues, killed his jokes and humiliated him in front of forty million people.

That was Toby Temple, too.

Someone asked O'Hanlon what Toby Temple was really like, and O'Hanlon replied, 'Do you remember the picture where Charlie Chaplin meets the millionaire? When the millionaire is drunk, he's Charlie Chaplin's buddy. When he's sober, he throws him out on his ass. That's Toby Temple, only without the liquor.'

Once during a meeting with the heads of a network, one of the junior executives hardly said a word. Later, Toby said to Clifton Lawrence, 'I don't think he liked me.'

'Who?'

'The kid at the meeting.'

'What do you care? He's a thirty-second Assistant Nobody.'

'He didn't say a word to me,' Toby brooded. 'He really doesn't like me.'

Toby was so upset that Clifton Lawrence had to track down the young executive. He called the bewildered man in the middle of the night and said, 'Do you have anything against Toby Temple?'

'*Me?* I think he's the funniest man in the whole world!'

'Then would you do me a favour, dear boy? Call him and tell him so.'

'*What?*'

'Call Toby and tell him you like him.'

'Well, sure. I'll call him first thing tomorrow.'

'Call him now.'

'It's three o'clock in the morning!'

'It doesn't matter. He's waiting for you.'

When the executive called Toby, the phone was answered immediately. He heard Toby's voice say, 'Hi.'

The young executive swallowed and said, 'I – I just wanted to tell you that I think you're great.'

'Thanks, pal,' Toby said, and hung up.

The size of Toby's entourage grew. Sometimes he would awaken in the middle of the night and telephone friends to come over for a gin game, or he would awaken O'Hanlon and Rainger and summon them to a story conference. He would often sit up all night running movies at home, with the three Macs and Clifton Lawrence and half a dozen starlets and hangers-on.

And the more people there were around him, the lonelier Toby became.

Chapter Twenty-two

It was November, 1963, and the autumn sunshine had given way to a thin, unwarming light from the sky. The early mornings were foggy and chilling now, and the first rains of winter had begun.

Jill Castle stopped in at Schwab's every morning, but it seemed to her that the conversations were always the same. The Survivors talked about who had lost a part and why. They gloated over each disastrous review that came out and deprecated the good ones. It was the threnody of losers, and Jill began to wonder if she were becoming like the rest of them. She was still sure that she was going to be Somebody, but as she looked around at the same familiar faces, she realized they all felt the same way about themselves. Was it possible they were all out of touch with reality, all of them gambling on a dream that was never going to happen? She could not bear the thought of it.

Jill had become the mother confessor to the group. They came to her with problems, and she listened and tried to help; with advice, a few dollars or a place to sleep for a week or two. She seldom dated because she was absorbed in her career and she had not met anyone who interested her.

Whenever Jill was able to put a little money aside, she sent it to her mother with long, glowing letters about how well she was doing. In the beginning, Jill's mother had written back urging Jill to repent and become a bride of God. But as Jill made occasional movies and sent more money home, her mother began to take certain reluctant pride in her daughter's career. She was no longer against Jill's being an actress but she pressed Jill to get parts in religious pictures. 'I'm sure Mr DeMille would give you a role if you explained your religious background to him,' she wrote.

Odessa was a small town. Jill's mother still worked for the Oil People, and she knew that her mother would talk about her, that sooner or later David Kenyon would hear of her success. And so, in her letters, Jill made up stories about all the stars she worked with, always careful to use their first names. She learned the bit players' trick of having the set photographer snap her picture as she stood next to the star. The photographer would give her two prints and Jill would mail one to her mother and keep the other. She made her letters sound as though she was just one step short of stardom.

It is the custom in Southern California, where it never snows, that three weeks before Christmas a Santa Claus Parade marches down Hollywood Boulevard and that each night after that until Christmas Eve a Santa Claus float makes the journey. The citizens of Hollywood are as conscientious about the celebration of the Christ child as are their neighbours in northern climes. They are not to be held responsible if 'Glory Be to God on High' and 'Silent Night' and 'Rudolph the Red-Nosed Reindeer' pour out of home and car radios in a community that is sweltering in a temperature of eighty-five or ninety degrees. They long for an old-fashioned white Christmas as ardently as other red-blooded, patriotic Americans, but because they know that God is not going to supply it, they have learned to create their own. They festoon the streets with Christmas lights and plastic Christmas trees and papier-mâché cut-outs of Santa Claus and his sled and his reindeer. Stars and character actors vie for the privilege of riding in the Santa Claus Parade; not because they are concerned about bringing holiday cheer to the thousands of children and adults who line the path of the parade, but because the parade is televised and their faces will be seen coast to coast.

Jill Castle stood on a corner, alone, watching the long parade of floats go by, the stars on top waving to their loving fans below. The Grand Marshal of the parade this year was Toby Temple. The adoring crowds cheered wildly as his float passed by. Jill caught a quick glimpse of Toby's beaming, ingenuous face and then he was gone.

There was music from the Hollywood High School Band, followed by a Masonic Temple float, and a marine corps band. There were equestrians in cowboy outfits and a Salvation Army band, followed by Shriners. There were singing groups carrying flags and streamers, a Knott's Berry Farm float with animals and birds made of flowers; fire engines, clowns and jazz bands. It might not have been the spirit of Christmas, but it was pure Hollywood spectacle.

Jill had worked with some of the character actors on the floats. One of them waved to her and called down, 'Hiya, Jill! How ya doin'?'

Several people in the crowd turned to look enviously at her, and it gave her a delightful feeling of self-importance that people knew she was in the Business. A deep, rich voice beside her said, 'Excuse me – are you an actress?'

Jill turned. The speaker was a tall blond, good-looking

boy in his middle twenties. His face was tanned and his teeth white and even. He wore a pair of old jeans and a blue tweed jacket with leather-patch elbows.

'Yes.'

'Me, too. An *actor,* I mean.' He grinned and added, 'Struggling.'

Jill pointed to herself and said, 'Struggling.'

He laughed. 'Can I buy you a cup of coffee?'

His name was Alan Preston and he came from Salt Lake City where his father was an elder in the Mormon Church. 'I grew up with too much religion and not enough fun,' he confided to Jill.

It's almost prophetic, Jill thought. *We have exactly the same kind of background.*

'I'm a good actor,' Alan said ruefully, 'but this is sure a rough town. Back home, everybody wants to help you. Here, it seems like everybody's out to *get* you.'

They talked until the coffee shop closed, and by that time they were old friends. When Alan asked, 'Do you want to come back to my place?' Jill hesitated only a moment. 'All right.'

Alan Preston lived in a boarding house off Highland Avenue, two blocks from the Hollywood Bowl. He had a small room at the back of the house.

'They ought to call this place The Dregs,' he told Jill. 'You should see the weirdos who live here. They all think they're going to make it big in show business.'

Like us, Jill thought.

The furniture in Alan's room consisted of a bed, a bureau, a chair and a small rickety table. 'I'm just waiting until I move into my place,' Alan explained.

Jill laughed. 'Same with me.'

Alan started to take her in his arms, and she stiffened. 'Please don't.'

He looked at her a moment and said gently, 'Okay,' and Jill was suddenly embarrassed. What was she doing here in this man's room, anyway? She knew the answer to that. She was desperately lonely. She was hungry for someone to talk to, hungry for the feel of a man's arms around her, holding her and reassuring her and telling her that everything was going to be wonderful. It had been so long. She thought of David Kenyon, but that was another life, another world. She wanted him so much that it was an ache. A little later, when Alan Preston put his arms around Jill again, she closed her eyes and it became David kissing her and undressing her and making love to her.

Jill spent the night with Alan, and a few days later he moved into her small apartment.

Alan Preston was the most uncomplicated man Jill had ever met. He was easygoing and relaxed, taking each day as it came, totally unconcerned with tomorrow. When Jill would discuss his way of life with him, he would say, 'Hey, remember *Appointment in Samarra?* If it's going to happen, it'll happen. Fate will find *you.* You don't have to go looking for it.'

Alan would stay in bed long after Jill had gone out looking for work. When she returned home, she would find him in an easy chair, reading or drinking beer with his friends. He brought no money into the house.

'You're a dope,' one of Jill's girlfriends told her. 'He's using your bed, eating your food, drinking your liquor. Get rid of him.'

But Jill didn't.

For the first time, Jill understood Harriet, understood

all her friends who clung desperately to men they did not love, men they hated.

It was the fear of being alone.

Jill was out of a job. Christmas was only a few days away and she was down to her last few dollars, yet she *had* to send her mother a Christmas present. It was Alan who solved the problem. He had left early one morning without saying where he was going. When he returned, he said to Jill, 'We've got a job.'

'What kind of job?'

'Acting, of course. We're actors, aren't we?'

Jill looked at him, filled with a sudden hope. 'Are you serious?'

'Of course I am. I ran into a friend of mine who's a director. He's got a picture starting tomorrow. There's parts for both of us. A hundred bucks apiece, for one day's work.'

'That's wonderful!' Jill exclaimed. 'A hundred dollars!' With that she could buy her mother some lovely English wool for a winter coat and have enough left over to buy a good leather purse.

'It's just a little indie. They're shooting it in back of someone's garage.'

Jill said, 'What can we lose? It's a part.'

The garage was on the south side of Los Angeles, in an area that in one generation had gone from exclusivity to middle-class gentility to seed.

They were greeted at the door by a short, swarthy man who took Alan's hand and said, 'You made it, buddy. Great.'

He turned to Jill and whistled appreciately. 'You told it like it is, pal. She's an eyeful.'

Alan said, 'Jill, this is Peter Terraglio. Jill Castle.'

'How do you do!' Jill said.

'Pete's the director,' Alan explained.

'Director, producer, chief bottle washer. I do a little of everything. Come on in.' He led them through the empty garage into a passageway that had at one time been servants' quarters. There were two bedrooms off the corridor. The door to one was open. As they approached it, they could hear the sound of voices. Jill reached the doorway, looked inside and stopped in shocked disbelief. In the middle of the room four naked people were lying on a bed; a black man, a Mexican man, and two girls, one white and one black. A cameraman was lighting the set while one of the girls practised fellatio on the Mexican. The girl paused for a moment, out of breath, and said, 'Come on, you cock. Get hard.'

Jill felt faint. She wheeled around in the doorway to start back down the passageway, and she felt her legs start to give way. Alan had his arm around her, supporting her.

'Are you all right?'

She could not answer him. Her head was suddenly splitting, and her stomach was filled with knives.

'Wait here,' Alan ordered.

He was back in a minute with a bottle of red pills and a pint of vodka. He took out two of the pills and handed them to Jill. 'These will make you feel better.'

Jill put the pills in her mouth, her head pounding.

'Wash it down with this,' Alan told her.

She did as he said.

'Here.' Alan handed her another pill. She swallowed it with vodka. 'You need to lie down a minute.'

He led Jill into the empty bedroom, and she lay down on the bed, moving very slowly. The pills were beginning to work. She started to feel better. The bitter bile had stopped coming up into her mouth.

Fifteen minutes later, her headache was fading away. Alan handed her another pill. Without even thinking about it, Jill swallowed it. She took another drink of vodka. It was such a blessing to have the pain disappear. Alan was behaving peculiarly, moving all round the bed. 'Sit still,' she said.

'I am sitting still.'

Jill thought that was funny and began to laugh. She laughed until the tears streamed down her face. 'What – what were those pills?'

'For your headache, honey.'

Terraglio peered into the room and said, 'How we doin'? Everybody happy?'

'Every – everybody's happy,' Jill mumbled.

Terraglio looked at Alan and nodded. 'Five minutes,' Terraglio said. He hurried off.

Alan was leaning over Jill, stroking her breast and her thighs, lifting her skirt and working his fingers between her legs. It felt marvellously exciting, and Jill suddenly wanted him inside her.

'Look, baby,' Alan said, 'I wouldn't ask you to do anything bad. You'd just make love to *me*. It's what we do anyway, only this time we get paid for it. Two hundred bucks. And it's all yours.'

She shook her head, but it seemed to take for ever to move it from side to side. 'I couldn't do that,' she said, fuzzily.

'Why not?'

She had to concentrate to remember. 'Because I'm –

I'm gonna be a star. Can't do porno films.'

'Would you like me to fuck you?'

'Oh, yes! I want you, David.'

Alan started to say something, then grinned. 'Sure, baby. I want you, too. Come on.' He took Jill's hand and lifted her off the bed. Jill felt as though she were flying.

They were in the hallway, then moving into the other bedroom.

'Okay,' Terraglio said as he saw them. 'Keep the same setup. We've got some fresh blood coming in.'

'Do you want me to change the sheets?' one of the crew asked.

'What the fuck do you think we are, MGM?'

Jill was clinging to Alan. 'David, there are people here.'

'They'll leave,' Alan assured her. 'Here.' He took out another pill and gave it to Jill. He put the bottle of vodka to her lips, and she swallowed the pill. From that point on, everything happened in a haze. David was undressing her and saying comforting things. Then she was on the bed with him. He moved his naked body close to her. A bright light came on, blinding her.

'Put this in your mouth,' he said, and it was David talking.

'Oh, yes.' She stroked it lovingly and started to put it in her mouth and someone in the room said something that Jill could not hear, and David moved away so that Jill was forced to turn her face into the light and squint in the glare. She felt herself being pushed down on her back and then David was inside her making love to her, and at the same time she had his penis in her mouth. She loved him so much. The lights bothered her and the talking in the background. She wanted to tell David to stop them, but she was in an ecstasy of delirium, having orgasm after orgasm until she thought that her body would tear itself apart. David loved *her,* not Cissy, and he had come back to her and they were married. They were having such a wonderful honeymoon.

'David . . .' she said. She opened her eyes and the Mexican was on top of her, moving his tongue down her body. She tried to ask him where David was, but she could not get the words out. She closed her eyes while the man did delicious things to her body. When Jill opened her eyes again, the man had somehow turned into a girl with long red hair and large bosoms trailing across Jill's belly. Then the woman started doing something with her tongue and Jill closed her eyes and fell into unconsciousness.

The two men stood looking down at the figure on the bed.

'She gonna be all right?' Terraglio asked.

'Sure,' Alan said.

'You really come up with 'em,' Terraglio said admiringly. 'She's terrific. Best looker yet.'

'My pleasure.' He held out his hand.

Terraglio pulled a thick wad of bills out of his pocket and peeled off two of them. 'Here y'are. Wanna drop by for a little Christmas dinner? Stella'd love to see you.'

'Can't,' Alan said. 'I'm spending Christmas with the wife and kids. I'm catching the next plane out to Florida.'

'We're gonna have a hell of a picture here.' Terraglio nodded towards the unconscious girl. 'What kind of billing should we give her?'

Alan grinned. 'Why don't you use her real name? It's Josephine Czinski. When the picture plays in Odessa, it'll give all her friends a real kick.'

Chapter Twenty-three

They had lied. Time was not a friend that healed all wounds; it was the enemy that ravaged and murdered youth. The seasons came and went and each season brought a new crop of Product to Hollywood. The competition hitch-hiked and came on motorcycles and trains and planes. They were all eighteen years old, as Jill had once been. They were long-legged and lithe, with fresh eager young faces and bright smiles that did not need caps. And with each new crop that came in, Jill was one year older. One day she looked in the mirror and it was 1964 and she had become twenty-five years old.

At first, the experience of making the pornographic film had terrified her. She had lived in dread that some casting director would learn about it and blackball her. But as the weeks went by and then the months, Jill gradually forgot her fears. But she had changed. Each succeeding year had left its mark upon her, a patina of hardness, like the annual rings on a tree. She began to hate all the people who would not give her a chance to act, the people who made promises they never kept.

She had embarked on an endless series of monotonous thankless jobs. She was a secretary and a receptionist and a short-order cook and a baby-sitter and a model and a waitress and a telephone operator and a salesgirl. Just until she got The Call.

But The Call never came. And Jill's bitterness grew.

She did occasional walk-ons and one-liners, but they never led to anything. She looked in the mirror and received Time's message: *Hurry.* Seeing her reflection was like looking back into layers of the past. There were still traces of the fresh young girl who had come to Hollywood seven endless years ago. But the fresh young girl had small wrinkles near the edges of her eyes and deeper lines that ran from the corners of her nose to her chin, warning signals of time fleeting and success ungrasped, the souvenirs of all the countless dreary little defeats. *Hurry, Jill, hurry!*

And so it was that when Fred Kapper, an eighteen-year-old assistant director at Fox, told Jill he had a good part for her if she would go to bed with him, she decided it was time to say yes.

She met Fred Kapper at the studio during his lunch hour.

'I only got half an hour,' he said. 'Lemme think where we can have some privacy.' He stood there a moment, frowning in deep thought, then brightened. 'The dubbing room. Come on.'

The dubbing room was a small, soundproof projection chamber where all the sound tracks were combined on one reel.

Fred Kapper looked around the bare room and said, 'Shit! They used to have a little couch in here.' He glanced at his watch. 'We'll have to make do. Get your clothes off, sweetheart. The dubbing crew'll be back in twenty minutes.'

Jill stared at him a moment, feeling like a whore, and she loathed him. But she did not let it show. She had tried it her way and had failed. Now she was going to do it *their* way. She took off her dress and pants. Kapper did not bother undressing. He merely opened his zipper and took out his tumescent penis. He looked at Jill and grinned, 'That's a beautiful ass. Bend over.'

Jill looked around for something to lean against. In front of her was the laugh machine, a console on wheels, filled with laugh-track loops controlled by buttons on the outside.

'Come on, bend over.'

Jill hesitated a moment, then leaned forward, propping herself up by her hands. Kapper moved in back of her and Jill felt his fingers spreading her cheeks. An instant later she felt the tip of his penis pressing against her anus. 'Wait!' Jill said. 'Not there! I – I can't – '

'Scream for me, baby!' and he plunged his organ inside her, ripping her with terrible pain. With each scream, he thrust deeper and harder. She tried frantically to get away, but he was grabbing her hips, shoving himself in and out, holding her fast. She was off balance now. As she reached out to get leverage, her fingers touched the buttons of the laugh machine, and instantly the room was filled with maniacal laughter As Jill squirmed in a burning agony, her hands pounded the machine, and a woman tittered and a small crowd guffawed and a girl giggled and a hundred voices crackled and chuckled and roared at some obscene, secret joke. The echoes bounced hysterically around the walls as Jill cried out with pain.

Suddenly she felt a series of quick shudders and a moment later the alien piece of flesh inside her was withdrawn, and slowly the laughter in the room died away. Jill stayed still, her eyes shut, fighting the pain. When finally she was able to straighten up and turn around, Fred Kapper was zipping up his fly.

'You were sensational, sweetheart. That screaming really turns me on.'

And Jill wondered what kind of an animal he would be when he was nineteen.

He saw that she was bleeding. 'Get yourself cleaned up and come over to Stage Twelve. You start working this afternoon.'

After that first experience, the rest was easy. Jill began to work regularly at all the studios: Warner Brothers, Paramount, MGM, Universal, Columbia, Fox. Everywhere, in fact, except at Disney, where sex did not exist.

The role that Jill created in bed was a fantasy, and she acted it out with skill, preparing herself as though she were playing a part. She read books on Oriental erotica and bought philtres and stimulants from a sex shop on Santa Monica Boulevard. She had a lotion that an airline stewardess brought her from the Orient, with the faintest touch of wintergreen in it. She learned to massage her lovers slowly and sensuously. 'Lie there and think about what I'm doing to your body,' she whispered. She rubbed the lotion across the man's chest and down his stomach towards his groin, making gentle, circling motions. 'Close you eyes and enjoy it.'

Her fingers were as light as butterfly wings, moving down his body, caressing him. When he began to have an erection, Jill would take his growing penis in her hand and softly stroke it, moving her tongue down between his legs until he was squirming with pleasure, then continuing down slowly, all the way to his toes. Then Jill would turn him over, and it all began again. When a man's organ was limp, she put the head of it just inside the lips of her vagina, and slowly drew him inside her, feeling it grow hard and stiff. She taught the men the waterfall, and how to peak and stop just before an orgasm and then build again and peak again, so that when they finally came, it was an ecstatic explosion. They had their pleasure and got dressed and left. No one ever stayed long enough to give her the loveliest five minutes in sex, the quiet holding afterwards, the peaceful oasis of a lover's arms.

Providing Jill with acting parts was a small price to pay for the pleasure she gave the casting men, the assistant directors, the directors and the producers. She became known around town as a 'red-hot piece of ass', and everyone was eager for his share. And Jill gave it. Each time she did, there was that much less self-respect and love in her, and that much more hatred and bitterness.

She did not know how, or when, but she knew that one day this town would pay for what it had done to her.

During the next five years, Jill appeared in dozens of movies and television shows and commercials. She was the secretary who said, 'Good morning, Mr Stevens', and the baby-sitter who said, 'Don't worry now, you two have a good evening. I'll put the children to bed', and the elevator operator who announced, 'Sixth floor next', and the girl in the ski outfit who confided, 'All my girlfriends use Dainties'. But nothing ever *happened*. She was a nameless face in the crowd. She was in the Business, and yet she was not, and she could not bear the thought of spending the rest of her life like this.

In 1969, Jill's mother died and Jill drove to Odessa for the funeral. It was late afternoon and there were fewer than a dozen people at the service, none of them the women her mother had worked for all those years. Some of the church-goers were there, the doom-saying revivalists. Jill remembered how terrified she had been at those meetings. But her mother had found some sort of solace in them, the exorcising of whatever demons had tormented her.

A familiar voice said quietly, 'Hello, Josephine.' She turned and he was standing at her side and she looked into his eyes and it was as though they had never been apart, as though they still belonged to each other. The years had stamped a maturity on his face, added a sprinkling of grey to his sideburns. But he had not changed, he was still David, her David. Yet they were strangers.

He was saying, 'I'm very sorry about your mother.'

And she heard herself replying, 'Thank you, David.'

As though they were reciting lines from a play.

'I have to talk to you. Can you meet me tonight?' There was an urgent pleading in his voice.

She thought of the last time they had been together and of the hunger in him then and the promise and the dreams. She said, 'All right, David.'

'The lake? Do you have a car?'

She nodded.

'I'll meet you there in an hour.'

Cissy was standing in front of a mirror, naked, getting ready to dress for a dinner party when David arrived home. He walked into her bedroom and stood there watching her. He could judge his wife with complete dispassion, for he felt no emotion whatsoever towards her. She was beautiful. Cissy had taken care of her body, keeping it in shape with diet and exercise. It was her primary asset and David had reason to believe that she was liberal in sharing it with others, her golf coach, her ski teacher, her flight instructor. But David could not blame her. It had been a long time since he had gone to bed with Cissy.

In the beginning, he had really believed that she would give him a divorce when Mama Kenyon died. But David's mother was still alive and flourishing. David had no way of knowing whether he had been tricked or whether a miracle had taken place. A year after their marriage, David had said to Cissy, 'I think it's time we talked about that divorce.'

Cissy had said, 'What divorce?' And when she saw the astonished look on his face she laughed. 'I *like* being Mrs David Kenyon, darling. Did you really think I was going to give you up for that little Polish whore?'

He had slapped her.

The following day he had gone to see his attorney. When David was finished talking, the attorney said, 'I can get you the divorce. But if Cissy is set on hanging on to you, David, it's going to be bloody expensive.'

'Get it.'

When Cissy had been served the divorce papers, she had locked herself in David's bathroom and had swallowed an overdose of sleeping pills. It had taken David and two servants to smash the heavy door. Cissy had hovered on the brink of death for two days. David had visited her in the private hospital where she had been taken.

'I'm sorry, David,' she had said. 'I don't want to live without you. It's as simple as that.'

The following morning, he had dropped the divorce suit.

That had been almost ten years ago, and David's marriage had become an uneasy truce. He had completely taken over the Kenyon empire and he devoted all of his energies to running it. He found physical solace in the strings of girls he kept in the various cities around the world to which his business carried him. But he had never forgotten Josephine.

David had no idea how she felt about him. He wanted to know, and yet he was afraid to find out. She had every reason to hate him. When he had heard the news about Josephine's mother, David had gone to the funeral parlour just to look at Josephine. The moment he saw her, he knew that nothing had changed. Not for him. The years had been swept away in an instant, and he was as much in love with her as ever.

I have to talk to you . . . meet me tonight.

All right, David . . .

The lake.

Cissy turned around as she saw David watching her in the pier glass. 'You'd better hurry and change, David. We'll be late.'

'I'm going to meet Josephine. If she'll have me, I'm going to marry her. I think it's time this farce ended don't you?'

She stood there, staring at David, her naked image reflected in the mirror.

'Let me get dressed,' she said.

David nodded and left the room. He walked into the large drawing room, pacing up and down, preparing for the confrontation. Surely after all these years, Cissy would not want to hang onto a marriage that was a hollow shell. He would give her anything she – He heard the sound of Cissy's car starting and then the scream of tyres as it careened down the driveway. David raced to the front door and looked out. Cissy's Maserati was racing towards the highway. Quickly, David got into his car, started the engine and gunned down the driveway after Cissy.

As he reached the highway, her car was just disappearing in the distance. He stepped down hard on the accelerator. The Maserati was a faster car than David's Rolls. He pressed down harder on the gas pedal: 70 . . . 80 . . .90. Her car was no longer in sight.

100 . . . 110 . . . still no sign of her.

He reached the top of a small rise, and there he saw the car, like a distant toy, careening around a curve. The torque was pulling the car to one side. the tyres fighting to hold their traction on the road. The Maserati swayed back and forth, yawing across the highway. Then it levelled off and made it past the curve. And suddenly the car hit the shoulder of the road and shot into the air like a catapult and rolled over and over across the fields.

David pulled Cissy's unconscious body out of the car moments before the ruptured gas tank exploded.

It was six o'clock the next morning before the chief surgeon came out of the operating room and said to David, 'She's going to live.'

Jill arrived at the lake just before sunset. She drove to the edge of the water. Turning off the motor, she gave herself up to the sounds of the wind and the air. *I don't know when I've ever been so happy,* she thought. And then she corrected herself, *Yes, I do. Here. With David.* And she remembered how his body had felt on hers and she grew faint with wanting. Whatever had spoiled their happiness was over. She had felt it the moment she had seen David. He was still in love with her. She knew it.

She watched the blood-red sun slowly drown in the distant water, and darkness fell. She wished that David would hurry.

An hour passed, then two, and the air became chilled. She sat in the car, still and quiet. She watched the huge dead-white moon float into the sky. She listened to the night sounds all around her and she said to herself, *David is coming.*

Jill sat there all night and, in the morning, when the sun began to stain the horizon, she started the car and drove home to Hollywood.

Chapter Twenty-four

Jill sat in front of her dressing table and studied her face in the mirror. She saw a barely perceptible wrinkle at the corner of her eye and frowned. *It's unfair,* she thought. *A man can completely let himself go. He can have grey hair, a pot-belly and a face like a road map, and no one thinks anything of it. But let a woman get one tiny wrinkle . . .* She began to apply her make-up. Bob Schiffer, Hollywood's top make-up artist, had taught her some of his techniques. Jill put on a pan-stick base instead of the powder base that she had once used. Powder dried the skin, while the pan-stick kept it moist. Next, she concentrated on her eyes, the make-up under the lower lids three or four shades lighter than her other make-up, so that the shadows were softened. She rubbed in a small amount of eye shadow to give her eyes more colour, then carefully applied false eyelashes over her own lashes, tilting them at the outer edges at a forty-five-degree angle. She brushed some Duo adhesive on her own outer lashes and joined them with the false lashes, making the eyes look larger. To give the lashes a fuller look, she drew fine dots on her lower eyelid beneath her own lashes. After that, Jill applied her lipstick, then powdered her lips before applying a second coat of lipstick. She applied a blusher to her cheeks and dusted her face with powder, avoiding the areas around the eyes where the powder would accentuate the faint wrinkles.

Jill sat back in her chair and studied the effect in the mirror. She looked beautiful. Someday, she would have to resort to the tape trick, but thank God that was still years away. Jill knew of older actresses who used the trick. They fastened tiny pieces of Scotch tape to their skin just below the hairline. Attached to these tapes were threads which they tied around their heads and concealed beneath their hair. The result was to pull the slackened skin of their faces taut, giving the effect of a face lift without the expense and pain of surgery. A variation was also used to disguise their sagging breasts. A piece of tape attached to the breast on one end and to the firmer flesh higher on the chest on the other provided a simple temporary solution to the problem. Jill's breasts were still firm.

She finished combing her soft, black hair, took one final look in the mirror, glanced at her watch and realized that she would have to hurry.

She had an interview for 'The Toby Temple Show'

Chapter Twenty-five

Eddie Berrigan, the casting director for Toby's show, was a married man. He had made arrangements to use a friend's apartment three afternoons a week. One of the afternoons was reserved for Berrigan's mistress and the other two afternoons were reserved for what he called 'old talent' and 'new talent'.

Jill Castle was new talent. Several buddies had told Eddie that Jill gave a fantastic 'trip around the world' and wonderful head. Eddie had been eager to try her. Now, a part in a sketch had come up that was right for her. All the character had to do was look sexy, say a few lines and exit.

Jill read for Eddie and he was satisfied. She was no Kate Hepburn, but the role didn't call for one. 'You're in,' he said.

'Thank you, Eddie.'

'Here's your script. Rehearsal starts tomorrow morning, ten o'clock sharp. Be on time, and know your lines.'

'Of course.' She waited.

'Er – how about meeting me this afternoon for a cup of coffee?'

Jill nodded.

'A friend of mine has an apartment at ninety-five thirteen Argyle. The Allerton.'

'I know where it is,' Jill said.

'Apartment Six D. Three o'clock.'

*

Rehearsals went smoothly. It was going to be a good show. That week's talent included a spectacular dance team from Argentina, a popular rock and roll group, a magician who made everything in sight disappear and a top vocalist. The only one missing was Toby Temple. Jill asked Eddie Berrigan about Toby's absence. 'Is he sick?'

Eddie snorted. 'He's sick like a fox. The peasants rehearse while old Toby has himself a ball. He'll show up Saturday to tape the show, and then split.'

Toby Temple appeared on Saturday morning, breezing into the studio like a king. From a corner of the stage, Jill watched him make his entrance, followed by his three stooges, Clifton Lawrence and a couple of old-time comics. The spectacle filled Jill with contempt. She knew all about Toby Temple. He was an egomaniac who, according to rumour, bragged that he had been to bed with every pretty actress in Hollywood. No one ever said no to him. Oh, yes, Jill knew about the Great Toby Temple.

The director, a short, nervous man named Harry Durkin, introduced the cast to Toby. Toby had worked with most of them. Hollywood was a small village, and the faces soon became familiar. Toby had not met Jill Castle before. She looked beautiful in a beige linen dress, cool and elegant.

'What are you doing, honey?' Toby asked.

'I'm in the astronaut sketch, Mr Temple.'

He gave her a warm smile and said, 'My friends call me Toby.'

The cast started to work. The rehearsal went unusually well, and Durkin quickly realized why. Toby was showing off for Jill. He had laid every other girl in the show, and Jill was a new challenge.

The sketch that Toby did with Jill was the high point of the show. Toby gave Jill a couple of additional lines and a funny piece of business. When rehearsal was over, Toby said to her, 'How about a little drink in my dressing room?'

'Thank you, I don't drink.' Jill smiled and walked away. She had a date with a casting director and that was more important than Toby Temple. *He* was a one-shot. A casting director meant steady employment.

When they taped the show that evening it was an enormous success, one of the best shows Toby had ever done.

'Another smash,' Clifton told Toby. 'That astronaut sketch was top drawer.'

Toby grinned, 'Yeah. I like that little chick in it. She's got something.'

'She's pretty,' Clifton said. Every week there was a different girl. They all had something, and they all went to bed with Toby and became yesterday's conversation piece.

'Fix it for her to have supper with us, Cliff.'

It was not a request. It was a command. A few years ago, Clifton would have told Toby to do it himself. But these days, when Toby asked you to do something, you did it. He was a king and this was his kingdom, and those who did not want to be exiled stayed in his favour.

'Of course, Toby,' Clifton said. 'I'll arrange it.'

Clifton walked down the hall to the dressing room where the girl dancers and female members of the cast changed. He rapped once on the door and walked in. There were a dozen girls in the room in various stages of undress. They paid no attention to him except to call out greetings. Jill had removed her make-up and was getting into her street clothes. Clifton walked up to her. 'You were very good,' he said.

Jill glanced at him in the mirror without interest. 'Thanks.' At one time she would have been excited to be this close to Clifton Lawrence. He could have opened every door in Hollywood for her. Now everyone knew that he was simply Toby Temple's stooge.

'I have some good news for you. Mr Temple wants you to join him for supper.'

Jill lightly tousled her hair with her fingertips and said, 'Tell him I'm tired. I'm going to bed.' And she walked out.

Supper that evening was a misery. Toby, Clifton Lawrence and Durkin, the director, were in La Rue's at a front booth. Durkin had suggested inviting a couple of the showgirls, but Toby had furiously rejected the idea.

The table captain was saying, 'Are you ready to order, Mr Temple?'

Toby pointed to Clifton and said, 'Yeah. Give the idiot here an order of tongue.'

Clifton joined the laughter of the others at the table, pretending that Toby was simply being amusing.

Toby snapped, 'I asked you to do a simple thing like inviting a girl to dinner. Who told you to scare her off?'

'She was tired,' Clifton explained. 'She said –'

'*No* broad is too tired to have dinner with me. You must have said something that pissed her off.' Toby had raised his voice. The people at the next booth had turned to stare. Toby gave them his boyish smile and said, 'This is a farewell dinner, folks.' He pointed at Clifton. 'He's donated his brain to the zoo.'

There was laughter from the other table. Clifton forced a grin, but under the table his hands were clenched.

'Do you want to know how dumb he is?' Toby asked the people at the adjoining booth. 'In Poland, they tell jokes about *him.*'

The laughter increased. Clifton wanted to get up and walk out, but he did not dare. Durkin sat there embarrassed, too wise to say anything. Toby now had the attention of several nearby booths. He raised his voice again, giving them his charming smile. 'Cliff Lawrence here gets his stupidity honestly. When he was born, his parents had a big fight over him. His mother claimed it wasn't her baby.'

Mercifully, the evening finally came to an end. But tomorrow Clifton Lawrence stories were going to be told all over town.

Clifton Lawrence lay in his bed that night, unable to sleep. He asked himself why he allowed Toby to humiliate him. The answer was simple: money. The income from Toby Temple brought him over a quarter of a million dollars a year. Clifton lived expensively and generously, and he had not saved a cent. With his other clients gone, he needed Toby. That was the problem. Toby knew it, and baiting Clifton had become a blood sport. Clifton had to get away before it was too late.

But he was aware that it was already too late.

He had been trapped into this situation because of his affection for Toby: he had really loved him. He had watched Toby destroy others – women who had fallen in love with him, comics who had tried to compete with him, critics who had panned him. But those were *others.*

Clifton had never believed that Toby would turn on him. He and Toby were too close, Clifton had done too much for him.

He dreaded to think about what the future held.

Ordinarily, Toby would not have given Jill Castle more than a second glance. But Toby was not used to being denied anything he wanted. Jill's refusal only acted as a goad. He invited her to dinner again. When she declined, Toby shrugged it off as some kind of stupid game she was playing and decided to forget about her. The irony was that if it had been a game, Jill would never have been able to deceive Toby, because Toby understood women too well. No, he sensed that Jill really did *not* want to go out with him, and the thought galled him. He was unable to get her out of his mind.

Casually, Toby mentioned to Eddie Berrigan that it might be a good idea to use Jill Castle on the show again. Eddie telephoned her. She told him she was busy doing a bit role in a Western. When Eddie reported back to Toby, the comedian was furious.

'Tell her to cancel whatever she's doing,' he snapped. 'We'll pay her more. For Christ's sake, this is the number one show on the air. What's the matter with that dizzy broad?'

Eddie called Jill again and told her how Toby felt. 'He really wants you back on the show, Jill. Can you make it?'

'I'm sorry,' Jill said. 'I'm doing a part at Universal. I can't get out of it.'

Nor would she try. An actress did not get ahead in Hollywood by walking out on a studio. Toby Temple meant nothing to Jill except a day's work. The following evening, the Great Man himself telephoned her. His voice on the telephone was warm and charming.

'Jill? This is your little old co-star, Toby.'

'Hello, Mr Temple.'

'Hey, come on! What's with the "mister" bit?' There was no response. 'Do you like baseball?' Toby asked. 'I've got box seats for – '

'No, I don't.'

'Neither do I.' He laughed. 'I was testing you. Listen, how about having dinner with me Saturday night? I stole my chef from Maxim's in Paris. He – '

'I'm sorry. I have a date, Mr Temple.' There was not even a flicker of interest in her voice.

Toby felt himself gripping the receiver more tightly. 'When *are* you free?'

'I'm a hard-working girl. I don't go out much. But thank you for asking me.'

And the line went dead. The bitch had hung up on him – a fucking bit player had hung up on Toby Temple! There was not a woman Toby had met who would not give a year of her life to spend one night with him – and this stupid cunt had turned him down! He was in a violent rage, and he took it out on everyone around him. Nothing was right. The script stank, the director was an idiot, the music was terrible and the actors were lousy. He summoned Eddie Berrigan, the casting director, to his dressing room.

'What do you know about Jill Castle?' Toby demanded.

'Nothing,' Eddie said instantly. He was not a fool. Like everyone else on the show, he knew exactly what was going on. Whichever way it turned out, he had no intention of getting caught in the middle.

'Does she sleep around?'

'No, sir,' Eddie said firmly. 'If she did, I'd know about it.'

'I want you to check her out,' Toby ordered. 'Find out if she's got a boyfriend, where she goes, what she does – you know what I want.'

'*Yes*, sir,' Eddie said earnestly.

At three o'clock the next morning, Eddie was awakened by the telephone at his bedside.

'What did you find out?' a voice asked.

Eddie sat up in bed, trying to blink himself awake. 'Who the hell – ?' He suddenly realized who was at the other end of the telephone. 'I checked,' Eddie said hastily. 'She's got a clean bill of health.'

'I didn't ask you for her fucking medical certificate,' Toby snapped. 'Is she laying anybody?'

'No, sir. Nobody. I talked to my buddies around town. They all like Jill and they use her because she's a fine actress.' He was talking faster now, anxious to convince the man at the other end of the phone. If Toby Temple ever learned that Jill had slept with Eddie – had chosen *him* over Toby Temple! – Eddie would never work in this town again. He *had* talked to his casting-director friends, and they were all in the same position he was. No one wanted to make an enemy of Toby Temple, so they had agreed on a conspiracy of silence. 'She doesn't play around with *anybody*.'

Toby's voice softened. 'I see. I guess she's just some kind of crazy kid, huh?'

'I guess she is,' said Eddie, relieved.

'Hey! I hope I didn't wake you up?'

'No, no, that's all right, Mr Temple.'

But Eddie lay awake a long time, contemplating what could happen to him if the truth ever came out.

For this was Toby Temple's town.

Toby and Clifton Lawrence were having lunch at the Hillcrest Country Club. Hillcrest had been created because few of the top country clubs in Los Angeles admitted Jews. This policy was so rigidly observed that Groucho Marx's ten-year-old child, Melinda, had been ordered out of the swimming pool of a club where a Gentile friend had taken her. When Groucho heard what had happened, he telephoned the manager of the club and said, 'Listen – my daughter's only *half*-Jewish. Would you let her go into the pool up to her waist?'

As a result of incidents like this, some affluent Jews who enjoyed golf, tennis, gin rummy and baiting anti-Semites got together and formed their own club, selling shares exclusively to Jewish members. Hillcrest was built in a beautiful park a few miles from the heart of Beverly Hills, and it quickly became famous for having the best buffet and the most stimulating conversation in town. The Gentiles clamoured to be admitted. In a gesture towards tolerance, the board ruled that a few non-Jews would be allowed to join the club.

Toby always sat at the comedians' table, where the Hollywood wits gathered to exchange jokes and top one another. But today Toby had other things on his mind. He took Clifton to a corner table. 'I need your advice, Cliff,' Toby said.

The little agent glanced up at him in surprise. It had been a long time since Toby had asked for his advice. 'Certainly, dear boy.'

'It's this girl,' Toby began, and Clifton was instantly ahead of him. Half the town knew the story by now. It was the biggest joke in Hollywood. One of the columnists had even run it as a blind item. Toby had read it and commented, 'I wonder who the schmuck is?' The great lover was hooked on a girl on the town who had turned him down. There was only one way to handle this situation.

'Jill Castle,' Toby was saying, 'remember her? The kid who was on the show?'

'Ah, yes, a very attractive girl. What's the problem?'

'I'll be goddamned if I know,' Toby admitted. 'It's like she's got something against me. Every time I ask her for a date, I get a turn-down. It makes me feel like some kind of shit-kicker from Iowa.'

Clifton took a chance. 'Why don't you stop asking her?'

'That's the crazy part, pal. I can't. Between you and me and my cock, I've never wanted a broad so much in my life. It's getting so I can't think about anything else.' He smiled self-consciously and said, 'I told you it was crazy. You've been around the track a few times, Cliff. What do I do?'

For one reckless moment, Clifton was tempted to tell Toby the truth. But he couldn't tell him that his dream girl was sleeping around town with every assistant casting director who could give her a day's work. Not if he wanted to keep Toby as a client. 'I have an idea,' Clifton suggested. 'Is she serious about her acting?'

'Yes. She's ambitious.'

'All right. Then, give her an invitation she *has* to accept.'

'What do you mean?'

'Have a party at your house.'

'I just told you, she won't – '

'Let me finish. Invite studio heads, producers, directors – people who could do her some good. If she's really interested in being an actress, she'll be dying to meet them.'

Toby dialled her number. 'Hello, Jill.'

'Who is this?' she asked.

Everyone in the country recognized his voice, and she was asking who it was!

'Toby. Toby Temple.'

'Oh.' It was a sound that could have meant anything.

'Listen, Jill, I'm giving a little dinner party at my home next Wednesday night and I' – he heard her start to refuse and hurried on – 'I'm having Sam Winters, head of Pan-Pacific, and a few other studio heads there, and some producers and directors. I thought it might be good for you to meet them. Are you free?'

There was the briefest of pauses, and Jill Castle said, 'Wednesday night. Yes, I'm free. Thank you, Toby.'

And neither of them knew that it was an appointment in Samarra.

On the terrace, an orchestra played, while liveried waiters passed trays of hors d'oeuvres and glasses of champagne.

When Jill arrived forty-five minutes late, Toby nervously hurried to the door to meet her. She was wearing a simple white silk dress, and her black hair fell softly against her shoulders. She looked ravishing. Toby could not take his eyes off her. Jill was aware that she looked beautiful. She had washed and styled her hair very carefully and had taken a long time with her makeup.

'There are a lot of people here I want you to meet.' Toby took Jill's hand and led her across the large reception hall into the formal drawing room. Jill stopped at the entrance, staring at the guests. Almost every face in the room was familiar to her. She had seen them on the cover of *Time* and *Life* and *Newsweek* and *Paris Match* and *OGGI* or on the screen. This was the *real* Hollywood. These were the picture makers. Jill had imagined this moment a thousand times, being with these people, talking with them. Now that the reality was here, it was difficult for her to realize that it was actually happening.

Toby was handing her a glass of champagne. He took her arm and led her to a man surrounded by a group of people. 'Sam, I want you to meet Jill Castle.'

Sam turned. 'Hello, Jill Castle,' he said pleasantly.

'Jill, this is Sam Winters, chief Indian of Pan-Pacific Studios.'

'I know who Mr Winters is,' Jill said.

'Jill's an actress, Sam, a damned clever actress. You could use her. Give your joint a little class.'

'I'll keep that in mind,' Sam said politely.

Toby took Jill's hand, holding it firmly. 'Come on, honey,' he said. 'I want everybody to meet you.'

Before the evening was over, Jill had met three studio heads, half a dozen important producers, three directors, a few writers, several newspaper and television columnists and a dozen stars. At dinner, Jill sat at Toby's right. She listened to the various conversations, savouring the feeling of being on the Inside for the first time.

'. . .the trouble with these epics is that if one of them flops, it can wipe out the whole studio. Fox is hanging on by its teeth, waiting to see what *Cleopatra* does.'

'. . . have you seen the new Billy Wilder picture yet? Sensational!'

'Yeah? I liked him better when he was working with Brackett. Brackett has class.'

'Billy has talent.'

'. . . so, I sent Peck a mystery script last week, and he's crazy about it. He said he'd give me a definite answer in a day or two.'

'. . . I received this invitation to meet the new guru, Krishi Pramananada. Well, my dear, it turned out I'd already met him; I attended his bar mitzvah.'

'. . . the problem with budgeting a picture at two is that by the time you have an answer print, the cost of inflation plus the goddamned unions has pushed it up to three or four.'

Millions, Jill thought excitedly. *Three or four millions.* She remembered the endless penny-ante conversations at Schwab's where the hangers-on, the Survivors, avidly fed each other crumbs of information about what the studios were doing. Well, the people at this table tonight were the *real* survivors, the ones who made everything in Hollywood happen.

These were the people who had kept the gates shut against her, who had refused to give her a chance. Any person at this table could have helped her, could have changed her life, but none of them had had five minutes to spare for Jill Castle. She looked over at the producer who was riding high with a big new musical picture. He had refused to give Jill even an interview.

At the far end of the table, a famous comedy director was in animated conversation with the star of his latest film. He had refused to see Jill.

Sam Winters was talking to the head of another studio. Jill had sent a telegram to Winters, asking him to watch her performance on a television show. He had never bothered answering.

They would pay for their slights and insults, they and everybody else in this town who had treated her so shabbily. Right now, she meant nothing to the people here, but she would. Oh, yes. One day she would.

The food was superb, but Jill was too preoccupied to notice what she ate. When dinner was over, Toby rose and said, 'Hey! We better hurry before they start the picture without us.' Holding Jill's arm, he led the way to the large projection room where they were to watch a movie.

The room was arranged so that sixty people could comfortably view the picture in couches and easy chairs. An open cabinet filled with candy bars stood at one side of the entrance. A popcorn machine stood on the other side.

Toby had seated himself next to Jill. She was aware that all through the screening his eyes were on her rather than on the movie. When the picture ended and the lights went up, coffee and cake were served. Half an hour later, the party began to dissolve. Most of the guests had early studio calls.

Toby was standing at the front door saying good night to Sam Winters when Jill walked up, wearing her coat. 'Where are you going?' Toby demanded. 'I'm gonna take you home.'

'I have my car,' Jill answered, sweetly. 'Thank you for a lovely evening, Toby.' And she left.

Toby stood there in disbelief, watching her drive away. He had made exciting plans for the rest of the evening. He was going to take Jill upstairs to the bedroom and – he had even picked out the tapes he was going to play! *Any woman here tonight would have been grateful to jump into my bed,* Toby thought. They were stars, too, not some dumb bit player. Jill Castle was just too damned stupid to know what she was turning down. It was over as far as Toby was concerned. He had learned his lesson.

He was never going to talk to Jill again.

Toby telephoned Jill at nine o'clock the next morning, and he was answered by a tape-recorded message. 'Hello, this is Jill Castle. I'm sorry I'm not at home now. If you'll leave your name and telephone number, I'll call you back when I return. Please wait until you hear the signal. Thank you.' There was a sharp beep.

Toby stood there clutching the telephone in his hand, then slammed down the receiver without leaving a message. He was damned if he was going to carry on a conversation with a mechanical voice. A moment later, he redialled the number. He listened to the recording again and spoke. 'You've got the cutest voice-over in town. You should package it. I don't usually call back girls who eat and run, but in your case, I've decided to make an exception. What are you doing for dinner to – ?' The phone went dead. He had talked too long for the goddamned tape. He froze, not knowing what to do, feeling like a fool. It infuriated him to have to call back again, but he dialled the number for the third time and said, 'As I was saying before the rabbi cut me off, how about dinner tonight? I'll wait for your call.' He left his number and hung up.

Toby waited restlessly all day and did not hear from her. By seven o'clock, he thought, *To hell with you. That was your last chance, baby.* And this time it was final. He took out his private phone book and began to thumb through it. There was no one in it who interested him.

Chapter Twenty-six

It was the most tremendous role in Jill's life.

She had no idea why Toby wanted her so much when he could have any girl in Hollywood, nor did the reason matter. The fact was that he did. For days Jill had been able to think of nothing but the dinner party and how everyone there – all those important people – had catered to Toby. They would do anything for him. Somehow, Jill had to find a way to make Toby do anything for *her*. She knew she had to be very clever. Toby's reputation was that once he took a girl to bed, he lost interest in her. It was the pursuit he enjoyed, the challenge. Jill spent a great deal of time thinking about Toby and about how she was going to handle him.

Toby telephoned her every day and she let a week go by before she agreed to have dinner with him again. He was in such a euphoric state that everyone in the cast and crew commented on it.

'If there were such an animal,' Toby told Clifton, 'I'd say I was in love. Every time I think about Jill I get an erection.' He grinned and added, 'And when I get an erection, pal, it's like putting up a billboard on Hollywood Boulevard.'

The night of their first date, Toby picked Jill up at her apartment and said, 'We have a table at Chasen's.' He was sure it would be a treat for her.

'Oh?' There was a note of disappointment in Jill's voice.

He blinked. 'Is there someplace else you'd rather go?' It was Saturday night, but Toby knew he could get a table anywhere: Perino's, the Ambassador, the Derby. 'Name it.'

Jill hesitated, then said, 'You'll laugh.'

'No, I won't.'

'Tommy's.'

Toby was getting a poolside massage from one of the Macs, while Clifton Lawrence looked on. 'You wouldn't believe it,' Toby marvelled. 'We stood in line at that hamburger joint for twenty minutes. Do you know where the hell Tommy's is? Downtown Los Angeles. The only people who go downtown Los Angeles are wetbacks. She's crazy. I'm ready to blow a hundred bucks on her with French champagne and the whole bit, and the evening costs me two dollars and forty cents. I wanted to take her to Pip's afterwards. Do you know what we did instead? We walked along the beach at Santa Monica. I got sand in my Guccis. No one walks along the beach at night. You get mugged by scuba divers.' He shook his head in admiration. 'Jill Castle. Do you believe her?'

'No,' Clifton said dryly

'She wouldn't come back to my place for a little nightcap, so I figured I'd get in the kip at *her* place, right?'

'Right.'

'Wrong. She doesn't even let me in the door. I get a kiss on my cheek and I'm on my way home, alone. Now what the hell kind of night out on the town is that for Charlie-superstar?'

'Are you gonna see her again?'

'Are you demented? You bet your sweet ass I am!'

After that, Toby and Jill were together almost every night. When Jill would tell Toby she could not see him because she was busy or had an early morning call, Toby would be in despair. He telephoned Jill a dozen times a day.

He took her to the most glamorous restaurants and the most exclusive private clubs in town. In return, Jill took him to the old boardwalks in Santa Monica and the Trancas Inn and the little French family restaurant called Taix and to Papa DeCarlos and all the other out-of-the-way places a struggling actress with no money learns about. Toby did not care where he went, as long as Jill was with him.

She was the first person he had ever known who made his feeling of loneliness vanish.

Toby was almost afraid to go to bed with Jill now, for fear the magic might disappear. And yet he wanted her more than he had ever desired any woman in his life. Once, at the end of an evening, when Jill was giving him a light good night kiss, Toby reached between her legs and said, 'God, Jill, I'll go crazy if I can't have you.' She pulled back and said coldly, 'If that's all you want, you can buy it anywhere in town for twenty dollars.' She slammed the door in his face. Afterwards, she leaned against the door, trembling, afraid that she had gone too far. She lay awake all night, worrying.

The next day Toby sent her a diamond bracelet, and Jill knew that everything was all right. She returned the bracelet with a carefully thought-out note. 'Thank you, anyway. You make me feel very beautiful.'

'It cost me three grand,' Toby told Clifton proudly, 'and she sent it back!' He shook his head incredulously. 'What do you think of a girl like that?'

Clifton could have told him exactly what he thought, but all he said was, 'She's certainly unusual, dear boy.'

'Unusual!' Toby exclaimed. 'Every broad in this town is on the make for everything they can get their hot little hands on. Jill is the first girl I've ever met who doesn't give a damn about material things. Do you blame me for being crazy about her?'

'No,' Clifton said. But he was beginning to get worried. He knew all about Jill, and he wondered if he should not have spoken up sooner.

'I wouldn't object if you wanted to take Jill on as a client,' Toby said to Clifton. 'I'll bet she could be a big star.'

Clifton parried it deftly but firmly. 'No, thanks, Toby. One superstar on my hands is enough.' He laughed.

That night Toby repeated the remark to Jill.

After his unsuccessful attempt with Jill, Toby was careful not to broach the subject of their going to bed together. Toby was actually proud of Jill for refusing him. All the other girls he had gone with had been doormats. But not Jill. When Toby did something Jill thought was out of line, she told him so. One night Toby tongue-lashed a man who was pestering him for an autograph. Later, Jill said, 'It's funny when you're sarcastic on stage, Toby, but you hurt that man's feelings.'

Toby had gone back to the man and apologized.

Jill told Toby that she thought his drinking so much was not good for him. He cut down on his consumption. She made a casually critical remark about his clothes, and he changed tailors. Toby allowed Jill to say things that he would not have tolerated from anyone else in the world. No one had ever dared boss him around or criticize him.

Except, of course, his mother.

Jill refused to accept money or expensive gifts from Toby, but he knew that she could not have much money, and her courageous behaviour made Toby even more proud of her. One evening at Jill's apartment, while Toby was waiting for her to finish dressing before dinner, he noticed a stack of bills in the living room. Toby slipped them into his pocket and the next day ordered Clifton to pay them. Toby felt as though he had scored a victory. But he wanted to do something big for Jill, something important.

And he suddenly knew what it was going to be.

'Sam – I'm going to do you a great big favour!'

Beware of stars bearing gifts, Sam Winters thought wryly.

'You've been going crazy looking for a girl for Keller's picture, right?' Toby asked. 'Well, I got her for you.'

'Anyone I know?' Sam inquired.

'You met her at my house. Jill Castle.'

Sam remembered Jill. Beautiful face and figure, black hair. Far too old to play the teenager in the Keller movie. But if Toby Temple wanted her to test for the part, Sam was going to oblige. 'Have her come in to see me this afternoon,' he said.

Sam saw to it that Jill Castle's test was carefully handled. She was given one of the studio's top cameramen, and Keller himself directed the test.

Sam looked at the rushes the following day. As he had

guessed, Jill was too mature for the part of the young girl. Aside from that, she was not bad. What she lacked was charisma, the magic that leaped out from the screen.

He telephoned Toby Temple. 'I looked at Jill's test this morning, Toby. She photographs well, and she can read lines, but she's not a leading lady. She could earn a good living playing minor roles, but if she has her heart set on becoming a star, I think she's in the wrong business.'

Toby picked up Jill that evening to take her to dinner being given for a celebrated English director who had just arrived in Hollywood. Jill had been looking forward to it.

She opened the door for Toby and the moment he entered she knew that something was wrong. 'You heard some news about my test,' she said.

He nodded reluctantly. 'I talked to Sam Winters.' He told her what Sam had said, trying to soften the blow.

Jill stood there listening, not saying a word. She had been so *sure*. The part had felt so *right*. Out of nowhere came the memory of the gold cup in the department-store window. The little girl had ached with the wanting and the loss; Jill felt the same feeling of despair now.

Toby was saying, 'Look, honey, don't worry about it. Winters doesn't know what he's talking about.'

But he *did* know! She was not going to make it. All the agony and the pain and the hope had been for nothing. It was as though her mother had been right and a vengeful God was punishing Jill for she knew not what. She could hear the preacher screaming. *See that little girl? She will burn in Hell for her sins if she does not give her soul up to God and repent.* She had come to this town with love and dreams, and the town had degraded her.

She was overcome with an unbearable feeling of

sadness and she was not even aware that she was sobbing until she felt Toby's arm around her.

'Sh! It's all right,' he said, and his gentleness made her cry all the harder.

She stood there while he held her in his arms and she told him about her father dying when she was born, and about the gold cup and the Holy Rollers and the headaches and the nights filled with terror while she waited for God to strike her dead. She told him about the endless, dreary jobs she had taken in order to become an actress and the series of failures. Some deep-rooted instinct kept her from mentioning the men in her life. Although she had started out playing a game with Toby, she was now beyond pretence. It was in this moment of her naked vulnerability that she reached him. She touched a chord deep within him that no one else had ever struck.

He took out his pocket handkerchief and dried her tears. 'Hey, if you think *you* had it tough,' he said, 'listen to *this*. My old man was a butcher and . . .'

They talked until three o'clock in the morning. It was the first time in his life Toby had talked to a girl as a human being. He understood her. How could he not; she was *him*.

Neither of them ever knew who made the first move. What had started as a gentle, understanding comforting slowly became a sensual, animal wanting. They were kissing hungrily, and he was holding her tightly. She could feel his maleness pressing against her. She needed him and he was taking off her clothes, and she was helping him and then he was naked in the dark beside her, and there was an urgency in both of them. They went to the floor. Toby entered her and Jill moaned once at the enormous size of him, and Toby started to withdraw. She pulled him closer to her, holding him fiercely. He began to make love to her then, filling her, completing her, making her body whole. It was gentle and loving and it kept building and became frantic and demanding and suddenly it was beyond that. It was an ecstasy, an unbearable rapture, a mindless animal coupling, and Jill was screaming, 'Love me, Toby! Love me, love me!' His pounding body was on her, in her, was part of her, and they were one.

They made love all night and talked and laughed, and it was as though they had belonged together always.

If Toby had thought he cared for Jill before, he was insane about her now. They lay in bed, and he held her in his arms protectively, and he thought wonderingly. *This is what love is.* He turned to gaze at her. She looked warm and dishevelled and breathtakingly beautiful, and he had never loved anyone so much. He said, 'I want to marry you.'

It was the most natural thing in the world.

She hugged him tightly and said, 'Oh, yes, Toby.' She loved him and she was going to marry him.

And it was not until hours later that Jill remembered why all this had started in the first place. She had wanted Toby's power. She had wanted to pay back all the people who had used her, hurt her, degraded her. She had wanted vengeance.

Now she was going to have it.

Chapter Twenty-seven

Clifton Lawrence was in trouble. In a way, he supposed, it was his own fault for letting things get this far. He was seated at Toby's bar, and Toby was saying, 'I proposed to her this morning, Cliff, and she said yes. I feel like a sixteen-year-old kid.'

Clifton tried not to let the shock show on his face. He had to be extremely careful about the way he handled this. He knew one thing: he could not let that little tramp marry Toby Temple. The moment the wedding announcement was made, every cocksman in Hollywood would crawl out of the woodwork, announcing that he had gotten in there first. It was a miracle that Toby had not found out about Jill before now, but it could not be kept from him for ever. When he learned the truth, Toby would kill. He would lash out at everyone around him, everyone who had let this happen to him, and Clifton Lawrence would be the first to feel the brunt of Toby's rage. No, Clifton could not let this marriage take place. He was tempted to point out that Toby was twenty years older than Jill, but he checked himself. He looked over at Toby and said cautiously. 'It might be a mistake to rush things. It takes a long time to really get to know a person. You might change your –'

Toby brushed it aside. 'You're gonna be my best man. You think we should have the wedding here or up in Vegas?'

Clifton knew that he was wasting his breath. There was only one way to prevent this disaster from happening. He had to find a way to stop Jill.

That afternoon, the little agent telephoned Jill and asked her to come to his office. She arrived an hour late, gave him a cheek to kiss, sat down on the edge of the couch and said, 'I haven't much time. I'm meeting Toby.'

'This won't take long.'

Clifton studied her. It was a different Jill. She bore almost no resemblance to the girl he had first met a few months ago. There was a confidence about her now, an assurance that she had not had earlier. Well, he had dealt with girls like her before.

'Jill, I'm going to lay it on the line,' Clifton said. 'You're bad for Toby. I want you to get out of Hollywood.' He took a white envelope out of a drawer. 'Here's five thousand dollars cash. That's enough to take you anywhere you want to go.'

She stared at him a moment, a surprised expression on her face, then leaned back on the couch and began to laugh.

'I'm not joking,' Clifton Lawrence said. 'Do you think Toby would marry you if he found out you've laid everybody in town?'

She regarded Clifton for a long moment. She wanted to tell him that *he* was responsible for everything that had happened to her. He and all the other people in power who had refused to give her a chance. They had made her pay with her body, her pride, her soul. But she knew there was no way she could ever make him understand. He was trying to bluff her. He would not dare tell Toby about her; it would be Lawrence s word against hers.

Jill rose to her feet and walked out of the office.

One hour later, Clifton received a call from Toby.

Clifton had never heard Toby sound so excited. 'I don't know what you said to Jill, pal, but I have to hand it to you – she can't wait. We're on our way to Las Vegas to get married!'

The Lear jet was thirty-five miles from the Los Angeles International Airport, flying at 250 knots. David Kenyon made contact with the LAX approach control and gave them his position.

David was exhilarated. He was on his way to Jill.

Cissy had recovered from most of her injuries suffered in the automobile accident, but her face had been badly lacerated. David had sent her to the best plastic surgeon in the world, a doctor in Brazil. She had been gone for six weeks, during which time she had been sending him glowing reports about the doctor.

Twenty-four hours ago, David had received a telephone call from Cissy, saying she was not returning. She had fallen in love.

David could not believe his good fortune.

'That's – that's wonderful,' he managed to stammer. 'I hope you and the doctor will be happy.'

'Oh, it's not the doctor,' Cissy replied. 'It's someone who owns a little plantation here. He looks exactly like you, David. The only difference is that he loves me.'

The crackling of the radio interrupted his thoughts. 'Lear Three Alpha Papa, this is Los Angeles Approach Control. You're clear for approach to Runway Twenty-five Left. There will be a United seven-oh-seven behind you. When you land, please taxi to the ramp on your right.

'Roger.' David began to make his descent, and his

heart started to pound. He was on his way to find Jill, to tell her he still loved her, to ask her to marry him.

He was walking through the terminal when he passed the news stand and saw the headline: 'TOBY TEMPLE WEDS ACTRESS'. He read the story twice and then turned and went into the airport bar.

He stayed drunk for three days and then flew back to Texas.

Chapter Twenty-eight

It was a storybook honeymoon. Toby and Jill flew in a private jet to Las Hadas, where they were the guests of the Patinos at their fairyland resort carved out of the Mexican jungle and beach. The newlyweds were given a private villa surrounded by cacti, hibiscus and brilliantly coloured bougainvillaea, where exotic birds serenaded them all night. They spent ten days exploring and yachting and being partied. They ate delicious dinners at the Legazpi prepared by gourmet chefs and swam in the fresh-water pools. Jill shopped at the exquisite boutiques at the Plaza.

From Mexico they flew to Biarritz where they stayed at L'Hôtel du Palais, the spectacular palace that Napoleon III built for his Empress Eugenie. The honeymooners gambled at the casinos and went to the bullfights and fished and made love all night.

From the Côte Basque they drove east to Gstaad, thirty-five hundred feet above sea level in the Bernese Oberland. They took sightseeing flights among the peaks, skimming Mont Blanc and the Matterhorn. They skied the dazzling white slopes and rode dog sleds and attended fondue parties and danced. Toby had never been so happy. He had found the woman to make his life complete. He was no longer lonely.

Toby could have continued the honeymoon for ever, but

Jill was eager to get home. She was not interested in any of these places, nor in any of these people. She felt like a newly crowned queen who was being kept from her country. Jill Castle was burning to return to Hollywood.

Mrs Toby Temple had scores to settle.

BOOK THREE

Chapter Twenty-nine

There is a smell to failure. It is a stench that clings like a miasma. Just as dogs can detect the odour of fear in a human being, so people can sense when a man is on his way down.

Particularly in Hollywood.

Everyone in the Business knew that Clifton Lawrence was finished, even before he knew it. They could smell it in the air around him.

Clifton had not heard from Toby or Jill in the week since they had returned from their honeymoon. He had sent an expensive gift and had left three telephone messages, which had been ignored. Jill. Somehow she had managed to turn Toby's mind against him. Clifton knew that he had to effect a truce. He and Toby meant too much to each other to let anyone come between them.

Clifton drove out to the house on a morning when he knew Toby would be at the studio. Jill saw him coming up the driveway and opened the door for him. She looked stunningly beautiful, and he said so. She was friendly. They sat in the garden and had coffee, and she told him about the honeymoon and the places they had been. She said, 'I'm sorry Toby hasn't returned your calls, Cliff. You can't believe how frantic it's been around here.' She smiled apologetically, and Clifton knew then that he had been wrong about her. She was not his enemy.

'I'd like us to start fresh and be friends,' he said.

'Thank you, Cliff. So would I.'

Clifton felt an immeasurable sense of relief. 'I want to give a dinner party for you and Toby. I'll take over the private room at the Bistro. A week from Saturday. Black tie, a hundred of your most intimate friends. How does that sound?'

'Lovely. Toby will be pleased.'

Jill waited until the afternoon of the party to telephone and say, 'I'm so sorry, Cliff. I'm afraid I'm not going to be able to make it tonight. I'm a little tired. Toby thinks I should stay home and rest.'

Clifton managed to hide his feelings. 'I'm sorry about that, Jill, but I understand. Toby will be able to come, won't he?'

He heard her sigh over the telephone. 'I'm afraid not, dear boy. He won't go anywhere without me. But you have a nice party.' And she hung up.

It was too late to call off the party. The bill was three thousand dollars. But it cost Clifton much more than that. He had been stood up by the guest of honour, his one and only client, and everyone there, the studio heads, the stars, the directors – all the people who mattered in Hollywood – were aware of it. Clifton tried to cover up by saying that Toby was not feeling well. It was the worst thing he could have done. When he picked up a copy of the *Herald Examiner* the next afternoon, there was a photograph of Mr and Mrs Toby Temple that had been taken at the Dodgers Stadium the night before.

Clifton Lawrence knew now that he was fighting for his life. If Toby dropped him, there would be no one around to pick him up. None of the big agencies would take him on, because he could bring them no clients; and he could not bear the thought of starting all over again on his own. It was too late for that. He *had* to find a way to make peace with Jill. He telephoned Jill and told her he would like to come to the house to talk to her.

'Of course,' she said. 'I was telling Toby last night that we haven't seen enough of you lately.'

'I'll be over in fifteen minutes,' Clifton said. He walked over to the liquor cabinet and poured himself a double Scotch. He had been doing too much of that lately. It was a bad habit to drink during a working day, but who was he kidding? What work? Every day he received important offers for Toby, but he could not get the great man to sit down and even discuss them with him. In the past, they had talked over everything. He remembered all the wonderful times they had had, the trips they had taken, the parties and the laughs and the girls. They had been as close as twins. Toby had needed him, had counted on him. And now . . . Clifton poured another drink and was pleased to see his hands were not trembling so much.

When Clifton arrived at the Temples' house, Jill was seated on the terrace, having coffee. She looked up and smiled as she saw him approach. *You're a salesman,* Clifton told himself. *Sell her on you.*

'It's nice to see you, Cliff. Sit down.'

'Thanks, Jill.' He took a seat across from her at a large wrought-iron table and studied her. She was wearing a white summer dress, and the contrast with her black hair and golden, tanned skin was stunning. She looked younger, and – the only word he could think of somehow – innocent. She was watching him with warm, friendly eyes.

'Would you like some breakfast, Cliff?'

'No, thanks. I ate hours ago.'

'Toby isn't here.'

'I know. I wanted to talk to you alone.'

'What can I do for you?'

'Accept my apology,' Clifton urged. He had never begged anyone for anything in his life, but he was begging now. 'We – I got off on the wrong foot. Maybe it was my fault. It probably was. Toby's been my client and friend for so long that I – I wanted to protect him. Can you understand that?'

Jill nodded, her brown eyes fixed on him, and said, 'Of course, Cliff.'

He took a deep breath. 'I don't know whether he ever told you the story, but I'm the one who got Toby started. I knew he was going to be a big star the first time I saw him.' He saw that he had her full attention. 'I handled a lot of important clients then, Jill. I let them all go so that I could concentrate on Toby's career.'

'Toby's talked to me about how much you've done for him,' she said.

'Has he?' He hated the eagerness in his voice.

Jill smiled. 'He told me about the day he pretended that Sam Goldwyn telephoned you and how you went to see Toby anyway. That was nice.'

Clifton leaned forward and said, 'I don't want anything to happen to the relationship that Toby and I have. I need you in my corner. I'm asking you to forget everything that happened between us. I apologize for being out of line. I thought I was protecting Toby. Well, I was wrong. I think you're going to be great for him.'

'I want to be. Very much.'

'If Toby drops me, I – I think it would kill me. I'm not

just talking about business. He and I have – he's been like a son to me. I love him.' He despised himself for it, but he heard himself begging again. 'Please, Jill, for God's sake . . .' He stopped, his voice choked.

She looked at him a long moment with those deep brown eyes and then held out her hand. 'I don't hold grudges,' Jill said. 'Can you come to dinner tomorrow night?'

Clifton took a deep breath and then smiled happily and said, 'Thanks.' He found that his eyes were suddenly misty. 'I – I won't forget this. Ever.'

The following morning, when Clifton arrived at his office, there was a registered letter notifying him that his services had been terminated and that he no longer had the authority to act as Toby Temple's agent.

Chapter Thirty

Jill Castle Temple was the most exciting thing to hit Hollywood since Cinemascope. In a company town where everyone played the game of admiring the emperor's clothes, Jill used her tongue like a scythe. In a city where flattery was the daily currency of conversation, Jill fearlessly spoke her mind. She had Toby beside her and she brandished his power like a club, attacking all the important studio executives. They had never experienced anything like it before. They did not dare offend Jill, because they did not want to offend Toby. He was Hollywood's most bankable star, and they wanted him, needed him.

Toby was bigger than ever. His television show was still number one in the Nielsen Ratings every week, his movies were enormous money makers, and when Toby played Las Vegas, the casinos doubled their profits. Toby was the hottest property in show business. They wanted him for guest shots, record albums, personal appearances, merchandising, benefits, movies, they wanted they wanted they wanted.

The most important people in town fell all over themselves to please Toby. They quickly learned that the way to please Toby was to please Jill. She began to schedule all of Toby's appointments herself and to organize his life so that there was room in it only for those of whom she approved. She put up an impenetrable barricade around him, and none but the rich and famous and the powerful were allowed to go through it. She was the keeper of the flame. The little Polish girl from Odessa, Texas, entertained and was entertained by governors, ambassadors, world-renowned artists and the President of the United States. This town had done terrible things to her. But it would never do them again. Not as long as she had Toby Temple.

The people who were in real trouble were the ones on Jill's hate list.

She lay in bed with Toby and made sensuous love to him. When Toby was relaxed and spent, she snuggled in his arms and said, 'Darling, did I ever tell you about the time I was looking for an agent and I went to this woman – what was her name? – oh, yes! Rose Dunning. She told me she had a part for me and she sat down on her bed to read with me.'

Toby turned to look at her, his eyes narrowing. 'What happened?'

Jill smiled. 'Stupid innocent that I was, while I was reading, I felt her hand go up my thigh.' Jill threw back her head and laughed. 'I was so frightened out of my wits. I've never run so fast in my life.'

Ten days later, Rose Dunning's agency licence was permanently revoked by the City Licensing Commission.

The following weekend, Toby and Jill were at their house in Palm Springs. Toby was lying on a massage table in a patio, a heavy Turkish towel under him, while Jill gave him a long, relaxing massage. Toby was on his back, cotton pads protecting his eyes against the strong rays of the sun. Jill was working on his feet, using a soft creamy lotion.

'You sure opened my eyes about Cliff,' Toby said. 'He was nothing but a parasite, milking me. I hear he's going around town trying to get himself a partnership deal. No one wants him. He can't get himself arrested without me.'

Jill paused a moment and said, 'I feel sorry for Cliff.'

'That's the goddamned trouble with you, sweetheart. You think with your heart instead of your head. You've got to learn to be tougher.'

Jill smiled quietly. 'I can't help it. I'm the way I am.' She started to work on Toby's legs, moving her hands slowly up towards his thighs with light, sensuous movements. He began to have an erection.

'Oh, Jesus,' he moaned.

Her hands were moving higher now, moving towards Toby's groin, and the hardness increased. She slid her hands between his legs, underneath him, and slipped a creamy finger inside him. His enormous penis was rock hard.

'Quick, baby,' he said. 'Get on top of me.'

They were at the marina, on the *Jill*, the large motor-sailer Toby had bought for her. Toby's first television show of the new season was to tape the following day.

'This is the best vacation I've had in my whole life,' Toby said. 'I hate to go back to work.'

'It's such a wonderful show,' Jill said. 'I had fun doing it. Everyone was so nice.' She paused a moment, then added lightly, '*Almost* everyone.'

'What do you mean?' Toby's voice was sharp. 'Who wasn't nice to you?'

'No one, darling. I shouldn't have even mentioned it.'

But she finally allowed Toby to worm it out of her, and the next day Eddie Berrigan, the casting director, was fired.

In the months that followed, Jill told Toby little fictions about other casting directors on her list, and one by one they disappeared. Everyone who had ever used her was going to pay. It was, she thought, like the rite of mating with the queen bee. They had all had their pleasure, and now they had to be destroyed.

She went after Sam Winters, the man who had told Toby she had no talent. She never said a word against him; on the contrary, she praised him to Toby. But she always praised other studio heads just a little more . . . The other studios had properties better suited for Toby . . . directors who really understood him. Jill would add that she could not help thinking that Sam Winters did not really appreciate Toby's talent. Before long, Toby began feeling the same way. With Clifton Lawrence gone, Toby had no one to talk to, no one he could trust, except Jill. When Toby decided to make his movies at another studio, he believed that it was his own idea. But Jill made certain that Sam Winters knew the truth.

Retribution.

There were those around Toby who felt that Jill could not last, that she was simply a temporary intruder, a passing fancy. So they tolerated her or treated her with a thinly veiled contempt. It was their mistake. One by one, Jill eliminated them. She wanted no one around who had been important in Toby's life or who could influence him against her. She saw to it that Toby changed his lawyer and his public-relations firm and she hired people of her own choosing. She got rid of the three Macs and Toby's entourage of stooges. She replaced all the servants. It was *her* house now and she was the mistress of it.

A party at the Temples' had become the hottest ticket in town. Everyone who was anybody was there. Actors mingled with socialites and governors and heads of powerful corporations. The press was always there in full force, so that there was a bonus for the lucky guests. Not only did they go to the Temples' and have a wonderful time, but everyone *knew* that they had been to the Temples' and had a wonderful time.

When the Temples were not hosts, they were guests. There was an avalanche of invitations. They were invited to premieres, charity dinners, political affairs, openings of restaurants and hotels.

Toby would have been content to stay at home alone with Jill, but she liked going out. On some evenings, they had three or four parties to attend, and she rushed Toby from one to the other.

'Jesus, you should have been a social director at Grossinger's,' Toby laughed.

'I'm doing it for you, darling.' Jill replied.

Toby was making a movie for MGM and had a gruelling schedule. He came home late one night, exhausted, to find his evening clothes laid out for him. 'We're not going out *again*, baby? We haven't been home one night the whole fucking year!'

'It's the Davises' anniversary party. They'd be terribly hurt if we didn't show up.

Toby sat down heavily on the bed. 'I was looking

forward to a nice hot bath and a quiet evening. Just the two of us.'

But Toby went to the party. And because he always had to be 'on', always had to be the centre of attention, he drew on his enormous reservoir of energy until everyone was laughing and applauding and telling everyone else what a brilliantly funny man Toby Temple was. Late that night, lying in his bed, Toby was unable to sleep, his body drained, but his mind reliving the triumphs of the evening line by line, laugh by laugh. He was a very happy man. And all because of Jill.

How his mother would have adored her.

In March they received an invitation to the Cannes Film Festival.

'No way,' Toby said, when Jill showed him the invitation. 'The only Cannes I'm going to is the one in my bathroom. I'm tired, honey. I've been working my butt off.'

Jerry Guttman, Toby's public-relations man, had told Jill that there was a good chance that Toby's movie would win the Best Picture Award and that it would help if Toby were there. He felt that it was important for Toby to go.

Lately, Toby had been complaining that he was tired all the time and was unable to sleep. At night he took sleeping pills, which left him groggy in the morning. Jill counteracted the feeling of tiredness by giving him benzedrine at breakfast so that Toby would have enough energy to get through the day. Now, the cycle of uppers and downers seemed to be taking its toll on him.

'I've already accepted the invitation,' Jill told Toby, 'but I'll cancel. No problem, darling.'

'Let's go down to the Springs for a month and just lie around in the soap.'

She looked at him. 'What?'

He sat there, very still. 'I meant *sun*. I don't know why it came out *soap*.'

She laughed. 'Because you're funny.' Jill squeezed his hand. 'Anyway, Palm Springs sounds wonderful. I love being alone with you.'

'I don't know what's wrong with me,' Toby sighed. 'I just don't have the juice anymore. I guess I'm getting old.'

'You'll never get old. You can wear me out.'

He grinned. 'Yeah? I guess my pecker will live long after I die.' He rubbed the back of his head and said, 'I think I'll take a little nap. To tell the truth, I'm not feeling so hot. We don't have a date tonight, do we?'

'Nothing that I can't put off. I'll send the servants away and cook dinner myself tonight. Just us.'

'Hey, that'll be great.'

He watched her leave, and he thought, *Jesus, I'm the luckiest guy who ever lived.*

They were lying in bed late that night. Jill had given Toby a warm bath and a relaxing massage, kneading his tired muscles, soothing away his tensions.

'Ah, that feels wonderful,' he murmured. 'How did I ever get along without you?'

'I can't imagine.' She nestled close to him. 'Toby, tell me about the Cannes Film Festival. What's it like? I've never been to one.'

'It's just a mob of hustlers who come from all over the world to sell their lousy movies to one another. It's the biggest con game in the world.'

'You make it sound exciting,' Jill said.

'Yeah? Well, I guess it is kind of exciting. The place is filled with characters.' He studied her for a moment. 'Do you really want to go to that stupid film festival?'

She shook her head quickly. 'No. We'll go to Palm Springs.'

'Hell, we can go to Palm Springs anytime.'

'Really, Toby, it's not important.'

He smiled. 'Do you know why I'm so crazy about you? Any other woman in the world would have been pestering me to take her to the festival. You're dying to go, but do you say anything? No. You want to go to the Springs with me. Have you cancelled that acceptance?'

'Not yet, but – '

'Don't. We're going to India.' A puzzled look came over his face. 'Did I say India? I meant – Cannes.'

When their plane landed at Orly, Toby was handed a cablegram. His father had died in the nursing home. It was too late for Toby to go back for the funeral. He arranged to have a new wing added to the rest home, named after his parents.

The whole world was at Cannes.

It was Hollywood and London and Rome, all mixed together in a glorious, many-tongued cacophony of sound and fury, in Technicolor and Panavision. From all over the globe, picture makers flocked to the French Riviera, carrying cans of dreams under their arms, rolls of celluloid made in English and French and Japanese and Hungarian and Polish, that were going to make them rich and famous overnight. The *croisette* was packed with professionals and amateurs, veterans and tyros, comers and hasbeens, all competing for the prestigious prizes.

Being awarded a prize at the Cannes Film Festival meant money in the bank; if the winner had no distribution deal, he could get one, and if he already had one, he could better it.

Every hotel in Cannes was filled, and the overflow had spilled up and down the coast to Antibes, Beaulieu, Saint-Tropez and Menton. The residents of the small villages gaped in awe at the famous faces that filled their streets and restaurants and bars.

Every room had been reserved for months ahead, but Toby Temple had no difficulty getting a large suite at the Carlton. Toby and Jill were fêted everywhere they went. News photographers' cameras clicked incessantly, and their images were sent around the world. The Golden Couple, the King and Queen of Hollywood. The reporters interviewed Jill and asked for her opinions on everything from French wines to African politics. It was a far cry from Josephine Czinski of Odessa, Texas.

Toby's picture did not win the award, but two nights before the festival was to end, the Judges Committee announced that they were presenting a special award to Toby Temple for his contribution to the field of entertainment.

It was a black-tie affair, and the large banquet hall at the Carlton Hotel overflowed with guests. Jill was seated on the dais next to Toby. She noticed that he was not eating. 'What's the matter, darling?' she asked.

Toby shook his head. 'Probably had too much sun today. I feel a little woozy.'

'Tomorrow I'm going to see that you rest.' Jill had scheduled interviews for Toby with *Paris Match* and the London *Times* in the morning, luncheon with a group of television reporters, followed by a cocktail party. She decided she would cancel the least important.

At the conclusion of dinner, the mayor of Cannes rose to his feet and introduced Toby. '*Mesdames, messieurs, et invités distingués, c'est un grand privilège de vous présenter un homme dont l'oeuvre a donné plaisir et bonheur au monde entier. J'ai l'honneur de lui présenter cette medaille spéciale, un signe de notre affection et de notre appréciation.*' He held up a gold medal and ribbon and bowed to Toby. 'Monsieur Toby Temple!' There was an enthusiastic burst of applause from the audience, as everyone in the great banquet hall rose to his feet in a standing ovation. Toby was seated in his chair, not moving.

'Get up,' Jill whispered.

Slowly, Toby rose, pale and unsteady. He stood there a moment, smiled, then started towards the microphone. Halfway there, he stumbled and fell to the floor, unconscious.

Toby Temple was flown to Paris in a French air force transport jet and rushed to the American Hospital, where he was put in the intensive-care ward. The finest specialists in France were summoned, while Jill sat in a private room at the hospital, waiting. For thirty-six hours she refused to eat or drink or take any of the phone calls that were flooding into the hospital from all over the world.

She sat alone, staring at the walls, neither seeing nor hearing the stir of activity around her. Her mind was focused on only one thing: *Toby had to get well.* Toby was her sun, and if the sun went out, the shadow would die. She could not allow that to happen.

It was five o'clock in the morning when Doctor Duclos,

the chief of staff, entered the private room Jill had taken so she could be near Toby.

'Mrs Temple – I am afraid there is no point in trying to soften the blow. Your husband has suffered a massive stroke. In all probability, he will never be able to walk or speak again.'

Chapter Thirty-one

When they finally allowed Jill into Toby's hospital room in Paris, she was shocked by his appearance. Overnight, Toby had become old and desiccated, as if all his vital fluids had drained out of him. He had lost partial use of both arms and legs, and though he was able to make grunting animal noises, he could not speak.

It was six weeks before the doctors would permit Toby to be moved. When Toby and Jill arrived back in California, they were mobbed at the airport by the press and television media and hundreds of well-wishers. Toby Temple's illness had caused a major sensation. There were constant phone calls from friends inquiring about Toby's health and progress. Television crews tried to get into the house to take pictures of him. There were messages from the President and senators, and thousands of letters and postcards from fans who loved Toby Temple and were praying for him.

But the invitations had stopped. No one was calling to find out how *Jill* felt, or whether she would like to attend a quiet dinner or take a drive or see a movie. Nobody in Hollywood cared a damn about *Jill*.

She had brought in Toby's personal physician, Dr Eli Kaplan, and he had summoned two top neurologists, one from UCLA Medical Centre and the other from Johns Hopkins. Their diagnosis was exactly the same as that of Dr Duclos, in Paris.

'It's important to understand,' Dr Kaplan told Jill, 'that Toby's mind is not impaired in any way. He can hear and understand everything you say, but his speech and motor functions are affected. He can't respond.'

'Is – is he always going to be like this?'

Dr Kaplan hesitated. 'It's impossible to be absolutely certain, of course, but in our opinion, his nervous system has been too badly damaged for therapy to have any appreciable effect.'

'But you don't know for sure.'

'No . . .'

But Jill knew.

In addition to the three nurses who tended Toby round the clock, Jill arranged for a physiotherapist to come to the house every morning to work with Toby. The therapist carried Toby into the pool and held him in his arms, gently stretching the muscles and tendons, while Toby feebly tried to kick his legs and move his arms about in the warm water. There was no progress. On the fourth week, a speech therapist was brought in. She spent one hour every afternoon trying to help Toby learn to speak again, to form the sounds of words.

After two months, Jill could see no change. None at all. She sent for Dr Kaplan.

'You've got to do something to help him,' she demanded. 'You can't leave him like this.'

He looked at her helplessly. 'I'm sorry, Jill. I tried to tell you . . .'

Jill sat in the library, alone, long after Dr Kaplan had gone. She could feel one of the bad headaches beginning, but there was no time to think of herself now. She went upstairs.

Toby was propped up in bed, staring at nothingness. As Jill walked up to him, Toby's deep blue eyes lit up. They followed Jill, bright and alive, as she approached his bed and looked down at him. His lips moved and some unintelligible sound came out. Tears of frustration began to fill his eyes. Jill remembered Dr Kaplan's words, *It's important to understand that his mind is not impaired in any way.*

Jill sat down on the edge of the bed. 'Toby, I want you to listen to me. You're going to get out of that bed. You're going to walk and you're going to talk.' The tears were running down the sides of his cheeks now. 'You're going to do it,' Jill said. 'You're going to do it for me.'

The following morning, Jill fired the nurses, the physiotherapist and the speech therapist. As soon as he heard the news, Dr Eli Kaplan hurried over to see Jill.

'I agree with you about the physiotherapist, Jill – but the *nurses!* Toby has to have someone with him twenty-four hours a –'

'I'll be with him.'

He shook his head. 'You have no idea what you're letting yourself in for. One person can't –'

'I'll call you if I need you.

She sent him away.

The ordeal began.

Jill was going to attempt to do what the doctors had assured her could not be done. The first time she picked Toby up and put him into his wheelchair, it frightened her to feel how weightless he was. She took him downstairs in the elevator that had been installed and began to work with him in the swimming pool, as she had seen the physiotherapist do. But what happened now was different. Where the therapist had been gentle and coaxing, Jill was stern and unrelenting. When Toby tried to speak, signifying that he was tired and could not bear any more, Jill said, 'You're not through. One more time. For me, Toby.'

And she would force him to do it one more time.

And yet again, until he sat mutely crying with exhaustion.

In the afternoon, Jill set to work to teach Toby to speak again. 'Ooh . . . oooooooh.

'Ahaaahh . . . aaaaaaaaagh . . .

'No! Ooooooooh. Round your lips, Toby. Make them obey you. Oooooooh.'

'Aaaaaaaaagh . . .'

'No, goddamn you! You're going to speak! Now, say it – Ooooooooh!'

And he would try again.

Jill would feed him each night. and then lie in his bed, holding him in her arms. She drew his useless hands slowly up and down her body, across her breasts and down the soft cleft of her legs. 'Feel that, Toby,' she whispered. 'That's all yours, darling. It belongs to you. I want you. I want you to get well so we can make love again. I want you to fuck me, Toby.'

He looked at her with those alive, bright eyes and made incoherent, whimpering sounds.

'Soon, Toby, soon.'

Jill was tireless. She discharged the servants because she did not want anyone around. After that, she did all the cooking herself. She ordered her groceries by phone and never left the house. In the beginning, Jill had been kept busy answering the telephones, but the calls had soon dwindled to a trickle, then ceased. Newscasters had stopped giving bulletins on Toby Temple's condition. The world knew that he was dying. It was just a question of time.

But Jill was not going to let Toby die. If he died, she would die with him.

The days blended into one long, endless round of drudgery. Jill was up at six o'clock in the morning. First, she would clean Toby. He was totally incontinent. Even though he wore a catheter and a diaper, he would befoul himself during the night and the bedclothes would sometimes have to be changed, as well as Toby's pyjamas. The stench in the bedroom was almost unbearable. Jill filled a basin with warm water, took a sponge and soft cloth and cleaned the faeces and urine from Toby's body. When he was clean, she dried him off and powdered him, then shaved him and combed his hair.

'There. You look beautiful, Toby. Your fans should see you now. But they'll see you soon. They'll fight to get in to see you. The President will be there – everybody will be there to see Toby Temple.'

Then Jill prepared Toby's breakfast. She made oatmeal or cream of wheat or scrambled eggs, food she could spoon into his mouth. She fed him as though he were a baby, talking to him all the time, promising that he was going to get well.

'You're Toby Temple,' she intoned. 'Everybody loves you, everybody wants you back. Your fans out there are waiting for you, Toby. You've got to get well for them.'

And another long, punishing day would begin.

She wheeled his useless, crippled body down to the pool for his exercises. After that, she massaged him and worked on his speech therapy. Then it was time for her to prepare his lunch, and after lunch it would begin all over again. Through it all, Jill kept telling Toby how wonderful he was, how much he was loved. He was Toby Temple, and the world was waiting for him to come back to it. At night she would take out one of his scrapbooks and hold it up so he could see it.

'There we are with the Queen. Do you remember how they all cheered you that night? That's the way it's going to be again. You're going to be bigger than ever, Toby, bigger than ever.'

She tucked him in at night and crawled into the cot she had put next to his bed, drained. In the middle of the night, she would be awakened by the noisome stench of Toby's bowel movement in bed. She would drag herself from her cot and change Toby's diaper and clean him. By then it would be time to start fixing his breakfast and begin another day.

And another. In an endless march of days.

Each day Jill pushed Toby a little harder, a little further. Her nerves were so frayed that, if she felt Toby was not trying, she would slap him across the face. 'We're going to beat them,' she said fiercely. 'You're going to get well.'

Jill's body was exhausted from the punishing routine she was putting herself through, but when she lay down at night, sleep eluded her. There were too many visions dancing through her head, like scenes from old movies.

She and Toby mobbed by reporters at the Cannes Festival . . . The President at their Palm Springs home, telling Jill how beautiful she was . . . Fans crowding around Toby and her at a premiere . . . The Golden Couple . . . Toby stepping up to receive his medal and falling . . . falling . . . Finally, she would drift off to sleep.

Sometimes, Jill would awaken with a sudden, fierce headache that would not go away. She would lie there in the loneliness of the dark, fighting the pain, until the sun would come up, and it was time to drag herself to her feet.

And it would begin all over again. It was as though she and Toby were the lone survivors of some long-forgotten holocaust. Her world had shrunk to the dimensions of this house, these rooms, this man. She drove herself relentlessly from dawn until past midnight.

And she drove Toby, her Toby imprisoned in hell, in a world where there was only Jill, whom he must blindly obey.

The weeks, dreary and painful, dragged by and turned into months. Now, Toby would begin to cry when he saw Jill coming towards him, for he knew he was going to be punished. Each day Jill became more merciless. She forced Toby's flopping, useless limbs to move, until he was in unbearable agony. He made horrible gurgling pleas for her to stop, but Jill would say, 'Not yet. Not until you're a man again, not until we show them all.' She would go on kneading his exhausted muscles. He was a helpless, full-grown baby, a vegetable, a nothing. But when Jill looked at him, she saw him as he was going to be, and she declared. 'You're going to walk!'

She would lift him to his feet and hold him up while she forced one leg after the other, so that he was moving in a grotesque parody of motion, like a drunken, disjointed marionette.

Her headaches had become more frequent. Bright lights or a loud noise or sudden movement would set them off. *I must see a doctor,* she thought. *Later, when Toby is well again.* Now there was no time or room for herself.

Only Toby.

It was as though Jill were possessed. Her clothes hung loosely on her, but she had no idea of how much weight she had lost or how she looked. Her face was thin and drawn, her eyes hollow. Her once beautiful shiny black hair was lustreless and stringy. She did not know, nor would she have cared.

One day Jill found a telegram under the door asking her to phone Dr Kaplan. No time. The routine must be kept.

The days and nights became a Kafkaesque blur of bathing Toby and exercising him and changing him and shaving him and feeding him.

And then starting all over again.

She got a walker for Toby and fastened his fingers around it and moved his legs, holding him up, trying to show him the motions, walking him back and forth across the room until she was asleep on her feet, not knowing any longer where or who she was, or what she was doing.

Then, one day, Jill knew that it had all come to an end.

She had been up with Toby half the night and had finally gone into her own bedroom, where she had fallen into a dazed slumber just-before dawn. When Jill awakened, the sun was high in the sky. She had slept long past noon. Toby had not been fed or bathed or changed. He was lying in his bed, helpless, waiting for her, probably panicky. Jill started to rise and found that she could not move. She was filled with such a bottomless, bone-deep weariness that her exhausted body would no longer obey her. She lay there, helpless, knowing that she had lost, that it had all been wasted, all the days and nights of hell, the months of agony, none of it had meant anything. Her body had betrayed her, as Toby's had betrayed him. Jill had no strength left to give him anymore, and it made her want to weep. It was finished.

She heard a sound at her bedroom door and she raised her eyes. Toby was standing in the doorway, by himself, his trembling arms clutching his walker, his mouth making unintelligible slobbering noises, working to say something.

'Jiiiiiiiigh . . . Jiiiiiigh . . .'

He was trying to say 'Jill'. She began to sob uncontrollably, and she could not stop.

From that day on, Toby's progress was spectacular. For the first time, *he* knew he was going to get well. He no longer objected when Jill pushed him beyond the limits of his endurance. He welcomed it. He wanted to get well for *her*. Jill had become his goddess; if he had loved her before, he worshipped her now.

And something had happened to Jill. Before, it had been her own life she was fighting for; Toby was merely the instrument she was forced to use. But somehow, that had changed. It was as though Toby had become part of her. They were one body and one mind and one soul, obsessed with the same purpose. They had gone through a purging crucible. His life had been in her hands, and she had nurtured it and strengthened it, and saved it, and out of that had grown a kind of love. Toby belonged to her, just as she belonged to him.

Jill changed Toby's diet, so that he began to regain the weight he had lost. He spent time in the sun every day and took long walks around the grounds, using the walker, then a cane, building up his strength. When the day came that Toby could walk by himself, the two of them celebrated by having a candlelight dinner in the dining room.

Finally, Jill felt that Toby was ready to be seen. She telephoned Dr Kaplan, and his nurse put him on the phone immediately.

'Jill! I've been terribly worried. I've tried to telephone you and there was never any answer. I sent a telegram, and when I didn't hear, I assumed you had taken Toby away somewhere. Is he – has he – ?'

'Come and see for yourself, Eli.'

Dr Kaplan could not conceal his astonishment. 'It's unbelievable,' he told Jill. 'It's – it's a miracle.'

'It is a miracle,' Jill said. *Only in this life you made your own miracles, because God was busy elsewhere.*

'People still call me to ask about Toby,' Dr Kaplan was saying. 'Apparently they've been unable to get through to you. Sam Winters calls at least once a week. Clifton Lawrence has been calling.'

Jill dismissed Clifton Lawrence. But Sam Winters! That was good. Jill had to find a way to let the world know that Toby Temple was still a superstar, that they were still the Golden Couple.

Jill telephoned Sam Winters the next morning and asked him if he would like to come and visit Toby. Sam arrived at the house an hour later. Jill opened the front door to let him in, and Sam tried to conceal his shock at her appearance. Jill looked ten years older than when he had last seen her. Her eyes were hollow brown pools and her face was etched with deep lines. She had lost so much weight that she looked almost skeletal.

'Thank you for coming, Sam. Toby will be pleased to see you.'

Sam had been prepared to see Toby in bed, a shadow of the man he had once been, but he was in for a stunning surprise. Toby was lying on a pad alongside the pool and, as Sam approached, Toby rose to his feet, a little slowly, but steadily, and held out a firm hand. He appeared tanned and healthy, better than he had looked before his stroke. It was as though through some arcane alchemy, Jill's health and vitality had flowed into Toby's body, and the sick tides that had ravaged Toby had ebbed into Jill.

'Hey! It's great to see you, Sam.'

Toby's speech was a little slower and more precise than before, but it was clear and strong. There was no sign of the paralysis Sam had heard about. There was still the same boyish face with the bright blue eyes. Sam gave Toby a hug and said, 'Jesus, you really had us scared.'

Toby grinned and said, 'You don't have to call me "Jesus" when we're alone.'

Sam looked at Toby more closely and marvelled. 'I honestly can't get over it. Damn it, you look *younger*. The whole town was making funeral arrangements.'

'Over my dead body,' Toby smiled.

Sam said, 'It's fantastic what the doctors today can – '

'No doctors.' Toby turned to look at Jill and naked adoration shone from his eyes. 'You want to know who did it? Jill. Just Jill. With her two bare hands. She threw everybody out and made me get on my feet again.'

Sam glanced at Jill, puzzled. She had not seemed to him the kind of girl capable of such a selfless act. Perhaps he had misjudged her. 'What are your plans?' he asked Toby. 'I suppose you'll want to rest and – '

'He's going back to work,' Jill said. 'Toby's too talented to be sitting around doing nothing.'

'I'm raring to go,' Toby agreed.

'Perhaps Sam has a project for you,' Jill suggested.

They were both watching him. Sam did not want to discourage Toby, but neither did he want to hold out any false hopes. It was not possible to make a picture with a star unless you got insurance on him, and no company was going to insure Toby Temple.

'There's nothing in the shop at the moment,' Sam said carefully. 'But I'll certainly keep an eye open.'

'You're afraid to use him, aren't you?' It was as though she was reading his mind.

'Certainly not.' But they both knew he was lying.

No one in Hollywood would take a chance on using Toby Temple again.

Toby and Jill were watching a young comedian on television.

'He's rotten,' Toby snorted. 'Damn it, I wish I could get back on the air. Maybe I oughta get an agent. Somebody who could check around town and see what's doing.'

'No!' Jill's tone was firm. 'We're not going to let anyone peddle you. You're not some bum looking for a job. You're Toby Temple. We're going to make them come to you.'

Toby smiled wryly and said, 'They're not beating down the doors, baby.'

'They will be,' Jill promised. 'They don't know what shape you're in. You're better now than you ever were. We just have to show them.'

'Maybe I should pose in the nude for one of those magazines.'

Jill was not listening. 'I have an idea,' she said slowly. 'A one-man show.'

'Huh?'

'A one-man show.' There was a growing excitement in her voice. 'I'm going to book you into the Huntington Hartford Theatre. Everybody in Hollywood will come. After *that,* they'll start beating down the doors!'

And everybody in Hollywood did come: producers, directors, stars, critics – all the people in show business who mattered. The theatre on Vine Street had long since been sold out, and hundreds of people had been turned away. There was a cheering mob outside the lobby when Toby and Jill arrived in a chauffeur-driven limousine. He was *their* Toby Temple. He had come back to them from the dead, and they adored him more than ever.

The audience inside the theatre was there partly out of respect for a man who had been famous and great, but mostly out of curiosity. They were there to pay final tribute to a dying hero, a burnt-out star.

Jill had planned the show herself. She had gone to O'Hanlon and Rainger, and they had written some brilliant material, beginning with a monologue kidding the town for burying Toby while he was still alive. Jill had approached a song-writing team that had won three Academy Awards. They had never written special material for anyone, but when Jill said, 'Toby insists you're the only writers in the world who . . .'

Dick Landry, the director, flew in from London to stage the show.

Jill had assembled the finest talent she could find to back up Toby, but in the end everything would depend on the star himself. It was a one-man show, and he would be alone on that stage.

The moment finally arrived. The house lights dimmed, and the theatre was filled with that expectant hush that precedes the ringing up of the curtain, the silent prayer that on this night magic would happen.

It happened.

As Toby Temple strolled out onto the stage, his gait strong and steady, that familiar impish smile lighting up that boyish face, there was a momentary silence and then a wild explosion of applause and yelling, a standing ovation that rocked the theatre for a full five minutes.

Toby stood there, waiting for the pandemonium to subside, and when the theatre was finally still, he said, 'You call *that* a reception?' And they roared.

He was brilliant. He told stories and sang and danced, and he attacked everybody, and it was as though he had never been gone. The audience could not get enough of him. He was still a superstar, but now he was something more; he had become a living legend.

The *Variety* review the next day said, 'They came to bury Toby Temple, but they stayed to praise him and cheer him. And how he deserved it! There is no one in show business who has the old master's magic. It was an evening of ovations, and no one who was fortunate enough to be there is likely ever to forget that memorable . . .'

The *Hollywood Reporter* reviewer said, 'The audience

was there to see a great star come back, but Toby Temple proved he had never been away.'

All the other reviews were in the same panegyric vein. From that moment on, Toby's phones rang constantly. Letters and telegrams poured in with invitations and offers.

They were beating the doors down.

Toby repeated his one-man show in Chicago and in Washington and New York; everywhere he went, he was a sensation. There was more interest in him now than there had ever been. In a wave of affectionate nostalgia, Toby's old movies were shown at art theatres and at universities. Television stations had a Toby Temple Week and ran his old variety shows.

There were Toby Temple dolls and Toby Temple games and Toby Temple puzzles and jokebooks and T-shirts. There were endorsements for coffee and cigarettes and toothpaste.

Toby did a cameo in a musical picture at Universal and was signed to do guest appearances on all the big variety shows. The networks had writers at work, competing to develop a new Toby Temple Hour.

The sun was out once more, and it was shining on Jill.

There were parties again, and receptions and this ambassador and that senator and private screenings and . . . Everybody wanted them for everything. They were given a dinner at the White House, an honour usually reserved for heads of state. They were applauded wherever they appeared.

But now it was Jill they were applauding, as well as Toby. The magnificent story of what she had done, her feat of singlehandedly nursing Toby back to health against all odds, had stirred the imagination of the world. It was hailed by the press as the love story of the century. *Time* Magazine put them both on the cover, with a glowing tribute to Jill in the accompanying story.

A five-million-dollar deal was made for Toby to star in a new weekly television variety show, starting in September, only twelve weeks away.

'We'll go to Palm Springs so that you can rest until then,' Jill said.

Toby shook his head. 'You've been shut in long enough. We're going to live a little.' He put his arms around her and added, 'I'm not very good with words, baby, unless they're jokes. I don't know how to tell you what I feel about you. I – I just want you to know that I didn't start living until the day I met you.'

And he abruptly turned away, so that Jill could not see the tears in his eyes.

Toby arranged to tour his one-man show in London, Paris and – the greatest coup of all – Moscow. Everyone was fighting to sign him. He was as big a cult figure in Europe as he was in America.

They were out on the *Jill,* on a sunny, sparkling day, headed for Catalina. There were a dozen guests aboard the boat, among them Sam Winters and O'Hanlon and Rainger, who had been selected as the head writers on Toby's new television show. They were all in the salon, playing games and talking. Jill looked around and noticed that Toby was missing. She went out on deck.

Toby was standing at the railing, staring at the sea. Jill walked up to him and said, 'Are you feeling all right?'

'Just watching the water, baby.'

'It's beautiful, isn't it?'

'If you're a shark.' He shuddered. 'That's not the way I want to die. I've always been terrified of drowning.'

She put her hand in his. 'What's bothering you?'

He looked at her. 'I guess I don't want to die. I'm afraid of what's out there. *Here,* I'm a big man. Everybody knows Toby Temple. But out there . . . ? You know my idea of Hell? A place where there's no audience.'

The Friars Club gave a Roast with Toby Temple as the guest of honour. A dozen top comics were on the dais, along with Toby and Jill, Sam Winters and the head of the network that Toby had signed with. Jill was asked to stand up and take a bow. It became a standing ovation.

They're cheering me, Jill thought. *Not Toby. Me!*

The master of ceremonies was the host of a famous night-time television talk show. 'I can't tell you how happy I am to see Toby here,' he said. 'Because if we weren't honouring him *here* tonight, we'd be holding this banquet at Forest Lawn.'

Laughter.

'And believe me, the food's terrible there. Have you ever eaten at Forest Lawn? They serve leftovers from the Last Supper.'

Laughter.

He turned to Toby. 'We really are proud of you, Toby. I mean that. I understand you've been asked to donate a part of your body to science. They're going to put it in a jar at the Harvard Medical School. The only problem so far is that they haven't been able to find a jar big enough to hold it.'

Roars.

When Toby got up for his rebuttal, he topped them all.

Everyone agreed that it was the best Roast the Friars had ever held.

Clifton Lawrence was in the audience that night.

He was seated at a table in the back of the room near the kitchen with the other unimportant people. He had been forced to impose on old friendships to get even this table. Ever since Toby Temple had fired him, Clifton Lawrence had worn the label of a loser. He had tried to make a partnership deal with a large agency. With no clients, however, he had nothing to offer. Then Clifton had tried the smaller agencies, but they were not interested in a middle-aged has-been; they wanted aggressive young men. In the end, Clifton had settled for a salaried job with a small new agency. His weekly salary was less than what he had once spent in one evening at Romanoff's.

He remembered his first day at the new agency. It was owned by three aggressive young men – no, *kids* – all of them in their late twenties. Their clients were rock stars. Two of the agents were bearded, and they all wore jeans and sports shirts and tennis shoes without socks. They made Clifton feel a thousand years old. They spoke in a language he did not understand. They called him 'Dad' and 'Pop' and he thought of the respect he had once commanded in this town, and he wanted to weep.

The once dapper, cheerful agent had become seedy-looking and bitter. Toby Temple had been his whole life, and Clifton talked about those days compulsively. It was all he thought about. That and Jill. Clifton blamed her for everything that had happened to him. Toby could not help himself; he had been influenced by that bitch. But, oh, how Clifton hated Jill.

He was sitting in the back of the room watching the

crowd applaud Jill Temple when one of the men at the table said, 'Toby's sure a lucky bastard. I wish I had a piece of that. She's great in bed.'

'Yeah?' someone asked, cynically. 'How would *you* know?'

'She's in that porno flick at the Pussycat Theatre. Hell, I thought she was going to suck the guy's liver out of him.'

Clifton's mouth was suddenly so dry that he could hardly get out the words. 'Are you – are you sure it was Jill Castle?' he asked.

The stranger turned to him. 'Sure, I'm sure. She used another name – Josephine something. A crazy Polack name.' He stared at Clifton and said, 'Hey! Didn't you used to be Clifton Lawrence?'

There is an area of Santa Monica Boulevard, bordering between Fairfax and La Cienega, that is County territory. Part of an island surrounded by the City of Los Angeles, it operates under County ordinances, which are more lenient than those of the City. In one six-block area, there are four movie houses that run only hard-core pornography, half a dozen bookshops where customers can stand in private booths and watch movies through individual viewers and a dozen massage parlours staffed with nubile young girls who are experts at giving everything except massages. The Pussycat Theatre sits in the midst of it all.

There were perhaps two dozen people in the darkened theatre, all of them men except two women who sat holding hands. Clifton looked around at the audience and wondered what drove these people to darkened caverns in the middle of a sunny day, to spend hours watching images of other people fornicating on film.

The main feature came on, and Clifton forgot everything except what was up on the screen. He leaned forward in his seat, concentrating on the face of each actress. The plot was about a young college professor who smuggled his female students into his bedroom for night classes. All of them were young, surprisingly attractive and incredibly endowed. They went through a variety of sexual exercises, oral, vaginal and anal, until the professor was as satisfied as his pupils.

But none of the girls was Jill. *She has to be there,* Clifton thought. This was the only chance he would ever have to avenge himself for what she had done to him. He would arrange for Toby to see the film. It would hurt Toby, but he would get over it. Jill would be destroyed. When Toby learned what kind of whore he had married, he would throw her out on her ass. Jill *had* to be in this film.

And suddenly, there she was – on the wide screen, in wonderful, glorious, living colour. She had changed a great deal. She was thinner now, more beautiful and more sophisticated. But it was Jill. Clifton sat there, drinking in the scene, revelling in it, rejoicing and feasting his senses, filled with an electrifying sense of triumph and vengeance.

Clifton remained in his seat until the credits came on There it was, *Josephine Czinski.* He got to his feet and made his way back to the projection booth. A man in shirt sleeves was inside the small room, reading a racing form. He glanced up as Clifton entered and said, 'No one's allowed in here, buddy.'

'I want to buy a print of that picture.'

The man shook his head. 'Not for sale.' He went back to his handicapping.

'I'll give you a hundred bucks to run off a dupe. No one will ever know.'

The man did not even look up.

'Two hundred bucks,' Clifton said.

The projectionist turned a page.

'Three hundred.'

He looked up and studied Clifton. 'Cash?'

'Cash.'

At ten o'clock the following morning, Clifton arrived at Toby Temple's house with a can of film under his arm. *No, not film,* he thought happily. *Dynamite. Enough to blow Jill Castle to hell.*

The door was opened by an English butler Clifton had not seen before.

'Tell Mr Temple that Clifton Lawrence is here to see him.'

'I'm sorry, sir. Mr Temple is not here.'

'I'll wait,' Clifton said firmly.

The butler replied, 'I'm afraid that won't be possible. Mr and Mrs Temple left for Europe this morning.'

Chapter Thirty-two

Europe was a succession of triumphs.

The night of Toby's opening at the Palladium in London, Oxford Circus was jammed with crowds frantically trying to get a glimpse of Toby and Jill. The entire area around Argyll Street had been cordoned off by the metropolitan police. When the mob got out of hand, mounted police were hastily summoned to assist. Precisely at the stroke of eight o'clock, the Royal Family arrived and the show began.

Toby exceeded everyone's wildest expectations. His face beaming with innocence, he brilliantly attacked the British government and its ol-school tie smugness. He explained how it had managed to become less powerful than Uganda and how it could not have happened to a more deserving country. They all roared with laughter, because they knew that Toby Temple was only joking. He did not mean a word of it. Toby loved them.

As they loved him.

The reception in Paris was even more tumultuous. Jill and Toby were guests at the President's Palace and were driven around the city in a state limousine. They could be seen on the front pages of the newspapers every day, and when they appeared at the theatre, extra police had to be called out to control the crowds. At the end of Toby's performance, he and Jill were being escorted towards their waiting limousine when suddenly the mob broke through the police guard and hundreds of Frenchmen descended on them, screaming, 'Toby, Toby . . . *on veut Toby!*' The surging crowd held out pens and autograph books, pressing forward to touch the great Toby Temple and his wonderful Jill. The police were unable to hold them back; the crowd swept them aside, tearing Toby's clothes, fighting to obtain a souvenir. Toby and Jill were almost crushed by the press of bodies, but Jill felt no fear. This riot was a tribute to *her*. She had done this for these people; she had brought Toby back to them.

Their last stop was Moscow.

Moscow in June is one of the loveliest cities in the world. Graceful white *berezka* and Lipa trees with yellow flowerbeds line the wide boulevards crowded with natives and visitors strolling in the sunshine. It is the season for tourists. Except for official visitors, all tourists to Russia are handled through Intourist, the government controlled agency which arranges transportation, hotels and guided sightseeing tours. But Toby and Jill were met at the Sheremetyevo International Airport by a large Zil limousine and driven to the Metropole Hotel, usually reserved for VIPs from satellite countries. The suite had been stocked with Stolichnaya vodka and black caviar.

General Yuri Romanovitch, a high party official, came to the hotel to bid them welcome. 'We do not run many American pictures in Russia, Mr Temple, but we have played your movies here often. The Russian people feel that genius transcends all boundaries.'

Toby had been booked to appear at the Bolshoi Theatre for three performances. Opening night, Jill shared in the ovation. Because of the language barrier, Toby did most of his act in pantomime, and the audience adored him. He gave a diatribe in his pseudo-Russian, and their laughter and applause echoed through the enormous theatre like a benediction of love.

During the next two days, General Romanovitch escorted Toby and Jill on a private sightseeing tour. They went to Gorky Park and rode on the giant ferris wheel, and saw the historic Saint Basil's Cathedral. They were taken to the Moscow State Circus and given a banquet at Aragvi, where they were served the golden roe caviar, the rarest of the eight caviars, *zakushki,* which literally means small bites, and *pashteet,* the delicate paté baked in a crust. For dessert, they ate *yoblochnaya,* the incredibly delicious apple charlotte pastry with apricot sauce.

And more sightseeing. They went to the Pushkin Art Museum and Lenin's Mausoleum and the Detsky Mir, Moscow's enchanting children's shop.

They were taken to places of whose existence most Russians were unaware. Granovsko Street, crowded with chauffeur-driven Chaikas and Volgas. Inside, behind a simple door marked 'Office of Special Passes', they were ushered into a store crammed with imported luxury foodstuffs from all over the world. This was where the 'Nachalstov', the Russian élite, were privileged to shop.

They went to a luxurious *dacha,* where foreign films were run in the private screening room for the privileged few. It was a fascinating insight into the People's State.

On the afternoon of the day Toby was to give his final performance, the Temples were getting ready to go out shopping. Toby said, 'Why don't you go alone, baby? I think I'll sack out for a while.'

She studied him for a moment. 'Are you feeling all right?'

'Great. I'm just a little tired. You go buy out Moscow.'

Jill hesitated. Toby looked pale. When this tour was over, she would see to it that Toby had a long rest before he began his new television show. 'All right,' she agreed. 'Take a nap.'

Jill was walking through the lobby towards the exit when she heard a man's voice call, 'Josephine', and even as she turned, she knew who it was, and in a split second the magic happened again.

David Kenyon was moving towards her, smiling and saying, 'I'm so glad to see you', and she felt as though her heart would stop. *He's the only man who has ever been able to do this to me,* Jill thought.

'Will you have a drink with me?' David asked.

'Yes,' she said.

The hotel bar was large and crowded, but they found a comparatively quiet table in a corner where they could talk.

'What are you doing in Moscow?' Jill asked.

'Our government asked me to come over. We're trying to work out an oil deal.'

A bored waiter strolled over to the table and took their order for drinks.

'How's Cissy?'

David looked at her a moment, then said, 'We got a divorce a few years ago.' He deliberately changed the subject. 'I've followed everything that's been happening to you. I've been a fan of Toby Temple's since I was a kid.' Somehow, it made Toby sound very old. 'I'm glad he's well again. When I read about his stroke, I was concerned about you.' There was a look in his eyes that Jill remembered from long ago, a wanting, a needing.

'I thought Toby was great in Hollywood and London,' David was saying.

'Were you there?' Jill asked, in surprise.

'Yes.' Then he added quickly, 'I had some business there.'

'Why didn't you come backstage?'

He hesitated. 'I didn't want to intrude on you. I didn't know if you would want to see me.'

Their drinks arrived in heavy, squat glasses.

'To you and Toby,' David said. And there was something in the way he said it, an undercurrent of sadness, a hunger . . .

'Do you always stay at the Metropole?' Jill asked.

'No. As a matter of fact, I had a hell of a time getting –' He saw the trap too late. He smiled wryly. 'I knew you'd be here. I was supposed to have left Moscow five days ago. I've been waiting, hoping to run into you.'

'Why, David?'

It was a long time before he replied. When he spoke, he said, 'It's all too late now, but I want to tell you anyway, because I think you have a right to know.'

And he told her about his marriage to Cissy, how she had tricked him, about her attempted suicide, and about the night when he had asked Jill to meet him at the lake. It all came out in an outpouring of emotion that left Jill shaken.

'I've always been in love with you.'

She sat listening, a feeling of happiness flowing through her body like a warm wine. It was like a lovely dream come true, it was everything she had wanted, wished for.

Jill studied the man sitting across from her, and she remembered his strong hands on her, and his hard demanding body, and she felt a stirring within herself. But Toby had become a part of her, he was her own flesh; and David . . .

A voice at her elbow said, 'Mrs Temple! We have been looking everywhere for you!' It was General Romanovitch.

Jill looked at David. 'Call me in the morning.'

Toby's last performance in the Bolshoi Theatre was more exciting than anything that had been seen there before. The spectators threw flowers and cheered and stamped their feet and refused to leave. It was a fitting climax to Toby's other triumphs. A large party was scheduled for after the show, but Toby said to Jill, 'I'm beat, goddess. Why don't you go? I'll return to the hotel and get some shut-eye.'

Jill went to the party alone, but it was as though David were at her side every moment. She carried on conversations with her hosts and danced and acknowledged the tributes they were paying to her, but all the time her mind was reliving her meeting with David. *I married the wrong girl. Cissy and I are divorced. I've never stopped loving you.*

At two o'clock in the morning, Jill's escort dropped her at her hotel suite. She went inside and found Toby lying on the floor in the middle of the room, unconscious, his right hand stretched out towards the telephone.

Toby Temple was rushed in an ambulance to the

Diplomatic Polyclinic at 3 Sverchkov Prospekt. Three top specialists were summoned in the middle of the night to examine him. Everyone was sympathetic towards Jill. The chief of the hospital escorted her to a private office, where she waited for news. *It's like a rerun,* Jill thought. *All this has happened before.* It had a vague, unreal quality.

Hours later, the door to the office opened and a short, fat Russian waddled in. He was dressed in an ill-fitting suit and looked like an unsuccessful plumber. 'I am Dr Durov,' he said. 'I am in charge of your husband's case.'

'I want to know how he is.'

'Sit down, Mrs Temple, please.'

Jill had not even been aware that she had stood up. 'Tell me!'

'Your husband has suffered a stroke – technically called a cerebral venous thrombosis.'

'How bad is it?'

'It is the most – what do you say? – hard-hitting, dangerous. If your husband lives – and it is too soon to tell – he will never walk or speak again. His mind is clear but he is completely paralysed.'

Before Jill left Moscow, David telephoned her.

'I can't tell you how sorry I am,' he said. 'I'll be standing by. Anytime you need me, I'll be there. Remember that.'

It was the only thing that helped Jill keep her sanity in the nightmare that was about to begin.

The journey home was a hellish déjà vu. The hospital litter in the plane, the ambulance from the airport to the house, the sickroom.

Except that this time it was *not* the same. Jill had

known it the moment they had allowed her to see Toby. His heart was beating, his vital organs functioning; in every respect he was a living organism. And yet he was not. He was a breathing, pulsating corpse, a dead man in an oxygen tent, with tubes and needles running into his body like antennae, feeding him the vital fluids that were necessary to keep him alive. His face was twisted in a horrifying rictus that made him look as though he were grinning, his lips pulled up so that his gums were exposed. *I am afraid I can offer you no hope,* the Russian doctor had said.

That had been weeks ago. Now they were back home in Bel-Air. Jill had immediately called in Dr Kaplan, and he had sent for specialists who had summoned more specialists, and the answer always came out the same: a massive stroke that had heavily damaged or destroyed the nerve centres, with very little chance of reversing the damage that had already been done.

There were nurses around the clock and a physiotherapist to work with Toby, but they were empty gestures.

The object of all this attention was grotesque. Toby's skin had turned yellow, and his hair was falling out in large tufts. His paralysed limbs were shrivelled and stringy. On his face was the hideous grin that he could not control. He was monstrous to look at, a death's head.

But his eyes were alive. And how alive! They blazed with the power and frustration of the mind trapped in that useless shell. Whenever Jill walked into his room, Toby's eyes would follow her hungrily, frantically, pleading. For what? For her to make him walk again? Talk again? To turn him into a man again?

She would stare down at him, silent, thinking: *A part of*

me is lying in that bed, suffering, trapped. They were bound together. She would have given anything to have saved Toby, to have saved herself. But she knew that there was no way. Not this time.

The phones rang constantly, and it was a replay of all those other phone calls, all those other offers of sympathy.

But there was one phone call that was different. David Kenyon telephoned. 'I just want you to know that whatever I can do – anything at all – I'm waiting.'

Jill thought of how he looked, tall and handsome and strong, and she thought of the misshapen caricature of a man in the next room. 'Thank you, David. I appreciate it. There's nothing. Not at the moment.'

'We've got some fine doctors in Houston,' he said. 'Some of the best in the world. I could fly them down to him.'

Jill could feel her throat tightening. Oh, how she wanted to ask David to come to her, to take her away from this place! But she could not. She was bound to Toby, and she knew that she could never leave him.

Not while he was alive.

Dr Kaplan had completed his examination of Toby. Jill was waiting for him in the library. She turned to face him as he walked through the door. He said, with a clumsy attempt at humour, 'Well, Jill, I have good news and I have bad news.'

'Tell me the bad news first.'

'I'm afraid Toby's nervous system is damaged too heavily to be rehabilitated. There's no question about it. Not this time. He'll never walk or talk again.'

She stared at him a long time, and then said, 'What's the good news?'

Dr Kaplan smiled. 'Toby's heart is amazingly strong. With proper care, he can live for another twenty years.'

Jill looked at him, unbelievingly. *Twenty years. That* was the *good* news! She thought of herself saddled with the horrible gargoyle upstairs, trapped in a nightmare from which there was no escape. She could never divorce Toby. Not as long as he lived. Because no one would understand. She was the heroine who had saved his life. Everyone would feel betrayed, cheated, if she deserted him now. Even David Kenyon.

David telephoned every day now, and he kept talking about her wondcrful loyalty and her selflessness, and they were both aware of the deep emotional current flowing between them.

The unspoken phrase was, *when Toby dies.*

Chapter Thirty-three

Three nurses attended Toby around the clock in shifts. They were crisp and capable and as impersonal as machines. Jill was grateful for their presence, for she could not bear to go near Toby. The sight of that hideous, grinning mask repelled her. She found excuses to stay away from his room. When she did force herself to go to him, Jill could sense a change in him immediately. Even the nurses could feel it. Toby lay motionless and impotent, frozen in his spastic cage. Yet the moment Jill entered the room, a vitality began to blaze from those bright blue eyes. Jill could read Toby's thoughts as clearly as if he were speaking aloud. *Don't let me die. Help me! Help me!*

Jill stood looking down at his ruined body and thought, *I can't help you. You don't want to live like this. You want to die.*

The idea began to grow in Jill.

The newspapers were full of stories about terminally ill husbands whose wives had released them from their pain. Even some doctors admitted that they deliberately let certain patients die. Euthanasia, it was called. Mercy killing. But Jill knew that it could also be called murder, even though nothing lived in Toby any more but those damned eyes that would not stop following her around.

In the weeks that followed, Jill never left the house. Most

of the time, she shut herself away in her bedroom. Her headaches had returned, and she could find no relief.

Newspapers and magazines carried human-interest stories about the paralysed superstar and his devoted wife, who had once nursed him back to health. All the periodicals speculated about whether Jill would be able to repeat the miracle. But she knew that there would be no more miracles. Toby would never be well again.

Twenty years, Dr Kaplan had said. And David was out there waiting for her. She had to find a way to escape from her prison.

It began on a dark, gloomy Sunday. It rained in the morning and continued all day, drumming against the roof and the windows of the house until Jill thought she would go mad. She was in her bedroom, reading, trying to get the vicious tattoo of the falling rain out of her mind, when the night nurse walked in. Her name was Ingrid Johnson. She was starched and Nordic.

'The burner upstairs isn't working,' Ingrid announced. 'I'll have to go down to the kitchen to prepare Mr Temple's dinner. Could you stay with him for a few minutes?'

Jill could sense the disapproval in the nurse's voice. She thought it strange for a wife not to go near her husband's sick-bed. 'I'll look after him,' Jill said.

She put down her book and went down the hall to Toby's bedroom. The moment Jill walked into the room, her nostrils were assailed by the familiar stench of sickness. In an instant, every fibre of her being was flooded with memories of those long, dreadful months she had fought to save Toby.

Toby's head was propped up on a large pillow. As he

watched Jill enter, his eyes suddenly came alive, flashing out frantic messages. *Where have you been? Why have you stayed away from me? I need you. Help me!* It was as though his eyes had a voice. Jill looked down at the loathsome, twisted body with the grinning death's mask and she felt nauseated. *You'll never get well, damn you! You've got to die! I want you to die!*

As Jill stared at Toby, she watched the expression in his eyes change. They registered shock and disbelief and then they began to fill with such hatred, such naked malevolence, that Jill involuntarily took a step away from the bed. She realized then what had happened. She had spoken her thoughts aloud.

She turned and fled from the room.

In the morning, the rain stopped. Toby's old wheelchair had been brought up from the basement. The day nurse, Frances Gordon, was wheeling Toby out in his chair to the garden to get some sun. Jill listened to the sound of the wheelchair moving down the hall towards the elevator. She waited a few minutes, then she went downstairs. She was passing the library when the phone rang. It was David, calling from Washington.

'How are you today?' He sounded warm and caring.

She had never been so glad to hear his voice. 'I'm fine, David.'

'I wish you were with me, darling.'

'So do I. I love you so much. And I want you. I want you to hold me in your arms again. Oh, David . . .'

Some instinct made Jill turn. Toby was in the hallway, strapped in the wheelchair where the nurse had left him for a moment. His blue eyes blazed at Jill with such loathing, such malice that it was like a physical blow. His mind was speaking to her through his eyes, screaming at her, *I'm going to kill you!* Jill dropped the telephone in panic.

She ran out of the room and up the stairs, and she could feel Toby's hatred pursuing her, like some violent, evil force. She stayed in her bedroom all day, refusing food. She sat in a chair, in a trance-like state, her mind going over and over the moment at the telephone. Toby knew. He knew. She could not face him again.

Finally, night came. It was the middle of July, and the air still held the heat of the day. Jill opened her bedroom windows wide to catch whatever faint breeze there might be.

In Toby's room, Nurse Gallagher was on duty. She tiptoed in to take a look at her patient. Nurse Gallagher wished she could read his mind, then perhaps she might be able to help the poor man. She tucked the covers around Toby. 'You get a good night's sleep now,' she said, cheerily. 'I'll be back to check on you.' There was no reaction. He did not even move his eyes to look at her.

Perhaps it's just as well I can't read his mind, Nurse Gallagher thought. She took one last look at him and retired to her little sitting room to watch some late-night television. Nurse Gallagher enjoyed the talk shows. She loved to watch movie stars chat about themselves. It made them terribly *human,* just like ordinary, everyday people. She kept the sound low, so that it would not disturb her patient. But Toby Temple would not have heard it in any case. His thoughts were elsewhere.

The house was asleep, safe in the guarded fastness of the Bel-Air woods. A few faint sounds of traffic drifted up from Sunset Boulevard far below. Nurse Gallagher was watching a late-night movie. She wished they would run an old Toby Temple film. It would be so exciting to watch Mr Temple on television and know that he was here in person, just a few feet away.

At four a.m., Nurse Gallagher dozed off in the middle of a horror film.

In Toby's bedroom there was a deep silence.

In Jill's room, the only sound that could be heard was the ticking of the bedside clock. Jill lay in her bed, naked, sound asleep, one arm hugging a pillow, her body dark against the white sheets. The street noises were muffled and far away.

Jill turned restlessly in her sleep and shivered. She dreamed that she and David were in Alaska on their honeymoon. They were on a vast frozen plain and a sudden storm had come up. The wind was blowing the icy air into their faces, and it was difficult to breathe. She turned towards David, but he was gone. She was alone in the frigid Arctic, coughing, fighting to get her breath. It was the sound of someone choking that woke Jill up. She heard a horrid gasping wheeze, a death rattle, and she opened her eyes, and the sound was coming from her own throat. She could not breathe. An icy cloak of air covered her like some obscene blanket, caressing her nude body, stroking her breasts, kissing her lips with a frigid, malodorous breath that reeked of the grave. Jill's heart was pounding wildly now, as she fought for air. Her lungs felt seared from the cold. She tried to sit up, and it was as though there was an invisible weight holding her down. She knew this had to be a dream, but at the same time she could hear that hideous rattle from her throat as she fought for breath. She was dying. But could a person die during a nightmare? Jill could feel the cold tendrils exploring her body, moving in between her legs, inside her now, filling her, and with a heart-stopping suddenness, she realized it was Toby. Somehow, by some means, it was Toby. And the quick rush of terror in Jill gave her the strength to claw her way to the foot of the bed, gasping for breath, mind and body fighting to stay alive. She reached the floor and struggled to her feet and ran for the door, feeling the cold pursuing her, surrounding her, clutching at her. Her fingers found the door knob and twisted it open. She ran out into the hallway, panting for air, filling her starved lungs with oxygen.

The hallway was warm, quiet, still. Jill stood there, swaying, her teeth chattering uncontrollably. She turned to look into her room. It was normal and peaceful. She had had a nightmare. Jill hesitated a moment, then slowly walked back through the doorway. Her room was warm. There was nothing to be afraid of. Of *course,* Toby could not harm her.

In her sitting room, Nurse Gallagher awakened and went in to check on her patient.

Toby Temple was lying in his bed, exactly as she had left him. His eyes were staring at the ceiling, focused on something that Nurse Gallagher could not see.

After that the nightmare kept recurring regularly, like a black omen of doom, a prescience of some horror to come. Slowly, a terror began to build up in Jill. Wherever she went in the house, she could feel Toby's presence. When the nurse took him out, Jill could hear him. Toby's wheelchair had developed a high-pitched creak, and it got on Jill's nerves every time she heard it. *I must have it fixed,* she thought. She avoided going anywhere near Toby's room, but it did not matter. He was everywhere, waiting for her.

The headaches were constant now, a savage rhythmic pounding that would not let her rest. Jill wished that the pain would stop for an hour, a minute, a second. She *had* to sleep. She went into the maid's room behind the kitchen, as far away from Toby as she could get. The room was warm and quiet. Jill lay down on the bed and closed her eyes. She was asleep almost instantly.

She was awakened by the fetid, icy air, filling the room, clutching at her, trying to entomb her. Jill leaped up and ran out the door.

The days were horrible enough, but the nights were terrifying. They followed the same pattern. Jill would go to her room and huddle in her bed, fighting to stay awake, afraid to go to sleep, knowing that Toby would come. But her exhausted body would take over and she would finally doze off.

She would be awakened by the cold. She would lie shivering in her bed, feeling the icy air creeping towards her, an evil presence enveloping her like a terrible malediction. She would get up and flee in silent terror.

It was three a.m.

Jill had fallen asleep in her chair, reading a book. She came out of her sleep gradually, slowly, and she opened her eyes in the pitch-black bedroom, knowing that something was terribly wrong. Then she realized what it was. *She had gone to sleep with all the lights on.* She felt her heart begin to race and she thought, *There's nothing to be afraid of. Nurse Gallagher must have come in and turned out the lights.*

Then she heard the sound. It was coming down the hallway, *creak . . . creak . . .* Toby's wheelchair, moving towards her bedroom door. Jill began to feel the hairs rise on the back of her neck. *It's only a tree branch against the roof, or the house settling,* she told herself. Yet she knew that it wasn't true. She had heard that sound too many times before. *Creak . . . creak . . .* like the music of death coming to get her. *It can't be Toby,* she thought. *He's in his bed, helpless. I'm losing my mind.* But she could hear it coming closer and closer. It was at her door now. It had stopped, waiting. And suddenly there was the sound of a crash, and then silence.

Jill spent the rest of the night huddled in her chair in the dark, too terrified to move.

In the morning, outside her bedroom door, she found a broken vase on the floor, where it had been knocked over from a hallway table.

She was talking to Dr Kaplan. 'Do you believe that the – the mind can control the body?' Jill asked.

He looked at her, puzzled. 'In what way?'

'If Toby wanted – wanted *very* much to get out of his bed, could he?'

'You mean unaided? In his present condition?' He gave her a look of incredulity. 'He has absolutely no mobility at all. None whatsoever.'

Jill was still not satisfied. 'If – if he was really *determined* to get up – if there was something he felt he had to do . . .'

Dr Kaplan shook his head. 'Our mind gives commands to the body, but if your motor impulses are blocked, if there are no muscles to carry out those commands, then nothing can happen.'

She had to find out. 'Do you believe that objects can be moved by the mind?'

'You mean psychokinesis? There are a lot of experiments being done, but no one has ever come up with any proof that's convinced me.'

There was the broken vase outside her bedroom door.

Jill wanted to tell him about that, about the cold air that kept following her, about Toby's wheelchair at her door, but he would think she was crazy. *Was she? Was something wrong with her? Was she losing her mind?*

When Dr Kaplan left, Jill walked over to look at herself in the mirror. She was shocked by what she saw. Her cheeks were sunken and her eyes enormous in a pale, bony face. *If I go on this way,* Jill thought, *I'll die before Toby.* She looked at her stringy, dull hair and her broken, cracked fingernails. *I must never let David see me looking like this. I have to start taking care of myself. From now on,* she told herself, *you're going to the beauty parlour once a week, and you're going to eat three meals a day and sleep eight hours.*

The following morning, Jill made an appointment at the beauty parlour. She was exhausted, and under the warm, comfortable hum of the hair drier, she dozed off, and the nightmare began. She was in bed, asleep. She could hear Toby come into her bedroom in his wheelchair . . . *creak* . . . *creak*. Slowly, he got out of the chair and rose to his feet and moved towards her, grinning, his skeletal hands reaching for her throat. Jill awoke screaming wildly, throwing the beauty shop into an uproar. She fled without even having her hair combed out.

After that experience, Jill was afraid to leave the house again.

And afraid to remain in it.

*

Something seemed to be wrong with her head. It was no longer just headaches. She was beginning to forget things. She would go downstairs for something and walk into the kitchen and stand there, not knowing what she had come for. Her memory began to play strange tricks on her. Once Nurse Gordon came in to speak to her; Jill wondered what a nurse was doing there, and then suddenly remembered. The director was waiting on the set for Jill. She tried to recall her line. *Not very well, I'm afraid, Doctor.* She must speak to the director and find out how he wanted her to read it. Nurse Gordon was holding her hand, saying, 'Mrs Temple! Mrs Temple! Are you feeling all right?' And Jill was back in her own surroundings, again in the present, caught up in the terror of what was happening to her. She knew she could not go on like this. She had to find out whether there was something wrong with her mind or whether Toby was able to somehow move, whether he had found a way to attack her, to try to murder her.

She had to see him. She forced herself to walk down the long hall towards Toby's bedroom. She stood outside a moment, steeling herself, and then Jill entered Toby's room.

Toby was lying in his bed, and the nurse was giving him a sponge bath. She looked up, saw Jill and said, 'Why, here's Mrs Temple. We're just having a nice bath, aren't we?'

Jill turned to look at the figure on the bed.

Toby's arms and legs had shrivelled into stringy appendages attached to his shrunken, twisted torso. Between his legs, like some long, indecent snake, lay his useless penis, flaccid and ugly. The yellow cast had gone from Toby's face, but the gaping idiot grin was still there. The body was dead, but the eyes were frantically alive. Darting, seeking, weighing, planning, hating; cunning blue eyes filled with their secret plans, their deadly determination. It was Toby's mind she was seeing. *The important thing to remember is that his mind is unimpaired,* the doctor had told her. His mind could think and feel and hate. That mind had nothing to do but plan its revenge, figure out a way to destroy her. Toby wanted her dead, as she wanted him dead.

As Jill looked at him now, staring into those eyes blazing with loathing, she could hear him saying, *I'm going to kill you,* and she could feel the waves of abhorrence hitting her like physical blows.

Jill stared into those eyes, and she remembered the broken vase and she knew that none of the nightmares had been illusions. He had found a way.

She knew now that it was Toby's life against hers.

Chapter Thirty-four

When Dr Kaplan finished his examination of Toby, he went to find Jill. 'I think you should stop the therapy in the swimming pool,' he said. 'It's a waste of time. I was hoping we might get some slight improvement in Toby's musculature, but it's not working. I'll talk to the therapist myself.'

'No!' It was a sharp cry.

Dr Kaplan looked at her in surprise. 'Jill, I know what you did for Toby last time. But this time it's hopeless. I –'

'We can't give up. Not yet.' There was a desperation in her voice.

Dr Kaplan hesitated, then shrugged. 'Well, if it means that much to you, but –'

'It does.'

At that moment, it was the most important thing in the world. It was going to save Jill's life.

She knew now what she had to do.

The following day was Friday. David telephoned Jill to tell her that he had to go to Madrid on business.

'I may not be able to call over the weekend.'

'I'll miss you,' Jill said. 'Very much.'

'I'll miss you, too. Are you all right? You sound strange. Are you tired?'

Jill was fighting to keep her eyes open, to forget the terrible pain in her head. She could not remember the last time she had eaten or slept. She was so weak that it was difficult to stand. She forced energy into her voice. 'I'm fine, David.'

'I love you, darling. Take care of yourself.'

'I'm going to, David. I love you, please know that.' *No matter what happens.*

She heard the physiotherapist's car turn into the driveway, and Jill started downstairs, her head pounding, her trembling legs barely able to support her. She opened the front door as the physiotherapist was about to ring the bell.

'Morning, Mrs Temple,' he said. He started to enter, but Jill blocked his way. He looked at her in surprise.

'Dr Kaplan has decided to discontinue Mr Temple's therapy treatments,' Jill said.

The physiotherapist frowned. It meant he had made an unnecessary trip out here. Someone should have told him earlier. Ordinarily he would have complained about the way it had been handled. But Mrs Temple was such a great lady, with such big problems. He smiled at her and said, 'It's okay, Mrs Temple. I understand.'

And he got back into his car.

Jill waited until she heard the car drive away. Then she started back up the stairs. Halfway up, a wave of dizziness hit her again, and she had to cling to the banister until it passed. She could not stop now. If she did, she would be dead.

She walked to the door of Toby's room, turned the knob and entered. Nurse Gallagher was seated in an easy chair working on needlepoint. She looked up in surprise as she saw Jill standing in the doorway. 'Well!' she said. 'You've come to visit us. Isn't that nice?' She turned towards the bed. 'I know Mr Temple is pleased. Aren't we, Mr Temple?'

Toby was sitting up in bed, propped upright by pillows, his eyes carrying his message to Jill. *I'm going to kill you.*

Jill averted her eyes and walked over to Nurse Gallagher. 'I've decided that I haven't been spending enough time with my husband.'

'Well, now, that's exactly what I've been thinking,' Nurse Gallagher chirped. 'But then I could see that you've been ill yourself, and so I said to myself – '

'I'm feeling much better now,' Jill interrupted. 'I'd like to be alone with Mr Temple.'

Nurse Gallagher gathered up her needlepoint paraphernalia and got to her feet. 'Of course,' she said. 'I'm sure we'll enjoy that.' She turned towards the grinning figure on the bed. 'Won't we, Mr Temple?' To Jill, she added, 'I'll just go down to the kitchen and fix myself a nice cup of tea.'

'No. You're off duty in half an hour. You can leave now. I'll stay here until Nurse Gordon arrives.' Jill gave her a quick, reassuring smile. 'Don't worry. I'll be here with him.'

'I suppose I *could* get some shopping done, and – '

'Fine,' Jill said. 'You run along.'

Jill stood there, immobile, until she heard the front door slam and Nurse Gallagher's car going down the driveway. When the sounds of the motor had died away on the summer air, Jill turned to look at Toby.

His eyes were focused on her face in an unwavering, unblinking stare. Forcing herself to move closer to the bed, she pulled back the covers and looked down at the wasted, paralysed frame, the limp, useless legs.

The wheelchair was in a corner. Jill moved it over to the

bedside and positioned the chair so that she could roll Toby onto it. She reached towards him, and stopped. It took every ounce of her willpower to touch him. The grinning, mummified face was only inches away from her, the mouth smiling idiotically and the bright blue eyes spewing venom. Jill leaned forward and forced herself to lift Toby by his arms. He was almost weightless, but in Jill's exhausted condition, she could barely manage it. As she touched his body, Jill could feel the icy air begin to envelop her. The pressure inside her head was becoming unbearable. There were bright coloured spots before her eyes, and they began to dance around, faster and faster, making her dizzy. She felt herself starting to faint, but she knew that she must not allow that to happen. Not if she wanted to live. With a superhuman effort, she dragged Toby's limp body onto the wheelchair and strapped him in. She looked at her watch. She had only twenty minutes.

It took Jill five minutes to go into her bedroom and change into a bathing suit and return to Toby's room.

She released the brake on the wheelchair and began to wheel Toby down the corridor, into the elevator. She stood behind him as they rode down, so that she could not see his eyes. But she could feel them. And she could feel the damp cold of the noxious air that began to fill the elevator, smothering her, caressing her, filling her lungs with its putrescence until she began to choke. She could not breathe. She fell to her knees, gasping, fighting to stay conscious, trapped in there with him. As she started to feel herself blacking out, the elevator door opened. She crawled into the warm sunlight and lay there on the ground, breathing deeply, sucking in the fresh air, slowly getting back her energy. She turned towards the elevator. Toby was seated in the wheelchair, watching, waiting. Jill quickly pushed the chair out of the elevator. She started towards the swimming pool. It was a beautiful, cloudless day, warm and balmy, the sun sparkling on the blue, filtered water.

Jill rolled the wheelchair to the edge of the deep end of the pool and set the brake. She walked around to the front of the chair. Toby's eyes were fixed on her, watchful, puzzled. Jill reached for the strap holding Toby into the chair, and tightened it as hard as she could, pulling on it, – yanking it with all that was left of her strength, feeling herself growing dizzy again with the effort. Suddenly it was done. Jill watched Toby's eyes change as he realized what was happening, and they began to fill with a wild demonic panic.

Jill released the brake, grasped the handle of the wheelchair and started to push it towards the water. Toby was trying to move his paralysed lips, trying to scream, but no sound came out, and the effect was terrifying. She could not bear to look into his eyes. She did not want to know.

She shoved the wheelchair to the very edge of the pool.

And it stuck. It was held back by the cement lip. She pushed harder, but it would not go over. It was as though Toby were holding the chair back by sheer willpower. Jill could see him straining to rise out of the chair, fighting for his life. He was going to get loose, free himself, reach out for her throat with his bony fingers . . . She could hear his voice screaming, *I don't want to die . . . I don't want to die,* and she did not know whether it was her imagination or whether it was real, but in a rush of panic, she found a sudden strength ahd shoved as hard as she could against the back of the wheelchair. It lurched forward, upward into the air, and hung there, motionless, for what seemed an eternity, then rolled into the pool, hitting with a loud splash. The wheelchair seemed to float on top of the water for a long time, then slowly began to sink. The eddies of the water turned the chair around, so that the last thing Jill saw was Toby's eyes damning her to hell as the water closed over them.

She stood there for ever, shivering in the warm noonday sun, letting the strength flow back into her mind and body. When she was finally able to move again, she walked down the steps of the swimming pool to wet her bathing suit.

Then she went into the house to telephone the police.

Chapter Thirty-five

Toby Temple's death made newspaper headlines all over the world. If Toby had become a folk hero, then Jill had become a heroine. Hundreds of thousands of words were printed about them, their photographs appeared in all the media. Their great love story was told and retold, the tragic ending giving it an even greater poignancy. Letters and telegrams of condolence streamed in from heads of state, housewives, politicians, millionaires, secretaries. The world had suffered a personal loss; Toby had shared the gift of his laughter with his fans, and they would always be grateful. The air waves were filled with praise for him, and each network paid tribute to him.

There would never be another Toby Temple.

The inquest was held at the Criminal Court Building on Grand Avenue in downtown Los Angeles, in a small compact courtroom. An inquest examiner was in charge of the hearings, guiding the panel of six jurors.

The room was packed to overflowing. When Jill arrived, the photographers and reporters and fans mobbed her. She was dressed in a simple black tailored wool suit. She wore no makeup and she had never looked more beautiful. In the few days that had elapsed since Toby's death, Jill had miraculously bloomed into her old self again. For the first time in months, she was able to sleep soundly and dreamlessly. She had a voracious appetite and her headaches had disappeared. The demon that had been draining her life away was gone.

Jill had talked to David every day. He had wanted to come to the inquest, but Jill insisted that he stay away. They would have enough time together later.

'The rest of our lives,' David had told her.

There were six witnesses at the inquest. Nurse Gallagher, Nurse Gordon and Nurse Johnson testified about the general routine of their patient and his condition. Nurse Gallagher was giving her testimony.

'What time were you supposed to go off duty on the morning in question?' the inquest examiner asked.

'At ten.'

'What time did you actually leave?'

Hesitation. 'Nine-thirty.'

'Was it your custom, Mrs Gallagher, to leave your patient before your shift was up?'

'No, sir. That was the first time.'

'Would you explain how you happened to leave early on that particular day?'

'It was Mrs Temple's suggestion. She wanted to be alone with her husband.'

'Thank you. That's all.'

Nurse Gallagher stepped down from the stand. *Of course Toby Temple's death was an accident,* she thought. *It's a pity that they had to put a wonderful woman like Jill Temple through this ordeal.* Nurse Gallagher looked over at Jill and felt a quick stab of guilt. She remembered the night that she had gone into Mrs Temple's bedroom and found her asleep in a chair. Nurse Gallagher had quietly turned out the lights and closed the door so that Mrs Temple would not be disturbed. In the dark hallway, Nurse Gallagher had brushed against a vase on a pedestal and it had fallen and broken. She had meant to tell Mrs Temple, but the vase had looked very expensive, and so, when Mrs Temple had not mentioned it, Nurse Gallagher decided to say nothing about it.

The physiotherapist was on the witness stand.

'You usually gave Mr Temple a treatment every day?'

'Yes, sir.'

'Did this treatment take place in the swimming pool?'

'Yes, sir. The pool was heated to a hundred degrees, and–'

'Did you give Mr Temple a treatment on the date in question?'

'No, sir.'

'Would you tell us why?'

'She sent me away.'

'By "she", you mean Mrs Temple?'

'Right.'

'Did she give you any reason?'

'She said Dr Kaplan didn't want him to have no more treatments.'

'And so you left without seeing Mr Temple?'

'That's correct. Yeah.'

Dr Kaplan was on the stand.

'Mrs Temple telephoned you after the accident, Dr Kaplan. Did you examine the deceased as soon as you arrived at the scene?'

'Yes. The police had pulled the body out of the swimming pool. It was still strapped into the wheelchair. The police surgeon and I examined the body and determined that it was too late for any attempt at resuscitation. Both lungs were filled with water. We could detect no vital signs.'

'What did you do then, Dr Kaplan?'

'I took care of Mrs Temple. She was in a state of acute hysteria. I was very concerned about her.'

'Dr Kaplan, did you have a previous discussion with Mrs Temple about discontinuing therapy treatments?'

'I did. I told her I thought they were a waste of time.'

'What was Mrs Temple's reaction to that?'

Dr Kaplan looked over at Jill Temple and said, 'Her reaction was very unusual. She insisted that we keep trying.' He hesitated. 'Since I am under oath and since this inquest jury is interested in hearing the truth, I feel there is something I am obliged to say.'

A complete hush had fallen over the room. Jill was staring at him. Dr Kaplan turned toward the jury box.

'I would like to say, for the record, that Mrs Temple is probably the finest and bravest woman I have ever had the honour to know.' Every eye in the courtroom turned towards Jill. 'The first time her husband suffered a stroke, none of us thought he had a chance of recovery. Well, she nursed him back to health single-handedly. She did for him what no doctor I know could have done. I could never begin to describe to you her devotion or dedication to her husband.' He looked over to where Jill was sitting and said, 'She is an inspiration to all of us.'

The spectators broke out into applause.

'That will be all, Doctor,' the inquest examiner said. 'I would like to call Mrs Temple to the stand.'

They watched as Jill rose and slowly walked over to the witness stand to be sworn in.

'I know what an ordeal this is for you, Mrs Temple, and I will try to get it over with as quickly as possible.'

'Thank you.' Her voice was low.

'When Dr Kaplan said he wanted to discontinue the therapy treatments, why did you want to go ahead with them?'

She looked up at him and he could see the deep pain in her eyes. 'Because I wanted my husband to have every chance to get well again. Toby loved life, and I wanted to bring him back to it. I – ' her voice faltered, but she went on. 'I had to help him myself.'

'On the day of your husband's death, the physiotherapist came to the house, and you sent him away.'

'Yes.'

'Yet, earlier, Mrs Temple, you said you wanted those treatments to continue. Can you explain your action?'

'It's very simple. I felt that our love was the only thing strong enough to heal Toby. It had healed him before . . .' She broke off, unable to continue. Then, visibly steeling herself, she continued in a harsh voice, 'I had to let him know how much I loved him, how much I wanted him to get well again.'

Everyone in the courtroom was leaning forward, straining to hear every word.

'Would you tell us what happened on the morning of the accident?'

There was a silence that lasted for a full minute while Jill gathered her strength, and then she spoke. 'I went into Toby's room. He seemed so glad to see me. I told him that I was going to take him to the pool myself, that I was going to make him well again. I put on a bathing suit so that I could work with him in the water. When I started to lift him off the bed into his wheelchair, I – I became faint. I suppose I should have realized then that I wasn't physically strong enough to do what I was trying to do.

But I couldn't stop. Not if it was going to help him. I put him in the wheelchair and talked to him all the way down to the pool. I wheeled him to the edge . . .'

She stopped, and there was a breathless hush in the room. The only sound was the susurration of the reporters' pens as they frantically scribbled on their shorthand pads.

'I reached down to undo the straps that held Toby in the wheelchair, and I felt faint again and started to fall. I – I must have accidentally released the brake. The chair started to roll into the pool. I tried to grab it, but it – it went into the pool with – with Toby strapped into it.' Her voice was choked. 'I jumped into the pool after him and fought to free him, but the straps were too tight. I tried to lift the chair out of the water, but it was – it was too heavy. It . . . was . . . just . . . too . . . heavy.' She closed her eyes a moment to hide her deep anguish. Then, almost in a whisper, 'I tried to help Toby, and I killed him.'

It took the inquest jury less than three minutes to reach a verdict: Toby Temple had died in an accident.

Clifton Lawrence sat in the back of the courtroom and listened to the verdict. He was certain that Jill had murdered Toby. But there was no way to prove it. She had gotten away with it.

The case was closed.

Chapter Thirty-six

The funeral was standing room only. It was held at Forest Lawn on a sunny August morning, on the day Toby Temple was to have started his new television series. There were thousands of people milling about the lovely, rolling grounds, trying to get a look at all the celebrities who were there to pay their last respects. Television cameramen photographed the funeral services in long shots and zoomed in for close-ups of the stars and producers and directors who were at the graveside. The President of the United States had sent an emissary. There were governors present, studio heads, presidents of large corporations, and representatives from every guild that Toby had belonged to: SAG and AFTRA and ASCAP and AGVA. The president of the Beverly Hills branch of the Veterans of Foreign Wars was there in full uniform. There were contingents from the local police and fire departments.

And the *little people* were there. The grips and prop men and extras and stunt men who had worked with Toby Temple. The wardrobe mistresses and the best boys and the go-fers and the gaffers and the assistant directors. And there were others, and all of them had come to pay homage to a great American. O'Hanlon and Rainger were there, remembering the skinny little kid who had walked into their office at Twentieth Century-Fox. *I understand you fellas are going to write some jokes for me . . . He uses his hands like he's chopping wood. Maybe we would write a woodchopper act for him . . . He pushes too hard . . . Jesus, with that material – wouldn't you? . . . A comic opens funny doors. A comedian opens doors funny.* And Toby Temple had worked and learned and gone to the top. *He was a prick,* Rainger was thinking. *But he was our prick.*

Clifton Lawrence was there. The little agent had been to the barber and his clothes were freshly pressed, but his eyes gave him away. They were the eyes of a failure among his peers. Clifton was lost in memories, too. He was remembering that first preposterous phone call. *There's a young comic Sam Goldwyn wants you to see . . .* and Toby's performance at the school. *You don't have to eat the entire jar of caviar to know if it's good, right? . . . I've decided to take you on as a client, Toby . . . If you can put the beer drinkers in your pocket, the champagne crowd will be a pushover . . . I can make you the biggest star in the business.* Everyone had wanted Toby Temple: the studios, the networks, the nightclubs. *You've got so many clients that sometimes I think you don't pay enough attention to me . . . It's like a group fuck, Cliff. Somebody always gets left with a hard-on . . . I need your advice, Cliff . . . It's this girl . . .*

Clifton Lawrence had a lot to remember.

Next to Clifton stood Alice Tanner.

She was absorbed in the memory of Toby's first audition in her office. *Somewhere, hidden under all those movie stars, is a young man with a lot of talent . . . After seeing those pros last night, I – I don't think I have it.* And falling in love with him. *Oh, Toby, I love you so much . . . I love you, too, Alice . . .* Then he was gone. But she was grateful that she had once had him.

Al Caruso had come to pay tribute. He was stooped and grey and his brown Santa Claus eyes were filled with tears. He was remembering how wonderful Toby had been to Millie.

Sam Winters was there. He was thinking of all the pleasure Toby Temple had given to millions of people and he wondered how one measured that against the pain that Toby had given to a few.

Someone nudged Sam and he turned to see a pretty dark-haired girl, about eighteen. 'You don't know me, Mr Winters' – she smiled – 'but I heard you're looking for a girl for the new William Forbes movie. I'm from Ohio, and . . .'

David Kenyon was there. Jill had asked him not to come, but David had insisted. He wanted to be near her. Jill supposed that it could do no harm now. She was finished with her performance.

The play had closed and her part was over. Jill was so glad and so tired. It was as though the fiery ordeal she had gone through had burned away the hard core of bitterness within her, had cauterized all the hurts and the disappointments and the hatreds. Jill Castle had died in the holocaust and Josephine Czinski had been reborn in the ashes. She was at peace again, filled with a love for everyone and a contentment she had not known since she was a young girl. She had never been so happy. She wanted to share it with the world.

The funeral rites were ending. Someone took Jill's arm, and she allowed herself to be led to the limousine. When she reached the car, David was standing there, a look of adoration on his face. Jill smiled at him. David took her hands in his and they exchanged a few words. A press photographer snapped a picture of them.

Jill and David decided to wait five months before they got married, so that the public's sense of propriety would be satisfied. David spent a great part of that time out of the country, but they talked to each other every day. Four months after Toby's funeral, David telephoned Jill and said, 'I had a brainstorm. Let's not wait any longer. I have to go to Europe next week for a conference. Let's sail to France on the *Bretagne*. The captain can marry us. We'll honeymoon in Paris and from there we'll go anywhere you like for as long as you like. What do you say?'

'Oh, yes, David, yes!'

She took a long last look around the house, thinking of all that had happened here. Remembering her first dinner party there and all the wonderful parties later and then Toby's sickness and her fight to bring him to health. And then . . . there were too many memories.

She was glad to be leaving.

Chapter Thirty-seven

David's private jet plane flew Jill to New York, where a limousine was waiting to drive her to the Regency Hotel on Park Avenue. The manager himself ushered Jill to an enormous penthouse suite.

'The hotel is completely at your service, Mrs Temple,' he said. 'Mr Kenyon instructed us to see that you have everything you need.'

Ten minutes after Jill checked in, David telephoned from Texas. 'Comfortable?' he asked.

'It's a little crowded.' Jill laughed. 'It has *five bedrooms*, David. What am I going to do with them all?'

'If I were there, I'd show you,' he said.

'Promises, promises,' she teased. 'When am I going to see you?'

'The *Bretagne* sails at noon tomorrow. I have some business to wind up here. I'll meet you aboard the ship. I've reserved the honeymoon suite. Happy, darling?'

'I've never been happier,' Jill said. And it was true. Everything that had gone before, all the pain and the agony, it had all been worth it. It seemed remote and dim, now, like a half-forgotten dream.

'A car will pick you up in the morning. The driver will have your boat ticket.'

'I'll be ready,' Jill said.

Tomorrow.

*

It could have started with the photograph of Jill and David Kenyon that had been taken at Toby's funeral and sold to a newspaper chain. It could have been a careless remark dropped by an employee of the hotel where Jill was staying or by a member of the crew of the *Bretagne*. In any case, there was no way that the wedding plans of someone as famous as Jill Temple could have been kept secret. The first item about her impending marriage appeared in an Associated Press Bulletin. After that, it was a front-page story in newspapers across the country and in Europe.

The story was also carried in the *Hollywood Reporter* and *Daily Variety*.

The limousine arrived at the hotel precisely on the dot of ten o'clock. A doorman and three bellboys loaded Jill's luggage into the car. The morning traffic was light and the drive to Pier 90 took less than half an hour.

A senior ship's officer was waiting for Jill at the gangplank. 'We're honoured to have you aboard, Mrs Temple,' he said. 'Everything's ready for you. If you would come this way, please.'

He escorted Jill to the Promenade Deck and ushered her into a large, airy suite with its own private terrace. The rooms were filled with fresh flowers.

'The captain asked me to give you his compliments. He will see you at dinner this evening. He said to tell you how much he's looking forward to performing the wedding ceremony.'

'Thank you,' Jill said. 'Do you know whether Mr Kenyon is on board yet?'

'We received a telephone message. He's on his way

from the airport. His luggage is already here. If there is anything you need, please let me know.'

'Thank you,' Jill replied. 'There's nothing.' And it was true. There was not one single thing that she needed that she did not have. She was the happiest person in the world.

There was a knock at the cabin door and a steward entered, carrying more flowers. Jill looked at the card. They were from the President of the United States. Memories. She pushed them out of her mind and began to unpack.

He was standing at the railing on the Main Deck, studying the passengers as they came aboard. Everyone was in a festive mood, preparing for a holiday or joining loved ones aboard. A few of them smiled at him, but the man paid no attention to them. He was watching the gangplank.

At eleven-forty a.m., twenty minutes before sailing time, a chauffeur-driven Silver Shadow raced up to Pier 90 and stopped. David Kenyon jumped out of the car, looked at his watch and said to the chauffeur, 'Perfect timing, Otto.'

'Thank you, sir. And may I wish you and Mrs Kenyon a very happy honeymoon.'

'Thanks.' David Kenyon hurried towards the gangplank, where he presented his ticket. He was escorted aboard by the ship's officer who had taken care of Jill.

'Mrs Temple is in your cabin, Mr Kenyon.'

'Thank you.'

David could visualize her in the bridal suite, waiting

for him, and his heart quickened. As David started to move away, a voice called, 'Mr Kenyon . . .'

David turned. The man who had been standing near the railing walked over to him, a smile on his face. David had never seen him before. David had the millionaire's instinctive distrust of friendly strangers. Almost invariably, they wanted something.

The man held out his hand, and David shook it cautiously. 'Do we know each other?' David asked.

'I'm an old friend of Jill's,' the man said, and David relaxed. 'My name is Lawrence. Clifton Lawrence.'

'How do you do, Mr Lawrence.' He was impatient to leave.

'Jill asked me to come up and meet you,' Clifton said. 'She's planned a little surprise for you.'

David looked at him. 'What kind of surprise?'

'Come along, and I'll show you.'

David hesitated a moment. 'All right. Will it take long?'

Clifton Lawrence looked up at him and smiled. 'I don't think so.'

They took an elevator down to C deck, moving past the throngs of embarking passengers and visitors. They walked down a corridor to a large set of double doors. Clifton opened them and ushered David in. David found himself in a large, empty theatre. He looked around, puzzled. 'In here?'

'In here.' Clifton smiled.

He turned and looked up at the projectionist in the booth and nodded. The projectionist was greedy. Clifton had had to give him two hundred dollars before he would agree to assist him. 'If they ever found out, I would lose my job,' he had grumbled.

'No one will ever know,' Clifton had assured him. 'It's just a practical joke. All you have to do is lock the doors when I come in with my friend, and start running the film. We'll be out of there in ten minutes.'

In the end, the projectionist had agreed.

Now David was looking at Clifton, puzzled. 'Movies?' David asked.

'Just sit down, Mr Kenyon.'

David took a seat on the aisle, his long legs stretched out. Clifton took a seat across from him. He was watching David's face as the lights went down and the bright images started to flicker on the large screen.

It felt as though someone was pounding him in the solar plexus with iron hammers. David stared up at the obscene images on the screen and his brain refused to accept what his eyes were seeing. Jill, a young Jill, the way she had looked when he had first fallen in love with her, was naked on a bed. He could see every feature clearly. He watched, mute with disbelief, as a man got astride the girl on the screen and rammed his penis into her mouth. She began sucking it lovingly, caressingly, and another girl came into the scene and spread Jill's legs apart and put her tongue deep inside her. David thought he was going to be sick. For one wild, hopeful instant, he thought that this might be trick photography, a fake, but the camera covered every movement that Jill made. Then the Mexican came into the scene and got on top of Jill, and a hazy red curtain descended in front of David's eyes. He was fifteen years old again, and it was his sister Beth he was watching up there, his sister on top of the naked Mexican gardener in her bed, saying, *Oh, God, I love you, Juan. Keep fucking me. Don't stop!* and David standing in the doorway, unbelievingly, watching his beloved sister. He had been seized with a blind, overpowering rage, and had snatched up a steel letter opener from the desk and had run over to the bed and knocked his sister aside and plunged the opener into the gardener's chest, again and again, until the walls were covered with blood, and Beth was screaming, *Oh, God, no! Stop it, David! I love him. We're going to be married!* There was blood everywhere. David's mother had come running into the room and had sent David away. But he learned later that his mother had telephoned the district attorney, a close friend of the Kenyon family. They had had a long talk in the study, and the Mexican's body had been taken to the jail. The next morning, it was announced that he had committed suicide in his cell. Three weeks later, Beth had been placed in an institution for the insane.

It all flooded back into David now, the unbearable guilt for what he had done, and he went berserk. He picked up the man sitting across from him and smashed his fist into his face, pounding at him, screaming meaningless, senseless words, attacking him for Beth and for Jill, and for his own shame. Clifton Lawrence tried to defend himself, but there was no way that he could stop the blows. A fist smashed into his nose and he felt something break. A fist cannoned into his mouth and the blood started running like a river. He stood there helplessly, waiting for the next blow to strike him. But suddenly there were no more. There was no sound in the room but his tortured, stertorous breathing and the sensuous sounds coming from the screen.

Clifton pulled out a handkerchief to try to stem the bleeding. He stumbled out of the theatre, covering his nose and mouth with his handkerchief, and started towards Jill's cabin. As he passed the dining room, the swinging kitchen door opened for a moment, and he walked into the kitchen, past the bustling chefs and stewards and waiters. He found an ice-making machine and scooped up chunks of ice into a cloth and put them over his nose and mouth. He started out. In front of him was an enormous wedding cake with little spun-sugar figures of the bride and groom on top. Clifton reached out and twisted off the bride's head and crushed it in his fingers.

Then he went to find Jill.

The ship was under way. Jill could feel the movement as the fifty-five-thousand-ton liner began to slide away from the pier. She wondered what was keeping David.

As Jill was finishing her unpacking, there was a knock at the cabin door. Jill hurried over to the door and called out, 'David!' She opened it, her arms outstretched.

Clifton Lawrence stood there, his face battered and bloody. Jill dropped her arms and stared at him. 'What are you doing here? What – happened to you?'

'I just dropped by to say hello, Jill.'

She could hardly understand him.

'And to give you a message from David.'

Jill looked at him, uncomprehendingly. 'From *David?*'

Clifton walked into the cabin.

He was making Jill nervous. 'Where is David?'

Clifton turned to her and said, 'Remember what movies used to be like in the old days? There were the good guys in the white hats and the bad guys in the black hats and in the end you always knew the bad guys were going to get their just desserts. I grew up on those movies, Jill. I grew up believing that life was really like that, that the boys in the white hats always won.'

'I don't know what you're talking about.'

'It's nice to know that once in a while life works out like those old movies.' He smiled at her through battered bleeding lips and said, 'David's gone. For good.'

She stared at him in disbelief.

And at that moment, they both felt the motion of the ship come to a stop. Clifton walked out to the veranda and looked down over the side of the ship. 'Come here.'

Jill hesitated a moment, then followed him, filled with some nameless, growing dread. She peered over the railing. Far below on the water, she could see David getting on the pilot tug, leaving the *Bretagne*. She clutched the railing for support. '*Why?*' she demanded unbelievingly. '*What happened?*'

Clifton Lawrence turned to her and said, 'I ran your picture for him.'

And she instantly knew what he meant and she moaned, 'Oh, my God. No! Please, no! You've killed me!'

'Then we're even.'

'Get out!' she screamed. 'Get out of here!' She flung herself at him and her nails caught his cheeks and ripped deep gashes down the side. Clifton swung and hit her hard across the face. She fell to her knees, clutching her head in agony.

Clifton stood looking at her for a long moment. This was how he wanted to remember her. 'So long, Josephine Czinski,' he said.

Clifton left Jill's cabin and walked up to the boat deck,

keeping the lower half of his face covered with the handkerchief. He walked slowly, studying the faces of the passengers, looking for a fresh face, an unusual type. You never knew when you might stumble across new talent. He felt ready to go back to work again.

Who could tell? Maybe he would get lucky and discover another Toby Temple.

Shortly after Clifton left, Claude Dessard walked up to Jill's cabin and knocked at the door. There was no response, but the chief purser could hear sounds inside the room. He waited a moment, then raised his voice and said, 'Mrs Temple, this is Claude Dessard, the chief purser. I was wondering if I might be of service?'

There was no answer. By now Dessard's internal warning system was screaming. His instincts told him that there was something terribly wrong, and he had a premonition that it centred, somehow, around this woman. A series of wild, outrageous thoughts danced through his brain. She had been murdered or kidnapped or – He tried the handle of the door. It was unlocked. Slowly, Dessard pushed the door open. Jill Temple was standing at the far end of the cabin, looking out the porthole, her back to him. Dessard opened his mouth to speak, but something in the frozen rigidity of her figure stopped him. He stood there awkwardly for a moment, debating whether to quietly withdraw, when suddenly the cabin was filled with an unearthly, keening sound, like an animal in pain. Helpless before such a deep private agony, Dessard withdrew, carefully closing the door behind him.

Dessard stood outside the cabin a moment, listening to the wordless cry from within, then, deeply disturbed, turned and headed for the theatre on the main deck.

At dinner that evening, there were two empty seats at the captain's table. Halfway through the meal, the captain signalled to Dessard, who was hosting a party of less important passengers two tables away. Dessard excused himself and hurried over to the captain's table.

'Ah, Dessard,' the captain said, genially. He lowered his voice and his tone changed. 'What happened with Mrs Temple and Mr Kenyon?'

Dessard looked around at the other guests and whispered, 'As you know, Mr Kenyon left with the pilot at the Ambrose Lightship. Mrs Temple is in her cabin.'

The captain swore under his breath. He was a methodical man who did not like to have his routine interfered with. '*Merde!* All the wedding arrangements have been made,' he said.

'I know, Captain.' Dessard shrugged and rolled his eyes upward. 'Americans,' he said.

Jill sat alone in the darkened cabin, huddled in a chair, her knees pulled up to her chest, staring into nothingness. She was grieving, but it was not for David Kenyon or Toby Temple or even for herself. She was grieving for a little girl named Josephine Czinski. Jill had wanted to do so much for that little girl, and now all the wonderful magical dreams she had had for her were finished.

Jill sat there, unseeing, numbed by a defeat that was beyond comprehension. Only a few hours ago she had owned the world, she had everything she ever wanted, and now she had nothing. She became slowly aware that her headache had returned. She had not noticed it before because of the other pain, the agonizing pain that was tearing deep into her bowels. But now she could feel the band around her forehead tightening. She pulled her knees up closer against her chest, in the foetal position, trying to shut out everything. She was so tired, so terribly tired. All she wanted to do was to sit here for ever and not have to think. Then maybe the pain would stop, at least for a little while.

Jill dragged herself over to the bed and lay down and closed her eyes.

Then she felt it. A wave of cold, foul-smelling air moving towards her, surrounding her, caressing her. And she heard his voice, calling her name. *Yes,* she thought, *yes.* Slowly, almost in a trance, Jill got to her feet and walked out of her cabin, following the beckoning voice in her head.

It was two o'clock in the morning and the decks were deserted when Jill emerged from her cabin. She stared down at the sea, watching the gentle splashing of the waves against the ship as it cut through the water, listening to the voice. Jill's headache was worse now, a tight vice of agony. But the voice was telling her not to worry, telling her that everything was going to be fine. *Look down,* the voice said.

Jill looked down into the water and saw something floating there. It was a face. Toby's face, smiling at her, the drowned blue eyes looking up at her. The icy breeze began to blow, gently pushing her closer to the rail.

'I had to do it, Toby,' she whispered. 'You see that, don't you?'

The head in the water was nodding, bobbing, inviting her to come and join it. The wind grew colder and Jill's body began trembling. *Don't be afraid,* the voice told her. *The water is deep and warm . . . You'll be here with me . . . forever. Come, Jill.*

She closed her eyes a moment, but when she opened them, the smiling face was still there, keeping pace with the ship, the mutilated limbs dangling in the water. *Come to me*, the voice said.

She leaned over to explain to Toby, so that he would leave her in peace, and the icy wind pushed against her, and suddenly she was floating in the soft velvet night air, pirouetting in space. Toby's face was coming closer, coming to meet her, and she felt the paralysed arms go around her body, holding her. And they were together, for ever and ever.

Then there was only the soft night wind and the timeless sea.

And the stars above, where it had all been written.

Morning, Noon and Night

Sidney Sheldon

The Stanford family is one of the most respected in America - but behind the facade of fame and glamour lies a hidden web of blackmail, drugs and murder . . .

When Harry Stanford, one of the wealthiest men in the world, mysteriously drowns while cruising on his yacht, it sets off a chain of events that reverberates around the globe . . . At the family gathering following the funeral in Boston, a strikingly beautiful young woman appears. She claims to be Stanford's daughter and entitled to a share of the tycoon's estate. Is she genuine or is she an imposter?

Sweeping from the splendours of the Italian Riviera, to the fashion salons of Paris and New York, and the élite opulence of Boston and Florida, *Morning, Noon and Night* twists and turns its way through intrigue, smoke and mirrors to a surprise ending you'll never forget . . .

'Sheldon is a writer working at the height of his power . . . I hung on till the very end' *New York Times*

Nothing Lasts Forever
Sidney Sheldon

In the frenetic world of a big San Francisco hospital, events catapult three women doctors into a white-hot spotlight:

Dr Paige Taylor

She swore it was euthanasia, but when Paige inherited a million dollars from a patient, the District Attorney called it murder.

Dr Kat Hunter

She vowed never to let a man too close again - until she accepted the challenge of a deadly bet.

Dr Honey Taft

To make it in medicine, she knew she'd need something more than the brains God gave her.

Racing from the life and death decisions of the operating room to the tension-packed fireworks of a murder trial, *Nothing Lasts Forever* lays bare the ambitions and fears of healers and killers, lovers and betrayers in a heart-stopping story you wish would never end . . .

'Of all the popular novels I've read this summer this beats the lot for sheer storytelling mastery' *Today*

Bloodline
Sidney Sheldon

A daughter of privilege: Elizabeth Roffe possessed beauty, intelligence, youth, the adored daughter of a rich and powerful father.

At his death she had to obey his behest and take command of his mighty global empire. It made Elizabeth the richest girl in the world. But someone, somewhere, was determined that she must die . . .

In this story that spans three continents, Sidney Sheldon spins a hypnotic, exotic web – of love and ambition, of danger and death.

'Sheldon is a writer working at the height of his power . . . powerful enough to drag us along with him. I hung on till the very end.' *New York Times*

